BLOSSOMS of LUST

By LINDSEY FINCH

Blossoms of Lust

The Ivy & Bloom Trilogy: Book 3
A Dark Mafia Romance

By Lindsey Finch

AVIARY
PUBLICATIONS

ISBN: 978-1-966627-02-9 (eBook)
ISBN: 978-1-966627-17-3 (Paperback)

Blossoms of Lust is a work of fiction. Any references to historical events, real people, real places or crimes are used fictitiously. Names, characters, places, and events are products of the author's imagination. The author does not condone or support the horrible acts portrayed in this fictional work.

.

Front cover design and book design by Aviary Publications, LLC.

Printed in the United States of America.
First printing edition 2025.

www.instagram.com/aviarypublications

Books by Lindsey Finch

THE IVY & BLOOM TRILOGY

Petals of Sin
Thorns of Desire
Blossoms of Lust

THE WHITE LOTUS SERIES

The Keeper's Mark
The Keeper's Key
The Keeper's Reign
The Keeper's Empire
The Keeper's Legacy

THE CITADEL SERIES
(STANDALONES)

Silent Obsession
Surrendered Will
Crimson Chains
Possessive Claim
Dark Dominion

Disclaimer: this novel may contain elements not suited for every reader. If any of the following offends you, please do not read this book. This novel contains: elements of domination, submission, control, crossing personal boundaries, financial leverage, organized crime, and dark romance.

"It is in the chaos of shattered pieces that we find the strength to rebuild."
—Cassandra Clare

CHAPTER ONE

The gunshot rang out, sharp and unforgiving, and I watched the body fall again. The sound reverberated through the crumbled distillery, a cruel echo that refused to fade. Blood sprayed across the cold concrete floor, stark and vivid against the shadows. My chest heaved, but my legs refused to move, frozen in place as if bound by invisible chains.

Damien's lifeless eyes locked onto mine, unblinking and accusing. The betrayal in their empty depths seared into me, branding itself behind my eyelids. The coppery scent of blood filled the air, thick and suffocating, mingling with the acrid tang of gunpowder. My stomach twisted as the crimson pool beneath him spread like ink, its dark tendrils creeping outward, unstoppable.

I wanted to scream, to run, to do *something*. But I couldn't. My body was rooted in place, heavy with the weight of fear and disbelief. My pulse thundered in my ears, drowning out everything except the sharp clip of Cassian's footsteps as he approached, unbothered by his actions, or the murder of his father.

His voice, low and calm, cut through the haze, a blade slicing cleanly through my spiraling thoughts. "This is what loyalty costs," he murmured, his words laced with finality, each syllable a nail driven into the coffin of my

1

trust.

I turned to look at him—no, *forced* myself to look at him—but the face I knew was gone. His expression was impassive, his steel-gray eyes colder than I had ever seen them, devoid of the tenderness I had once foolishly believed was real. There was no remorse, no hesitation, just the unyielding presence of a man who had calculated every step, every consequence.

A sob clawed its way up my throat, but it refused to escape. My chest ached, the pressure unbearable, like I was suffocating under the weight of my own helplessness. "Why?" I wanted to ask, but the word never left my lips.

Damien's hand twitched, a final, involuntary spasm, before falling still. The sight broke something in me, a sharp crack that reverberated through my entire being. The bloodied walls of the conference room seemed to close in, the air thick and suffocating, trapping me in this waking nightmare.

And then Cassian's gaze turned to me.

"You knew this was coming," he said, his tone as smooth as velvet, yet devoid of any comfort. He stepped closer, the soles of his polished shoes clicking against the floor with a rhythm that matched the frantic pounding of my heart.

"I didn't..." I tried to speak, but the words felt heavy and broken, caught in the tangle of emotions choking me.

"You didn't *want* to see it," he corrected, tilting his head slightly, as though examining a curious artifact. "That's the difference."

His shadow stretched long over the bloodied floor, over Damien's lifeless form, over me. I couldn't breathe. The room darkened, the flames in the fireplace suddenly snuffed out, the edges of my vision closing in until all that remained was the crimson pool and Cassian's unyielding presence.

The blood crept closer, inching toward my feet, and I stumbled back, finally able to move. But no matter how far I retreated, it followed, relentless and unyielding.

I tried to close my eyes, to block out the scene, but the darkness behind my eyelids held no solace. The sound of the gunshot echoed again, louder this time, splitting the silence apart.

I woke up gasping, my heart clawing its way out of my chest.

The sound of my ragged breaths filled the room, and for a moment, I wasn't sure if I was awake or still trapped in that nightmare. My fingers dug into the bedsheets, the smooth fabric bunched tightly in my fists as though I could anchor myself to reality.

But the weight of Damien's gaze lingered, and Cassian's words were etched into my mind, haunting me even in the light of dawn.

The clock on the nightstand glared at me with its relentless red numbers: 5:13 a.m. It had been three weeks since I'd walked away from everything—Cassian, Ivy & Bloom, and the wreckage of who I thought I was. And yet, every night, the dreams brought me back to that warehouse.

I swung my legs over the side of the bed and sat there, my hands gripping the edge of the mattress. The cold floor against my bare feet was a small mercy, grounding me in the present. My chest felt heavy, like the weight of everything I'd been avoiding was pressing down harder with each breath.

The curtains were drawn, but I didn't need to look outside to know they were there—Marcus and Sierra, the ever-watchful bodyguards Cassian had stationed near my building. I'd changed the locks on my apartment again after the last time he let himself in. I wouldn't let him corner me, not here. Not anymore.

My phone buzzed on the nightstand, the screen lighting up with his name. I didn't need to check the message. It was the same as always—short, commanding, dripping with that quiet dominance he wielded so effortlessly.

"We need to talk."

I stared at the phone, the ache in my chest flaring. The urge to respond was there, sharp and undeniable, but I pushed it down. Ghosting him was the only thing I could control anymore.

Shoving the phone aside, I forced myself to stand. My reflection in the mirror across the room caught my eye, and I almost didn't recognize the woman staring back. Hollow eyes, dark circles, and tangled hair that hadn't seen a brush in days. My favorite old robe hung off my frame, the faded floral print a painful reminder of a time when my life felt simpler.

I wrapped the robe tighter around me and shuffled to the kitchen. The morning routine of the city outside was muted through the windows, and for a moment, I let the mundane ritual of brewing coffee distract me. The aroma filled the small space, comforting in its familiarity, but even that couldn't chase away the gnawing emptiness.

I hadn't set foot in Ivy & Bloom since the day I walked away from Cassian, convinced that seeing the shop would mean seeing him. It was easier to stay away, to bury myself in this half-life where the only company I had was my own guilt and the memories I couldn't escape.

The coffee maker sputtered, pulling me from my thoughts. I poured a mug, the warmth seeping into my hands as I held it close. But before I could take a sip, my phone buzzed again.

I stared at it from across the room, the glow of the screen taunting me. Another message. Another thread tying me to him. My chest tightened, and without thinking, I crossed the room and grabbed the phone.

The message was simple: *"You can't avoid me forever, Rosalie."*

A bitter laugh escaped me as I set the phone back down with a sharp click. He was wrong. Avoiding him was the only thing keeping me from completely falling apart.

Moving back to the kitchen, I leaned against the counter, the mug still warm in my hands, and stared out the window at the city waking up. Somewhere out there, Cassian Moreau was waiting. Watching. And I hated that some part of me wanted to let him in.

But I couldn't. Not after what I'd seen. Not after what he'd done.

I took a shaky breath and whispered to no one, "You

can't fix this, Cassian."

The words felt hollow, but I repeated them anyway, hoping that if I said them enough, I might start to believe them.

The silence in the apartment wrapped around me like a suffocating blanket, broken only by the annoying putter of the refrigerator and the occasional creak of the floorboards beneath my feet. I stayed rooted by the counter, clutching the coffee mug as if the warmth might seep deeper into my chilled bones. But it wouldn't.

It never did.

My gaze drifted back to the vase of flowers on the table, their brittle stems leaning precariously, petals curled inward as if retreating from the world. They mirrored how I felt—worn, lifeless, and incapable of holding any beauty that had once existed.

The vase hadn't moved since I'd brought it home, an afterthought from the shop when I thought I'd be back in a few days. Couldn't face the memories. Couldn't face him.

I set the mug down with a soft clink and ran a hand through my hair, wincing as my fingers caught on the tangles. My body felt heavy, leaden with exhaustion that no amount of sleep—or avoidance—seemed to ease. Even now, standing here, I wanted nothing more than to crawl back into bed, pull the covers over my head, and pretend the world outside didn't exist.

But the world did exist. And so did Cassian.

The phone buzzed again. He was persistent, unrelenting.

I didn't move this time, letting it vibrate against the nightstand until the sound faded into silence. The message wasn't going anywhere. Neither was he.

With a sigh, I grabbed the mug again and shuffled into the living room, the cluttered space feeling smaller with every passing day. I sank onto the couch, careful to avoid the stack of unopened mail teetering on the cushion beside me. My legs curled beneath me as I cradled my coffee, my eyes drifting to the window again.

What would it feel like to walk into Ivy & Bloom, to see

the flowers, the customers, the shop that had been my life for so long? The thought twisted something deep inside me. Ivy & Bloom had been in my family for as long as I could remember—until Cassian had tainted it, turned it into something I couldn't recognize.

I pressed the mug to my lips, letting the warmth burn my mouth, a small, grounding pain that distracted me for half a second. That's all it ever was now: distractions. Small, fleeting moments to keep me from drowning in the bigger picture.

I should clean. I should eat something. I should open one of those letters or call someone who might remind me what it felt like to live instead of just exist.

Instead, I sat there, the coffee growing cold in my hands, staring out the window and wondering how long I could keep avoiding everything before it finally caught up with me.

The truth was, it already had.

CHAPTER TWO

The shower was meant to wake me up, to shock my senses and force me into some semblance of normalcy. I stood under the spray, the hot water pounding against my shoulders as if it could wash away the layers of exhaustion clinging to me like a second skin. But the effort felt hollow. The water cascaded over me, down my back, pooling at my feet as I stared blankly at the tile, unmoving.

At some point, I turned off the shower and sank into the tub, letting it fill around me. The steam fogged the mirror and blurred the sharp edges of the bathroom, cocooning me in a hazy silence. I rested my head against the cool porcelain and closed my eyes, the water lapping softly against my skin.

It wasn't until the chill began to seep into my bones that I realized the water had turned cold. My fingers were pruned, and the goosebumps on my arms made me shiver as I finally forced myself to move. The sluggish pull of my body felt like wading through molasses, but I grabbed the detangling brush from the edge of the tub and began pulling it through my wet hair.

Each stroke of the brush tugged at the knots, and I winced at the sharp pricks of pain as it caught on tangles. The mirror, once fogged, cleared just enough to reflect the woman staring back at me.

Gaunt. Hollow. A shadow of who I'd been.

My cheekbones, always subtly pronounced, now jutted out sharply, the skin beneath them pale and stretched thin. My lips were dry and cracked, their natural blush faded into a muted pink that barely stood out against my sallow complexion. My eyes were the worst of it—dark, heavy shadows painted the skin beneath them, the kind that no amount of concealer could mask. They were glassy, distant, like they didn't belong to me anymore.

I leaned closer to the mirror, my damp hair falling forward to frame my face. My fingers brushed against my cheeks, tracing the hollows where fullness had once been. Even my collarbones seemed more pronounced, the ridges stark against the delicate curve of my neck.

The woman staring back wasn't someone I recognized.

I swallowed hard, forcing the lump in my throat down as I ran the brush through the last section of my hair, detangling it into submission. The process was automatic, mechanical—another distraction to fill the minutes of my day.

The urge to crawl back into bed whispered in the back of my mind, but something deeper stirred—a small flicker of rebellion against the monotony that had consumed me for weeks. My reflection stared at me, her eyes bleak but resolute, and for the first time in days, I listened to her.

I was going to leave this apartment.

I pulled on the first clothes I could find—a pair of faded jeans that hung looser on my hips than they used to, and a soft, oversized sweater that smelled faintly of lavender fabric softener. It was enough.

The air outside was damp and cool, the kind that hinted at the lingering grip of spring's early days. A light drizzle fell, the rain soft and gentle, soaking into the cracked pavement and darkening the edges of my jeans as I walked. The sweater I'd grabbed hung loose on my frame, but it was warm enough to keep the chill from sinking too deep into my skin. At the last moment, I'd grabbed a thin knee-length coat which had lost its form fitting appeal as well.

I didn't bother with an umbrella. The rain felt more

cleansing than oppressive, the tiny droplets cool against my face as I tucked my hands into my pockets and kept moving.

The corner coffee shop came into view, its familiar awning sagging slightly under the weight of rainwater. The soft glow of its interior lights spilled out onto the sidewalk, a warm invitation that drew me closer. I pushed the door open, the harsh chime of the doorbell blending with the low rumblings of chatter and the hiss of the espresso machine.

I'd spent a fair portion of my time surviving off of takeout and coffee—lots and lots of coffee.

My shoes squeaked slightly against the tile floor as I approached the counter, scanning the menu even though I already knew what I wanted.

"One medium black coffee and... a blueberry muffin," I said, my voice soft but steady as I handed over a crumpled bill.

The barista nodded, her polite smile not quite reaching her eyes, and I stepped aside to wait. My fingers traced the edge of my sweater sleeve as I stood there, feeling the damp fabric cling to my skin.

Out of the corner of my eye, I spotted them.

Marcus and Sierra.

They were seated at a small table near the back, their heads tilted slightly as if they were in conversation, but I knew better. Their presence was too deliberate, too coincidental. Even at this distance, I could feel their watchful gazes following my every move.

I turned back to the counter as the barista called my name, grabbing the coffee and the small paper bag containing the muffin. The warmth of the cup seeped into my hands once more.

Sliding into a booth by the window, I set the coffee and muffin on the table in front of me. The rain outside had picked up, streaking the glass and blurring the view of the street beyond. It gave the world a soft, dreamlike quality, as if everything outside this little coffee shop existed just out of reach.

I peeled the wrapper off the muffin slowly, my movements absent-minded as my thoughts were elsewhere—they always were these days. The smell of blueberries and sugar wafted up, sweet and nostalgic. I broke off a piece and brought it to my lips, letting the flavor linger on my tongue before setting the muffin back down.

One bite. That was all I could manage.

The coffee was easier. I cradled the cup in both hands, taking small sips, letting the warmth spread through me. It didn't fill the hollowness, but it dulled the edges, made it a little easier to sit still.

I could feel Marcus and Sierra even without looking. Their presence was like a weight pressing against my back, their eyes ensuring I wasn't truly alone. Cassian's shadows, always there, always watching. I wondered if he had sent them to protect me—or to make sure I hadn't run to the cops.

Although I had considered it, the thought hadn't resurfaced again. A nod to my corrupted moral compass.

Turning my gaze to the window, I let my mind wander, following the trails of raindrops as they slid down the glass. The streets outside were quiet, the occasional car passing by, its tires hissing against the wet pavement. A woman hurried by with a bright yellow umbrella, her laughter audible even through the rain.

For a moment, I envied her.

The corner coffee shop was my first step outside in weeks, my first attempt to feel human again. But even here, in this small bubble of warmth and normalcy, the weight of everything I'd left behind loomed large.

I gripped the coffee tighter and whispered to myself, "One step at a time." Having sat there for nearly an hour, I contemplated every possible excuse to prevent me from going there, but none of them seems worthy enough.

When the rain lightened up, I pushed open the coffee shop door, the bell giving a cheerful chime that didn't match the knot twisting in my stomach. The rain had softened to a mist, fine droplets clinging to my hair and coat as I stepped onto the sidewalk.

The muffin, still mostly whole, felt like a lead weight in my hand. With a sigh, I dropped it into the nearest trash can, its paper bag crumpling softly against the metal bin. The taste of blueberries lingered faintly on my tongue, bittersweet and hollow, much like everything else lately.

The coffee stayed in my grip, its warmth a small comfort as I walked aimlessly, letting the drizzle blur the edges of the city around me. I didn't need to look over my shoulder to know Marcus and Sierra were nearby, trailing me at a distance that wasn't far enough to forget but just far enough to pretend.

I wasn't sure if I could do this until I saw it: *Ivy & Bloom*.

The sight of the shop was a jolt to my system, like stepping into a puddle and realizing too late that the water was ice cold. The windows were just as I remembered, filled with carefully arranged blooms in every color. Roses, daisies, tulips—they looked vibrant, alive, and utterly out of place against the grayness of the day.

The coffee in my hand suddenly felt too hot, burning against my palm as I stood frozen on the sidewalk. My chest tightened, the ache sharp and familiar, as my gaze traced the curves of the painted sign above the door.

For a fleeting moment, I imagined pushing the door open, hearing the soft chime of the bell and breathing in the heady scent of flowers and earth. I could almost feel the smooth counters beneath my fingertips, hear the murmur of customers, and see the faint smile my mother always wore when she worked.

But the image shattered, replaced by the memory of Cassian standing in the center of the shop, his voice low and commanding as he unraveled the truth. My sanctuary, my mother's legacy, had been nothing more than a front for his schemes.

I took a step back, the motion instinctive, like touching a flame and realizing too late how much it burns. My heart was pounding, and the warmth from the coffee wasn't enough to steady my trembling hands.

I couldn't go in. Not yet.

With a sharp inhale, I turned on my heel and walked away, my footsteps quick and uneven against the wet pavement.

The walk back to my apartment felt heavier than it should have, the rain soaking into my coat and sweater and chilling me to the bone. By the time I reached my building, my fingers were stiff, and the coffee cup was cold and forgotten in my hand.

But it wasn't the rain or the chill that stopped me in my tracks. It was the single rose waiting for me, perched neatly in the center of my door.

The bloom was soft and delicate, its creamy white petals almost glowing against the dark wood. A black ribbon was tied in a neat bow around the stem, its stark contrast making the gesture feel more ominous than romantic.

I didn't need to touch it to know who had left it.

Cassian.

My pulse quickened, the sharp thrum of my heart pounding in my ears as I stared at the rose. It was elegant and deliberate, like that side of him that I fell in love with. White roses meant forgiveness—I knew that much. But this wasn't just about forgiveness. It was a message, one as clear as if he'd carved it into the door himself.

I reached for it hesitantly, my fingers brushing the ribbon. The softness of the petals under my touch felt wrong, too perfect for something that carried the weight of so many unspoken words.

A part of me wanted to throw it down, to toss it into the dumpster and let the rain wash it away. But I couldn't. Instead, I pulled it free, the stem cold and damp in my hand as I unlocked the door with trembling fingers.

The apartment was just as I'd left it—silent, stale, and suffocating. I placed the rose on the kitchen counter, the black bow unraveling slightly as it rested against the chipped surface.

I stood there for a long time, staring at it, the warmth of forgiveness and the chill of manipulation coiled tightly around its delicate petals.

Cassian always had a way of making his presence known, even when he wasn't there. And no matter how far I ran, he always seemed to find me.

CHAPTER THREE

I stared at my phone, Abram's name glowing on the screen, his call pulling me from the haze that had settled over me in the last few days. For a moment, I debated letting it ring, but guilt gnawed at me until I reluctantly answered.

"Dad," I said, my voice flat as I sank into the couch, tucking my legs beneath me.

"Rosalie," Abram said, his voice carrying a familiar warmth beneath its gruff exterior, the way it always did when he was trying not to worry too much. "I was starting to think I'd have to come knock on your door myself. You know, just to make sure you're still alive."

His attempt at lightness was painfully transparent, a thin veil over the concern I could hear plain as day.

I sighed, pressing a hand to my forehead. "I've been... busy."

"Busy doing what? Sitting in that apartment? I stopped by the shop the other day, they said you haven't been there in weeks." His voice carried a sharpness that I hadn't missed. "This isn't you, Rosalie. You used to be full of joy... and—" His words fell short, but anything else would have been the truth. "Now, look at you. You're just—"

"Don't." My voice cracked, and I cleared my throat, forcing the lump back down. "Please, don't do this right now."

Abram paused, the silence between us stretching long enough that I almost thought he'd hung up.

"You know," he said finally, softer this time, "you were happier when you were with him."

The words hit me like a punch to the gut, stealing the air from my lungs. I squeezed my eyes shut, the image of Cassian's face flashing in my mind—his intense gaze, the way he used to look at me like I was the only thing that mattered in the world.

"You didn't even like him," I shot back, my voice rising slightly.

"No," Abram admitted, "I didn't. And I still don't. But at least you weren't like this—hiding, sulking, wasting away."

I clenched my jaw, anger and hurt bubbling to the surface. "You don't get to say that to me. Not after everything."

Another pause. When Abram spoke again, his voice was softer, almost hesitant. "I'm worried about you, Rosalie. That's all. I just want my daughter back."

"I have to go," I said abruptly, standing and pacing the small space of my living room. "I'll call you later."

"Rosalie—"

I ended the call before he could say anything else, dropping the phone onto the couch and pressing the heels of my hands against my eyes. His words echoed in my head, louder than I wanted them to be.

You were happier when you were with him.

I took a deep breath, letting it out slowly as I lowered my hands. Abram was wrong. He had to be.

But as the quiet of the apartment settled over me again, I realized I couldn't sit here anymore. The suffocating weight of my own thoughts was too much.

I rifled through my closet, pulling out a black leather jacket and a pair of dark jeans. The sweater and jeans I'd been wearing for days felt like they were holding me back, a reminder of the inertia I'd been drowning in. I didn't want to feel it anymore.

Once dressed, I stood in front of the mirror and pulled

my hair into a loose French braid, smoothing the strands with trembling fingers. My reflection looked sharper now, more purposeful, even if the hollowness in my eyes remained.

Grabbing a small bag and slinging it over my shoulder, I turned off the lights and moved toward the window in my bedroom. The fire escape outside was barely used, the metal grates slick with rain from earlier in the evening. I opened the window carefully, the cool night air rushing in as I stepped out onto the fire escape.

I glanced down at the alley below, my heart thudding as I climbed down the steps. The thought of Marcus or Sierra catching me made my stomach twist, but I didn't hear the low hum of their SUV or see the flash of their silhouettes.

Once I reached the alley, I slipped into the shadows, the sounds of the city buzzing intoxicatingly around me. The air was cool and damp, the streets alive with the rhythm of traffic and the chatter of people moving from one place to another. I kept my head down, blending into the blur of the night.

The lights and sounds of downtown Chicago pulsed around me, the energy both overwhelming and grounding. For the first time in weeks, I felt something other than the weight of my own thoughts. The chaos of the city enveloped me, numbing the ache in my chest, even if just for a moment.

The rain fell softly at first, barely noticeable as it mingled with the mist rising from the pavement. I turned down one street, then another, following the shifting glow of neon signs and the faint strains of music escaping from bars and restaurants. My steps felt aimless, each one carrying me further from my apartment and the suffocating stillness I'd left behind.

By the time I glanced up again, the rain had turned heavier, soaking through my jacket as I walked, the drizzle from earlier now a steady patter against the pavement. My hair stuck to my neck, and my jeans clung uncomfortably to my legs. I didn't have a destination in mind, just the need to keep moving.

The streets shifted as I ventured further from my usual haunts, the familiar glow of coffee shops and corner stores replaced by dim alleyways and tightly packed buildings with facades that blurred in the rain. Neon lights reflected off the wet ground, their soft hum and electric colors cutting through the haze.

That's when I saw it.

A single, unassuming door tucked into the side of a building, its glossy black paint glinting under a narrow beam of light. Above it, the word *Nocturne* was etched in sleek silver letters, illuminated just enough to catch the eye. The name hummed with intrigue, and the faint sound of music—low, rhythmic, and intoxicating—seeped through the cracks.

I hesitated on the sidewalk, my breath fogging in the cool air. People moved in and out of the door with careless ease, their movements fluid, their expressions calm but guarded. The allure of the place tugged at me. I told myself it was curiosity, nothing more. But deep down, I knew it was the need to escape—if only for a little while—that pushed me forward.

The bouncer at the door gave me a quick once-over, his brow arching slightly. I straightened my back, forcing myself to meet his gaze, even as I felt out of place in my rain-dampened jacket and scuffed boots. He didn't say a word, just stepped aside and pushed the door open.

Warmth spilled out as I stepped inside, the low thrum of bass-heavy music pulsing through the air. The amber glow of pendant lights cast soft, flattering beauty over the space, illuminating deep forest-green booths and polished black tables scattered haphazardly to encourage conversation— or something more intimate.

The crowd was a mix that immediately put me on edge. Some were dressed to impress, their sharp suits and elegant dresses exuding effortless confidence, while others leaned casual but stylish, in fitted jeans, designer jackets, or crisp button-downs with the sleeves rolled up. A few groups clustered around the bar, their voices raised in laughter, while others lounged in booths, their movements languid and deliberate, as though they had all the time in the world.

The scent of expensive perfume mingled with the tang of spilled liquor and something musky I couldn't quite place. It wasn't unpleasant, but it added to the charged atmosphere that filled the room.

On one side of the club, a narrow stage was set up with low lighting, a DJ perched behind an impressive setup of turntables and equipment. The music was loud but not overwhelming, its rhythm thrumming through the floor and into my chest. It was upbeat, a mix of electronic and hip-hop, with the kind of energy that invited people to dance—or to disappear into a corner with someone under the pretense of conversation.

A group near the dance floor caught my eye—two women in glittering dresses laughing loudly, their drinks sloshing as they moved to the music, while a man in a tight v-neck and black blazer leaned close, his words lost in the noise. A few feet away, a couple stood pressed against a wall, their faces close, oblivious to everything around them.

The bar, however, was the center of it all. It stretched along the far wall, its glossy black surface catching the golden light from above. Bartenders moved in the controlled chaos with ease, shaking cocktails and sliding drinks across to waiting hands.

I hesitated near the entrance, feeling out of place in my damp jacket and jeans. My hair still clung to my neck from the rain, and I had none of the polished, put-together confidence the people here seemed to wear so easily.

But if I didn't adjust quickly, I'd stick out more than I already did.

Straightening my shoulders, I let my eyes drift over the room, feigning a casual disinterest while I took everything in. My fingers brushed my jacket's zipper as if debating whether to remove it, but I left it on for now—armor against the unfamiliar.

I headed toward the bar, keeping my pace steady and my expression neutral, as though I belonged here as much as anyone else. Around me, the conversations and laughter rose and fell, a symphony of energy and intent, but I couldn't shake the feeling of being watched.

I made my way to the bar, weaving through the crowd with measured steps. The energy in the room was infectious, and I could feel it creeping under my skin despite myself. Conversations hummed around me, snippets of laughter and raised voices blending into the rhythmic thrum of the music.

When I reached the bar, I leaned lightly against the sleek black surface, scanning the shelves of bottles glowing softly under the golden light. A bartender caught my eye and approached with an infectious smile.

"What can I get you?" he asked, his voice smooth, nearly drowned out by the noise.

"Whiskey sour," I said, louder than I intended, my voice cutting through the low hum around us. A smile slowly crept up as I realized that I had deliberately avoided anything with whisky until Cassian introduced me to it. His vice slowly became my own...

He nodded and turned to mix the drink. I glanced over my shoulder, letting my eyes roam the room. Groups gathered and scattered like shifting constellations, conversations flickering between laughter and low, urgent murmurs. The air was thick with the heady mix of expensive perfumes and sharp alcohol, undercut by the faint, unexpected sweetness of floral arrangements tucked into the darker corners. Their blooms were striking— nothing but black flowers, glossy and dramatic under the dim amber light. The combination was intoxicating, almost overwhelming, but strangely comforting in its indulgence. For once, the chaos around me felt easier to breathe in than the silence I'd left behind.

The bartender slid the drink toward me, the condensation already gathering on the outside of the glass. I handed him a bill, not bothering with change, and took a sip. The tart sweetness of lemon and the warmth of whiskey flooded my senses, igniting a fire in me as I turned from the bar and searched for a quieter spot.

I found it in a booth tucked into the farthest corner of

the room, partially obscured by shadows. Sliding into the seat, I positioned myself so I could see the crowd without being too conspicuous. The velvet fabric beneath me was cool and smooth, and the table had the faintest stickiness that came from countless spilled drinks, but I wasn't too bothered by it.

For a moment, I just watched.

The crowd moved like a living thing, shifting and undulating as people came together and broke apart. At one table, two men leaned close, their conversation intense and hurried. A few feet away, a woman in a red dress threw her head back in laughter, her companion leaning closer, clearly captivated. On the dance floor, the glittering dresses and sharp lines of jackets blurred into a kaleidoscope of movement under the shifting lights.

I took another sip of my drink, the warmth spreading through me as I leaned back against the booth. For the first time in weeks, the weight in my chest felt lighter, pushed aside by the buzz of the room and the whiskey loosening its hold.

A group near my booth caught my attention—a woman with a sleek ponytail and sharp cheekbones who radiated confidence, her laughter infectious as she leaned into the man beside her. They noticed me watching, and she offered a faint, knowing smile.

"You look like you've got a story," she said, her voice cutting through the music as she shifted slightly to face me.

I blinked, caught off guard. "I think everyone here does," I replied, my tone wry, the drink in my hand giving me a touch of boldness I wouldn't have found otherwise.

Her smile widened, and she raised her glass toward me. "Fair enough. I'm Lydia."

"Rosalie," I said, tipping my glass in return.

For the next few minutes—or maybe longer; time was slippery in this place—I found myself talking to Lydia and her companions. Their conversation was easy, light, filled with anecdotes and teasing jabs at one another. None of it felt pointed or prying, just the kind of banter that came from people who knew how to enjoy the night.

I let myself laugh, the sound unfamiliar in my throat but not unwelcome. The whiskey dulled the sharp edges of my thoughts, and for a little while, I forgot about Cassian, about the shop, about everything waiting for me outside of these walls.

The music changed, the beat slower and heavier, and Lydia turned back to her group, leaving me with a warm smile and a casual, "Come find us if you want more company."

The booth felt more comfortable now, or maybe it was just the whiskey. I wasn't sure how many I'd had—three or four? Maybe five? The glass in my hand was lighter than I remembered, the amber liquid inside dwindling faster with each sip. My stomach churned faintly, reminding me that I hadn't eaten dinner, but I ignored it. For the first time in weeks, I felt alive, like my body wasn't weighed down by the ache I'd been carrying.

The music had shifted again, slower now, with a pulsing rhythm that seemed to match the faint buzz in my veins. The dim amber light of the room blurred at the edges, softening the hard lines of the tables and the shadowy figures moving past. I leaned back in the booth, a faint, lazy smile tugging at my lips as I watched the people on the dance floor sway to the tantalizing music.

A man approached my booth, his confident stride cutting through the haze of the room. He was tall, with a cocky smile and sharp features that might have been charming if my head wasn't swimming. His dark shirt was unbuttoned at the collar, and he carried himself with the kind of casual arrogance that seemed to thrive in a place like this.

"Mind if I join you?" he asked, his voice smooth as he gestured to the empty seat across from me.

I shrugged, too relaxed—or maybe too tipsy—to argue. "Sure, but I'm not much for good company. I have a habit of attracting the wrong kind."

He slid into the booth, setting his drink on the table. "Or maybe the wrong kind are attracted to you, sweet, innocent enough, gorgeous ," he said, his tone light, his eyes scanning my face.

"I'm the magnet then, huh?" I replied, raising my glass with a wry smile. "Here's to attraction—the magnetic kind."

For a while, the conversation was pleasant enough. He asked where I was from, what brought me here, and I gave him vague answers, the kind that didn't invite too much prying. He laughed at my sarcasm, leaning in closer with each passing minute, the space between us shrinking.

The alcohol made it easier to talk, easier to smile, easier to forget the sinking feeling that always lingered at the edge of my thoughts. I felt a flicker of something I hadn't felt in a long time—lightness, freedom.

But then his hand brushed against mine, lingering for just a moment too long.

I tensed, the haze in my head clearing slightly as he leaned closer, his voice dropping into something softer, more intimate.

"You really are gorgeous, you know that, right?" he murmured, his breath warm against my cheek.

I shifted back instinctively, the smile slipping from my face. "Thanks," I said, my tone flat now, the warning clear in my voice.

He didn't seem to notice—or care. Before I could react, he leaned in, his lips aiming for mine.

I turned my head just in time, his kiss landing awkwardly near my temple. "Hey," I said sharply, my voice louder than I intended.

"Come on," he said, his hand moving to rest on my arm. "I thought we were having a good time."

Before I could respond, another voice cut through the air, low and commanding.

"She said no."

The man froze, his hand still on my arm as someone grabbed his wrist. The grip wasn't violent, but it was firm—unyielding.

I looked up, my heart skipping as my gaze locked onto Cassian.

He stood there, his sharp gray eyes a strange concoction of disarmingly cold and furious flames, a flicker of something dangerous dancing behind them. His fingers tightened just enough to make the man wince, forcing him to stand.

"Let go," the man hissed, his confidence crumbling under Cassian's steady gaze.

Cassian leaned in, his voice calm but laced with a quiet fury that sent a shiver down my spine. "You don't want to make me repeat myself. Fuck off."

The man hesitated, glancing between Cassian and me, before yanking his wrist free and stumbling away, muttering curses under his breath.

The booth felt impossibly small as Cassian turned to me, his presence filling the space. My chest tightened as his eyes met mine, the storm in his gaze softening slightly.

"Rosalie," he said, his voice lower now, but no less intense.

The sound of my name on his lips sent a rush of heat through me, cutting through the alcohol in my system like a blade. For a moment, I couldn't speak, couldn't move.

I would never forget the way he looked at me in that moment—like I was something fragile and precious, something he'd break the world to protect.

The chaos of the room faded, the music and voices becoming distant, drowned out by the weight of his gaze.

I swallowed hard, my voice barely above a whisper. "What are you doing here?"

Cassian didn't answer immediately. Instead, he slid into the booth across from me, his expression unreadable as he rested his forearms on the table, leaning closer.

"I should be asking you the same thing," he said finally, his tone soft but edged with something I couldn't quite place.

And just like that, the fragile peace I'd found tonight shattered, leaving me alone with the one person I'd been running from—and the emotions I could no longer ignore.

CHAPTER FOUR

The drink in my hand swirled lazily as I tilted the glass, watching the amber liquid catch the dim light. My vision blurred slightly, the room shimmering at the edges in a way that felt both intoxicating and precarious. The whiskey had wrapped me in a languid warmth, dulling the sharp corners of my thoughts. For the first time in weeks, the chasm between who I had been and who I had become didn't seem so suffocating.

Cassian's presence shattered that fragile balance.

He sat across from me, the space between us feeling both infinite and far too close. His sharp gray eyes followed my every move, filled with an ineffable mixture of frustration and concern. I wasn't sure which one irritated me more.

"Rosalie," he said, his voice low but firm, cutting through the haze that had settled over me. "You've had enough."

I scoffed, lifting the glass to my lips and taking another sip, savoring the burn that chased away his words. "You don't have any control over me anymore, Cassian. I'll drink until I have forgotten. And," I mumbled, "since when do you get to waltz in here, barking orders?" The words slurred just slightly at the edges, but they still hit their mark.

His jaw tightened, and he leaned forward, the light catching on the hard lines of his face. "Since you decided to make a spectacle of yourself in a place like this."

I laughed, the sound hollow and tinged with defiance. "A spectacle? Please." I waved my hand toward the room, gesturing at the clusters of people lost in their own amorous little dramas. "I'm not the one causing a scene, Cassian. You are."

The waiter appeared at my side, his polite smile faltering as his eyes darted nervously between us. "Another whiskey sour," I said, placing my glass on the table with a deliberate clink.

Before the waiter could respond, Cassian's voice cut through like a blade. "She's done for the night."

The waiter hesitated, his gaze flicking to Cassian and then to me. My chest tightened with a sudden, fiery compulsion to push back. "No," I said sharply, my tone daring him to disobey. "I'm not. Bring another."

Cassian leaned back in his chair, the movement deceptively casual. He tilted his head, his voice a dangerous murmur. "I don't think you understand. I said she's done."

The man's face paled, and he took an awkward step back, nodding quickly. "Of course, sir."

"Don't you dare!" I snapped, pushing myself upright, the room tilting slightly with the movement. "I'm not some fragile little doll you can control, Cassian. I'm a grown woman, and if I want another drink, I'll have one."

Cassian's gaze locked onto mine, the intensity in his eyes sending a frisson down my spine. "You're not thinking clearly," he said, his tone calm but unyielding. "I'm not going to let you drown yourself in bad decisions just to spite me."

My fists clenched, and I glared at him, anger bubbling up in a volatile mix of rebellion and hurt. "You don't get to decide what's best for me. Not anymore." My voice fell quieter, as if there was a part of myself that hated admitting, "I'm not your petal anymore—or your Queen."

His lips pressed into a thin line, and for a moment, I thought he might argue. Instead, he turned his attention back to the waiter, who lingered uncertainly nearby. "If you bring her another drink," Cassian said softly, his voice like velvet wrapped around steel, "You'll answer to me, and then Sebastian—who will no doubt hesitate to fire you after I explain that his waiters are plying women with alcohol beyond their measure."

The waiter nodded quickly and retreated, disappearing into the crowd.

My head buzzed with anger, the edges of my emotions fraying under the weight of the whiskey and Cassian's unrelenting control. "You can't keep doing this," I said, my voice cracking as I met his gaze. "You can't keep showing up and thinking you can fix me."

His expression softened, just barely, the frustration in his eyes giving way to something quieter, something almost tender. "I'm not trying to fix you, Rosalie. I'm trying to stop you from breaking any more than you already have."

The words hit me harder than I wanted to admit, piercing through the haze and the anger. For a moment, the room fell away, and it was just the two of us—Cassian, steady and unyielding, and me, teetering on the edge of something I couldn't name.

But I wasn't ready to face it. Not yet.

I grabbed my glass, draining the last of the whiskey in a single, defiant gulp. "Well, congratulations," I said bitterly, slamming the empty glass onto the table. "You've officially ruined my night."

His lips twitched, almost like he wanted to smile, but the weight in his eyes didn't budge. "If that's what it takes to keep you safe, I'll ruin every night you have."

I looked away, the knot in my chest tightening as his words settled over me. The warmth from the whiskey was gone, replaced by a cold, sinking feeling that I couldn't quite shake.

Before the silence could stretch too long, a figure appeared at the edge of the table. The man was sharply dressed, his blazer fitted perfectly over a dark button-up, and his expression was calm, almost too calm, as though nothing in the world could rattle him. There was a quiet allure to his presence, the kind that immediately demanded attention.

"Mr. Moreau," he said, his tone polite but firm. "Mr.

Salvatori would like to see you."

Cassian didn't look up right away, his attention still fixed on me as though he hadn't even registered the interruption. "Now isn't a good time," he replied coolly, his voice steady and controlled.

The man didn't flinch. If anything, his stance stiffened slightly, as though he'd anticipated Cassian's resistance. "Mr. Salvatori was very clear," he said. "It's urgent."

At that, Cassian finally turned his gaze toward the man, his eyes narrowing just slightly. The weight of his stare was palpable, a quiet dominance radiating off him that made the air feel heavier. "And I said, now isn't a good time," he repeated, his tone dripping with an almost dangerous calm, "Sabastian can wait until I've ensured she's getting home safely."

The man hesitated, his composure faltering for just a fraction of a second. "He insisted, sir," he said carefully. "Perhaps you could bring your... companion with. You know he wouldn't ask if it wasn't imperative."

Cassian's jaw tightened, and he turned back to me, his expression unreadable. For a moment, I thought he might refuse outright, but then he let out a slow, controlled breath. "Fine," he said, standing and gesturing for me to follow. "But this better be fucken important."

The man led us through the crowd, weaving effortlessly between the clusters of people as though he were immune to the chaos around him. Cassian stayed close, his hand brushing against the small of my back more than once as we moved, his touch a reminder of his protective instincts— or maybe just his need to control the situation.

Despite myself, I managed to snag another drink from a passing waiter, my fingers closing around the chilled glass before Cassian could stop me. He shot me a look, one that carried a resonance of exasperation and warning, but he didn't say anything. Not yet.

We stopped in front of a door at the far end of the club, its sleek black surface unmarked and imposing. The man knocked once before opening it, gesturing for us to enter.

The room beyond was a stark contrast to the main floor.

It was spacious and clean, the kind of space that spoke of deliberate luxury. The walls were lined with dark, ebony wood paneling, and a large desk sat at the far end of the room, flanked by shelves filled with leather-bound books and small, curated pieces of art. A low leather couch and a matching armchair were positioned near a sleek glass coffee table, completing the intimate yet imposing atmosphere.

Cassian stepped in first, his shoulders tense, his gaze sweeping the room with a practiced precision that spoke to years of experience in places like this. I followed, the drink in my hand already halfway gone as I sank onto the couch with a sigh, the soft leather cool against my skin.

"You could at least try not to antagonize me," Cassian said quietly, his voice low as he glanced at the glass in my hand.

I raised an eyebrow, tilting the glass slightly. "Antagonizing you seems to be the only fun I've had tonight."

His lips twitched, but whatever response he had was cut short as the door closed behind us, leaving us alone in the office. Cassian's attention shifted back to the room, his posture taut and unyielding as he waited for whatever Mr. Salvatori had deemed so important.

For my part, I leaned back against the couch, the alcohol settling into my system like a warm, languid wave. The room smelled faintly of leather and something faintly floral, but not in the overwhelming way the main floor had. Here, everything was deliberate, curated—a reflection of whoever owned this space.

I glanced at Cassian, noting the sharp lines of his face, the tension in his jaw as he stood by the desk, his eyes scanning the room like a predator waiting for a threat to emerge. There was something magnetic about him, something that made it impossible to look away, even when I wanted to.

The drink in my hand was nearly empty again, and I let my head fall back against the couch, a faint smile tugging at my lips. For all his control, for all his efforts to keep me in line, Cassian hadn't quite succeeded tonight, and I was enjoying it.

The door swung open with a quiet click, and Sebastian Salvatori stepped into the room, his presence as commanding as the name suggested. He was tall, with an elegant frame wrapped in a tailored charcoal suit that hinted at old money and effortless power. His dark hair was slicked back, and his olive-toned skin carried the faint sheen of someone who belonged under the glow of dim lights and whispered conversations.

"Cassian," Sebastian said, his voice smooth and resonant, the kind of voice that carried authority without the need to shout. His sharp eyes—almost as dark as his impeccably polished shoes—landed briefly on me before returning to Cassian. A flicker of amusement crossed his face. "I see you've brought company. Unexpected, but not unwelcome."

"Sebastian," Cassian greeted him curtly, his voice steady, but the tension in his posture didn't ease. "You said it was urgent."

"It is." Sebastian crossed the room, unbuttoning his suit jacket and easing into the armchair opposite the couch. His movements were painstakingly deliberate, as though time bent to accommodate him. He leaned back, his fingers steepled in front of him as he spoke. "I have a problem. A big one."

Cassian stayed by the desk, his stance controlled, his jaw tightening further. "Go on."

Sebastian's gaze flicked to me again, as if deciding how much to say in front of an outsider. Whatever conclusion he came to, it didn't deter him. "I've got a drug problem in the club," he said bluntly, his voice low but laced with frustration. "Someone's been sneaking product into my floors. It's laced with something new—some designer blend. I've had three overdoses this month. Two more tonight alone."

I froze, the warmth of the drink in my veins turning cold.

Sebastian's fingers tapped rhythmically against the armrest, a cadence of annoyance. "If I don't get this under control, the city will shut me down. And you know as well as I do, Cassian, that's not just a business problem. That's a spotlight on everyone tied to me."

Cassian's brow furrowed, and he glanced at the floor for a moment, as if calculating. Then his gaze snapped back to Sebastian. "You've tightened security?"

"As much as I can without scaring off the clientele," Sebastian replied, his voice dripping with irritation. "But whoever's doing this is slipping through the cracks. And now, I've got the health department sniffing around. If I can't stop this, it's only a matter of time before the cops start asking questions."

Sebastian leaned forward, the subtle shift in his posture making the air in the room feel heavier. "Which brings me to my next question. Is your cop still on the payroll? I forget his name..."

Cassian's expression darkened, and I noticed the slight twitch of his fingers where they rested against his arm. "Markson... and he is," Cassian said finally, his voice edged with caution. "But you know his reach has limits. He's not going to cover for negligence."

Sebastian let out a soft, sardonic laugh. "It's not negligence. It's sabotage. Someone's testing me, Cassian. They want to see how far they can push before I break."

Cassian's eyes narrowed, his jaw tightening as he processed the information. "Have you made any enemies recently?"

Sebastian's mouth curved into a wry smile, though it didn't reach his eyes. "Have you met me? Making enemies is practically my hobby."

Despite the tension, a faint laugh bubbled up in my chest, and I brought my drink to my lips, unable to help myself, but hesitated to take another sip, before setting the glass down. Sebastian's sharp gaze turned to me, a faint flicker of curiosity in his expression.

"And who's your charming companion?" he asked, his voice smoother now, as though testing my reaction.

Before I could respond, Cassian stepped in, his voice steady but carrying an undertone of authority. "This is

Rosalie, she's my…" Now it was Cassian's turn to hesitate. I wanted him to finish that sentence so badly, to say exactly what I was to him, because deep down, in some twisted, fucked up way, I wasn't ready to let him go. "…my colleague. She runs one of my shops, Ivy & Bloom."

The way he said *my* shop, it was like a dagger to the gut. *His* shop.

It was my fucken shop, my hard work and dream—not his. Cassian noticed the shift in my demeanor, and gave me a soft, apologetic gaze, but it was nothing in comparison to the anger I felt rising.

"Rosalie, this is Sebastian Salvatori—we go way back."

Sebastian raised an eyebrow, a small, beguiling smile playing at his lips. "Clearly, she's part of something more. But pleasure to meet you." He gave a brief nod of acknowledgement from behind his desk, before turning his attention back to Cassian. "I trust you'll keep this confidential, and discreet."

Cassian didn't respond, his focus locked on Sebastian. "I'll make some calls," he said, his voice low and deliberate. "But if this goes deeper than your floors, we're going to have a bigger problem."

Sebastian leaned back in his chair, his fingers resuming their rhythmic tapping. "You let me worry about that. Just give me a name."

The room fell into a tense silence, the weight of Sebastian's words lingering. My head swam slightly, the effects of the whiskey pulling me into a soft haze, but I couldn't ignore the gravity of what was unfolding around me.

Cassian finally pushed away from the desk, his movements deliberate as he crossed to where I sat. He didn't say a word, but the look in his eyes—the mix of frustration, protection, and something unspoken—sent a shiver through me.

My chest tightened, and the room felt smaller, the tension suffocating me. The edges of my vision blurred as the effects of the whiskey mingled with the weight of Cassian's gaze. It was too much—Sebastian's cold amusement, Cassian's protective dominance, and the realization that I'd let myself become tangled in something far more dangerous than I could handle.

"I think I'm going to be sick," I mumbled, barely loud enough for anyone to hear.

CHAPTER FIVE

I pushed off the couch, wobbling slightly as I stood. Cassian's hand darted toward me, his reflexes sharp as ever, but I stepped out of his reach before he could steady me. I didn't need his help—not now, not ever. At least that's what I told myself as I stumbled toward the door, ignoring the soft buzz of their voices behind me.

The hallway outside the office was dim, the bass-heavy music from the main floor vibrating subtly through the walls. My stomach churned as I clutched the cool metal handle of the door leading back into the club, sucking in a breath of the airily floral-scented oxygen.

I had barely made it to the bar before the room tilted dangerously, and I grabbed the edge of the counter to steady myself. A concerned bartender glanced in my direction, but I waved him off with a weak shake of my head. My pride demanded I keep moving, even if my body begged for stillness.

I ducked into the nearest restroom, the quiet hum of the club muffled by the heavy door. The cold water from the sink splashed onto my face, shocking my senses enough to slow the spinning in my head. I gripped the edge of the counter, staring at my reflection in the mirror. My mascara had smudged, and my eyes were glassy, the weight of the night etched into every line of my face.

What the hell was I doing?

The question echoed in my mind as I leaned forward, letting the water drip from my chin. My anger at Cassian still simmered, but it was dulled now by exhaustion and the faint sting of humiliation. I'd come here to forget—to escape—but I'd only found myself deeper in his orbit, drowning in a world that was as alluring as it was suffocating.

A knock at the door startled me, and before I could respond, it creaked open slightly. Cassian's voice slipped through the gap, low and deliberate. "Rosalie, are you okay?"

"Fine," I snapped, the word sharper than I intended. I didn't want him to see me like this—vulnerable, unraveling, pathetic.

I barely made it to the toilet before my stomach betrayed me, unraveling in violent, heaving spasms. My hands clung weakly to the edges of the cold porcelain as my body purged every drop of whiskey I had so defiantly consumed. The sour taste burned my throat, and my head spun, the room tilting precariously with each ragged breath.

A warm, steady hand swept my hair away from my face, and I froze, my shame curling tightly around me. I didn't need to look to know it was Cassian—his presence was unmistakable, grounding even in the chaos. He crouched beside me, his movements measured, holding my hair back as I retched again.

"Breathe, Rosalie," he said quietly, his voice low and steady. "Just breathe."

I wanted to shove him away, to tell him to leave me alone, but I couldn't muster the strength. My pride was in tatters, mingling with the cold sweat that slicked my skin. The room felt oppressive, the dim light too harsh, the air too thin. My fingers trembled against the floor, and my head dipped forward as a wave of lightheadedness washed over me.

"I think..." I whispered, my voice barely audible, "I'm going to faint."

Cassian moved with precision, his arm slipping around

my waist as he pulled me upright. "You're not fainting," he said firmly, his tone leaving no room for argument. "Not here."

The next few moments were a blur as he guided me out of the restroom, his strength an unyielding anchor against my faltering steps. The cacophony of the bar hit me like a wall—music, laughter, and the faint scent of alcohol mingling with faint smell of vomit.

I blinked against the onslaught, my body leaning heavily against Cassian as he led me to a quiet corner at the bar.

"Sit," he ordered, his voice curt but not unkind.

I sank onto the stool, my head resting against my hand as the room tilted around me. The cool glass of water that appeared before me felt like salvation, and I gripped it tightly, forcing myself to take small, tentative sips.

Cassian stood beside me, his presence a mix of dominance and control, his fingers flying furiously across his phone's screen. Whatever he was typing, it wasn't good. His jaw was tight, the tension radiating off him in waves. I could see the faint flicker of frustration in his eyes when he glanced at me, as though weighing whether to say something or let the silence stretch.

"What are you doing?" I croaked, my voice rough from the strain of the night.

"Making sure this doesn't happen again," he replied sharply, his eyes not leaving his phone. "Texting Sebastian to get more eyes on the floors. And sending someone to take you home."

"I don't need anyone to take me home," I mumbled, the defiance in my voice undercut by the weakness in my limbs.

Cassian set his phone down with a deliberate click, his gaze pinning me to the stool. "Yes, you do. And whether you're in no position to be alone right now."

The words hung in the air, heavy and undeniable. My hands clenched around the glass of water, the cool condensation dampening my palms. "Why do you care?" I whispered, the question slipping out before I could stop it.

Cassian's expression softened just slightly, his sharp features losing some of their edge. He leaned forward, his voice dropping low enough that only I could hear. "I never stopped caring, Rosalie. Even when you make it difficult."

My chest tightened, the vulnerability in his words colliding with my own swirling emotions. I didn't know how to respond—didn't know if I could. The exhaustion and shame tugged at me, pulling me deeper into the haze of the moment.

I looked away, focusing on the water in my hands. The ice clinked softly against the glass as I took another sip, willing myself to ignore the way his words settled in my chest like an indelible mark I couldn't erase.

Cassian returned to his phone, his fingers resuming their furious tapping. I could feel the storm building behind his controlled demeanor, the volatile mix of frustration and protectiveness simmering just beneath the surface.

And despite everything—despite the mess I'd made of the night, of myself—I couldn't deny the faint, almost ethereal comfort his presence brought, as though he existed just beyond the tangible chaos, steady and unyielding.

For better or worse, Cassian Moreau was always there. And no matter how much I fought it, part of me wasn't sure I wanted him to leave.

Cassian didn't speak right away, his sharp gray eyes scanning me with an intensity that made me want to shrink under his gaze. I hated how easily he could see through me, past the defiance and the sarcasm, straight to the cracks I'd worked so hard to hide. His expression softened just slightly, his usual impassivity giving way to something quieter, something that felt almost... ardent.

"You're thinner," he said finally, his voice low but firm, cutting through the din of the bar. "You haven't been eating, have you?"

I looked away, my fingers tightening around the glass of water. "Not much of an appetite these days, but that's not your concern."

"It is when you're hurting yourself," he replied without hesitation. "You've been avoiding me, avoiding the shop, and now this—" He gestured toward me, his hand lingering in the air as if the words he wanted to say were just out of reach. "This destructive behavior. What the hell are you trying to prove?"

His words hit harder than they should have, peeling back layers I wasn't ready to confront. My chest tightened, and the lump in my throat grew unbearable as I stared into the glass, the ice melting into shapeless fragments. "I'm not trying to prove anything," I muttered, my voice trembling. "I'm just trying to forget."

"Forget what?" His voice was softer now, but it carried an ineffable weight, as though he already knew the answer but needed to hear me say it.

The dam I'd carefully constructed since that day finally cracked. The words tumbled out before I could stop them, unfiltered and raw. "Everything, Cassian. The shop, my father, Damien—him dying right in front of me. And you—using my shop, manipulating everything. I can't—I can't keep pretending like any of it makes sense, because it doesn't."

I sucked in a ragged breath, the admission cutting deeper than I expected. "I gave everything to Ivy & Bloom. It was all I had left of her. And you—you turned it into something I don't even recognize anymore. Something I can't even walk into without feeling like I've lost part of myself."

Cassian remained silent, his face unreadable as I continued, my voice cracking under the weight of my emotions. "And then there's you—showing up, pulling me back into your orbit like I don't have a choice. Like I'm just supposed to forgive you for all of it. But I can't, Cassian. I can't forgive you, and I can't forgive myself for letting it get this far."

My vision blurred, the tears threatening to spill over as the full breadth of everything I'd suppressed came crashing down. My shoulders shook as I finally let it all out, the water in my glass sloshing as my grip faltered.

Cassian reached across the small space between us, his hand covering mine. His touch was warm, grounding, but he didn't say a word. He just held my hand there, steady, as though he understood that words weren't what I needed.

"You've been suppressing these feelings, this *conflict* for so long," he said quietly after a moment, his voice a deep resonance that seemed to cut through the chaos in my head. "And it's killing you, Rosalie."

I closed my eyes, the tears slipping down my cheeks despite my best efforts to keep them at bay. "I don't know what else to do," I whispered, the confession barely audible.

He pushed the glass of water closer to me, his hand still covering mine. "Start with this," he said simply. "Drink the water. Take a breath. And then let yourself feel it all, instead of burying it. Get it off your chest, use me as a punching bag if you need to."

I hesitated, but the earnestness in his gaze was impossible to ignore. Slowly, I lifted the glass and took a small sip, the cool liquid soothing my dry throat. It wasn't much, but it was something.

Cassian didn't pull away, didn't press me for more. He just stayed there, watching me with an intensity that was as unsettling as it was comforting. For once, he wasn't trying to control me or fix me. He was just… there.

"You think I don't feel the weight of what I've done?" he said after a long silence, his voice almost a whisper. "I know I've hurt you. I know I've made mistakes. But I'm not ready to walk away from you; I'm incapable to existing without you, Rosalie. And you're not alone—not unless you choose to be."

The sincerity in his words settled over me like a balm, soothing the raw edges of my emotions. I didn't know if I could forgive him, or myself, but in that moment, it didn't matter. For the first time in weeks, I didn't feel entirely untethered.

Cassian's words hung in the air, heavy with a sincerity that felt impossible to escape. My mind buzzed, a haze of alcohol and emotion twisting into something I couldn't untangle. The water in my hand trembled as I brought it to my lips again, the cold liquid barely placating me against the storm brewing inside.

"You're too intoxicated to be out here alone," Cassian said softly, his voice firm but devoid of anger. It was calm in a way that only made the weight of his concern feel more profound. "You don't see the danger you've put yourself in."

A sardonic laugh escaped me, bitter and sharp. "Danger is nothing new to me, Cassian. You made sure of that."

His expression darkened, though he didn't rise to my provocation. "This isn't about me and the world I've introduced you to. It's about you—your refusal to take care of yourself, to face what's happening instead of running from it."

I glared at him, the heat of frustration bubbling beneath my skin. "I'm not running," I muttered, though the words sounded hollow even to me. My grip on the bar tightened as a wave of dizziness overtook me, the room seeming to ripple like water disturbed by a stone.

"Then what do you call this?" he asked, gesturing to me with a hand that hovered between exasperation and restraint. "Rosalie, look at yourself. This isn't you."

The words stung, more than I cared to admit. "I haven't been the same Rosalie since the day you walked into my shop," I bit back, my voice faltering. "You don't know me. Not anymore."

His gaze softened, though his intensity didn't waver. "I know enough," he said quietly. "I know you're hurting. And I know you can't keep doing this to yourself."

I wanted to argue, to throw his words back at him, but the room tilted again, and my balance faltered. My knees buckled beneath me, and I braced for the inevitable impact of the floor.

But Cassian was there, swift and unrelenting, catching me before I could fall. His arms enveloped me, steadying me with an ease that felt both infuriating and reassuring.

"Rosalie," he said, his voice quieter now, as though afraid I might shatter if he spoke too loudly. "Breathe, keep your eyes on me; I've got you."

I tried to look up at him, but my body felt heavy, my movements sluggish. My head lolled against his chest, and for a moment, I could hear the steady beat of his heart—a rhythm that was strangely soothing amidst my turmoil.

"Stay with me," he murmured, his tone gentle but

insistent. His eyes, when I finally managed to meet them, were penetrating, like they were seeing parts of me even I didn't understand.

His gaze held mine, the air between us thick with something unspoken. It felt infinite, this moment, stretching out in a way that made my chest ache.

But the dizziness was too much, pulling me under like a tide. My lips parted to say something—to apologize, maybe, or to fight him—but the words didn't come.

The last thing I saw was the concern etched across his face, vivid and undeniable, before the darkness claimed me completely.

CHAPTER SIX

When I opened my eyes, it took a moment for the blurry edges of my vision to sharpen. The familiar outline of my bedroom came into focus, and for a fleeting second, I thought I'd dreamed the entire night—the whiskey, the bar, Cassian. But the pounding in my skull and the queasy churn in my stomach were undeniable reminders that it had all been real.

Groaning softly, I shifted beneath the blankets. The cool sheets clung to my skin, and that's when I noticed: I wasn't wearing my clothes from the night before. My heart stuttered, and I glanced down. One of my oversized T-shirts and a pair of clean underwear. Nothing scandalous, but enough to send a flicker of unease through me.

Cassian.

Of course, it had to be him. No one else would've taken it upon themselves to undress me and tuck me into bed. I pressed my palms to my face, embarrassment mingling with the dull ache of my hangover.

Dragging myself upright was a herculean effort. My body protested every movement, my head throbbing in rhythm with my pulse. I shuffled out of the bedroom, each step feeling like an eternity, and made my way to the kitchen. The only thought in my mind was coffee—something strong enough to scrape away the remnants of last night.

When I reached the counter, my fingers instinctively reached for the machine, but I froze. The smell of freshly brewed coffee wafted through the air, warm and inviting. The pot was full, the dark liquid steaming faintly. My brows knitted together in confusion. I hadn't set it.

Grateful but too exhausted to question it, I grabbed a mug and poured myself a cup. The first sip burned my tongue slightly, but the bitterness was comforting, soothing the chaos in my head. I turned around, ready to lean against the counter and let the caffeine work its magic.

And that's when I saw him.

Cassian stood in the doorway, his presence as commanding as ever, his arms crossed over his chest. His gaze was steady, unreadable, but there was a quiet intensity behind it that sent a shiver down my spine. I startled, the mug slipping from my hands. Hot coffee splashed across the counter, the sharp sound of the ceramic striking the surface echoing in the silence.

"Dammit," I muttered, grabbing for a dishtowel to mop up the mess. My heart raced, not from the spill but from the way his sudden presence had caught me off guard. "What the hell are you doing here?"

Cassian didn't move, his stance as immovable as stone. "Making sure you're still breathing," he said simply, his voice low and deliberate.

I couldn't help the sarcastic laugh that bubbled up. "Congratulations, I'm alive. You can leave now."

He didn't respond immediately, his eyes watching me with that penetrating gaze that always seemed to strip away my defenses. Finally, he pushed off the doorway and stepped closer, his movements slow, measured.

"You scared me last night," he said, his tone softer now but still carrying a weight I couldn't ignore. "You're not taking care of yourself, Rosalie. Reckless, irresponsible, ignorant of the dangers around you. You think I'm just going to walk away and let that happen?"

I threw the damp dishtowel onto the counter and turned to face him fully. "What, so now you're my savior? My

41

guardian angel?" My voice was sharper than I intended, but the combination of my pounding headache and his overbearing concern had my patience running thin.

"No," he said calmly, his eyes never leaving mine. "I've never had much of a savior complex, but someone has to care, even if you don't."

His works struck a cord within me, but I refused to let him see it. "I didn't ask for your help, Cassian. I didn't ask for any of this."

He leaned forward slightly, his gaze locking onto mine with an intensity that made it impossible to look away. "No, you didn't. But that doesn't mean you don't need it."

I opened my mouth to retort, but the words caught in my throat. His nearness, the quiet determination in his voice, the way his eyes softened just enough to reveal a flicker of vulnerability—it was all too much. The tension between us was a tangible thing, crackling in the air like a live wire.

For a moment, neither of us spoke. The only sound was the faint drip of coffee onto the counter, forgotten in the charged silence. My chest ached with the weight of everything I wanted to say but couldn't. I hated how easily he got under my skin, how his presence seemed to pull at the threads of my carefully constructed walls.

"I can take care of myself," I said finally, my voice barely above a whisper.

Cassian's lips pressed into a thin line, but he didn't argue. Instead, he reached past me for another dishtowel, his movements deliberate as he wiped up the remaining coffee. His proximity sent a frisson of warmth through me, and I hated myself for the way my breath hitched when his hand brushed against mine.

"I disagree, and you and I both know it. You're a disaster, a beautiful disaster at that, but a mess nonetheless. You're stubborn," he murmured, his voice carrying a faint edge of amusement. "I'll give you that."

"And you're insufferable," I shot back, though there was no real bite in my words.

I stared at him, my pulse hammering in my ears as the meaning behind his words settled over me. Cassian didn't look away, his sharp gaze holding mine, unreadable yet laced with something dangerous, something tantalizing. His calm demeanor was unnerving, a controlled intensity that felt as much a threat as it did a promise.

He began to move toward me, his steps slow and deliberate. My breath caught in my throat, the air between us growing heavier with each second. The way he carried himself—the balance of power and restraint—made my stomach twist in an unfamiliar, almost dizzying way. He wasn't just walking; he was stalking, and I suddenly felt like prey.

When he reached me, he didn't say a word. His hand came up, brushing softly against my cheek as he tucked a stray strand of hair behind my ear. The contact sent a tremor through me, my body betraying me as heat spread across my skin. His touch was benign, almost gentle, but the look in his eyes told me there was nothing innocent about his intentions.

"Do you have any idea," he murmured, his voice barely more than a whisper, "what I would have done to you last night if you weren't in this state?"

My breath hitched, and my fingers gripped the edge of the counter behind me for balance. The low rasp of his voice was hypnotic, a mix of menace and allure that sent shivers down my spine. I should have pushed him away, should have told him to stop, but the words caught in my throat, tangled with the sudden surge of desire igniting deep within me.

He leaned in closer, his lips brushing against my ear, his breath warm against my skin. "If you'd been sober," he continued, his tone velvet-soft but unmistakably pugnacious, "I would've stripped you out of that shirt—slowly. Made you beg for every touch, every kiss, every breath."

My heart pounded, my body reacting instinctively to the vivid images his words conjured. I hated the way my knees weakened, the way my pulse quickened, the way my body leaned into him without my permission.

"But you weren't," he said, his tone shifting to something

quieter, almost reflective. "And I'm not that type of person. I know you see me as a monster, Rosalie, but even beasts know when the wait it worth it."

The heat pooling in my stomach was unbearable, and I bit my lip to keep from making a sound. His proximity, his voice, the intensity of his gaze—it was all too much. I felt like I was on the edge of something, teetering dangerously close to falling.

He pulled back slightly, just enough to meet my gaze, his hand still lingering near my face. His thumb brushed against my cheek, featherlight but searing. "But when you do come back to me," he added, his voice dipping even lower, "you won't walk away until I've had all of you."

The silence that followed was deafening, thick with tension and charged with an energy that made the air feel electric. My body betrayed me completely, leaning toward him as though it had a mind of its own. I wanted to respond, to say something clever or cutting, but my voice was gone, stolen by the chaos he had unleashed within me.

Cassian's lips quirked into the faintest smirk, as though he knew exactly what he was doing to me. Then he stepped back, his movements deliberate, the space between us suddenly unbearable.

"Now, go shower, Rosalie. You mess of alcohol and vomit," he said, his tone back to its commanding cadence.

Cassian's words stung, but I couldn't exactly argue. The acrid scent clinging to my skin was undeniable, and the sticky remnants of sweat and booze only amplified the feeling of disgust radiating from every pore. Without another word, I turned on my heel and stalked to the bathroom, slamming the door behind me.

The hot water cascaded over me like absolution, scalding away the shame and filth of the night before. I scrubbed at my skin with a fervor that bordered on desperate, the soap lathering into a fragrant foam that was a welcome contrast to the sourness lingering in my memory. As the steam enveloped me, I let my thoughts drift to Cassian's words—his promises, his threats, the heat that lingered in his voice. My hands paused mid-scrub, and I leaned against the tiled wall, exhaling shakily.

Why did he always manage to crawl under my skin? No matter how much I pushed him away, no matter how fiercely I tried to maintain my independence, Cassian Moreau had a way of making me feel tethered. And for reasons I couldn't fully reconcile, part of me didn't hate it.

After what felt like an eternity, I stepped out of the shower, wrapping myself in a towel. My head still throbbed faintly, but the fog from earlier had lifted enough for me to function. When I reentered the living room, the sight that greeted me made me pause.

Cassian was sitting at the dining table, freshly dressed in a crisp black shirt and tailored slacks, his earlier disheveled appearance replaced with his usual air of effortless control. A faint whiff of cologne reached me— clean, masculine, and undoubtedly him. Marcus must have dropped off a change of clothes, though I hadn't heard him come in.

"You clean up well," I muttered, tying my towel tighter around me.

"So do you," he replied, his gaze flicking over me with a faint smirk before gesturing toward the table. "Sit."

My stomach growled at the sight of the spread before me: Belgian waffles, eggs, toast, fresh fruit, and a steaming cup of coffee. The rich aroma was palatable, and despite my hangover, I couldn't deny how inviting it looked. Cassian leaned back in his chair, his fingers drumming lightly against the tabletop as he watched me.

"I'm not hungry," I said, even as my traitorous stomach growled again.

His expression hardened slightly, the commanding edge returning to his tone. "You're eating, Rosalie. You need it after last night. And you'd do good to gain back a few pounds."

I wanted to argue, to push back against his imperious demeanor, but the thought of food was too tempting. Reluctantly, I slid into the chair opposite him and picked up a piece of toast, nibbling on the corner.

"Happy?" I asked dryly.

"Not yet," he said, his voice cool but tinged with a faint amusement. "But I'll get there once you've finished your plate."

He sipped his coffee, his movements calm and precise, but his gaze never left me. It was unnerving, as though he were assessing me, trying to extricate something I wasn't ready to reveal.

After a moment, he leaned forward slightly, his voice dropping into something softer but no less resolute. "I have to take care of some things. Business with Sebastian."

I didn't bother to ask what "business" entailed. With Cassian, it could mean anything—nothing I wanted to be involved in. Instead, I focused on the plate in front of me, pretending the tension between us wasn't as thick as the steam rising from my coffee.

"I'll check in on you later," he continued, his tone gentler now. "Stay here. Rest. Eat. And don't do anything reckless."

My eyes snapped up to meet his, a flare of irritation sparking. "What, you think I'm going to burn the place down while you're gone?"

"Reckless," he repeated, ignoring my sarcasm. "And no, I don't think you'll burn it down. But I do think you're stubborn enough to try to prove me wrong about something. Just... don't."

He stood, his movements fluid as he adjusted the cuffs of his shirt. For a moment, he hesitated, as though he wanted to say more, but then he turned and headed for the door.

"Cassian," I called out impulsively, my voice softer than I meant it to be, giving way to the insecurities I felt as he reached the door.

He stopped, his hand resting on the doorknob, but he didn't look back. "What is it?"

I hesitated, my thoughts a jumble of conflicting emotions. "Thank you," I said finally, the words feeling both necessary and insufficient.

He nodded once, a slight tilt of his head, before opening the door and stepping out, leaving me alone with the remnants of breakfast and the echoes of everything unsaid.

CHAPTER SEVEN

The late afternoon light streamed through the dusty blinds, casting soft, fractured beams across the living room. I sat on the edge of the couch, a mug of lukewarm coffee in my hands, staring at the state of my apartment. It wasn't as though I hadn't noticed before—the dishes piling up in the sink, the laundry draped over the back of a chair, the faint layer of dust coating every flat surface. But today, for some reason, it all felt unbearable.

The apartment used to feel cozy, like an extension of myself. Now, it was a reflection of everything I'd been trying to avoid—the stagnation, the malaise, the growing weight of unresolved emotions I couldn't seem to escape. The chaos felt almost symbolic, a testament to the way my life had unraveled piece by piece since the day Cassian Moreau walked into Ivy & Bloom.

I set the mug down with a sigh, pushing myself to my feet. "Enough," I muttered under my breath, more to the walls than to myself. It was time to do something—anything—to reclaim even the smallest sense of control.

I started in the kitchen. The sink was full of plates and glasses, the remnants of hastily consumed meals that had left me feeling more desiccated than nourished. As the hot water ran over my hands, the sound of scrubbing plates became oddly soothing, a distraction from the ceaseless whirl of thoughts in my head.

By the time I moved to the living room, a small pile of trash bags had already accumulated by the door. I wiped down the surfaces, the once-dull wood gleaming under a light coating of polish. The air felt cleaner somehow, as though eradicating the dust and grime from my surroundings could purge the heaviness from my chest.

It wasn't until I started folding the laundry that I noticed my phone buzzing on the coffee table. I picked it up, the screen lighting up with a familiar name. Cassian.

He'd sent a text. And another. And another. The thread was a mix of check-ins and thinly veiled attempts to coax me into a response.

Cassian: Just checking in; how have you been?

Cassian: Have you been eating today?"

Cassian: The thought has cross my mind on more than one occasion, if you keep ignoring me, I may just have to send Sierra upstairs. I've tried to give you space, Rosalie— truly, but this silent treatment is insufferable.

I stared at the screen, my thumb hovering over the keyboard. My first instinct was to ignore him, like I'd done countless times over the past few weeks. But something about the messages—about the way his words carried a weight that felt almost... human—made me pause.

I'm fine, I typed. Then I deleted it.

My fingers hovered, the familiar ambivalence creeping back in. Finally, I settled on something else.

Rosalie: The apartment needed cleaning. Just finished.

It wasn't much, but it was enough.

The response came almost instantly.

Cassian: Good. I wasn't going to mention the chow mein stench when I was there, but I'm glad you have more energy to spare.

I stared at Cassian's reply, the corners of my lips twitching in a way that felt foreign. Was that... a joke? Coming from him? It shouldn't have softened me, but somehow, it did.

Rosalie: Careful, Moreau. You're starting to sound almost personal.

The response came quickly.

Cassian: I'll take that as progress.

Progress. The word lingered in my mind as I set my phone down and returned to folding the last of my laundry. I wasn't sure if it was progress or just exhaustion. Whatever it was, it felt strange—unnerving, even—but not entirely unwelcome.

The buzz of my phone startled me again.

Cassian: What else have you done today? Besides cleaning up the remnants of your hibernation, of course.

I hesitated, my fingers hovering over the screen. Sharing anything felt risky, like letting him into my thoughts was akin to leaving the door unlocked in a storm. But as much as I hated to admit it, I didn't want the conversation to end. Not yet.

Rosalie: Cleaned the kitchen. Took out the trash. Found the mug I thought I lost—it was under the couch.

Cassian: Under the couch? Impressive. Next, you'll tell me you found a family of raccoons living in your bathroom.

Rosalie: Funny. No raccoons. Just dust bunnies and a questionable sock.

Cassian: Progress indeed. I'll hold off on the exterminator.

I shook my head, an involuntary smile tugging at the corners of my lips. It felt... easy, like slipping into a rhythm we'd had before everything had unraveled. But then the lingering doubts crept back in, tightening my chest with the familiar sense of wariness.

Rosalie: I'm still angry, you know.

The pause this time was longer, as if he was choosing his words carefully.

Cassian: I know. And you have every right to be.

I swallowed hard, my throat suddenly dry. It was such a simple acknowledgment, but it carried more weight than I expected. For so long, I had built a fortress around my anger, using it to keep him at bay. Now, with just a few words, he was threatening to dismantle it brick by brick.

Rosalie: It's not just about the shop—and what you're using it for—Cassian. It's... everything. The way you keep things from me. The way you justify your actions. Even if you think it's for the right reasons, it scares me. I'm not sure I can trust you.

The words spilled out before I could second-guess them. My chest tightened as I hit send, half-expecting him to respond with defensiveness or dismissal. Instead, his reply was quiet, almost subdued.

Cassian: I can't change the past, Rosalie. But I can try to do better. I'm not perfect, but I'm not giving up on earning your trust.

I stared at the screen, the lump in my throat growing heavier. His words were earnest, maybe even cogent, and they stirred something inside me I wasn't sure I wanted to confront.

Rosalie: You're so sure this is worth it? Me, I mean?

Cassian: There's no doubt in my mind.

The simplicity of his response hit me harder than I wanted it to. For the first time in weeks, the ever-present knot in my chest loosened slightly, though I wasn't ready to admit that to him—or myself.

Rosalie: I need time.

Cassian: Not too much or I'll knock down your door under the guise of a wellness check.

I couldn't help the soft laugh that escaped me as I read his response. Typical Cassian—turning even the most serious of moments into something laced with his unrelenting confidence and mild threats. It was infuriating, but it was also comforting, in a way I didn't entirely hate. I had no doubt he would follow through on his promise.

Rosalie: You're exhausting. Now who is the reckless one?

Cassian: And yet, here we are, having a conversation like normal humans. What was that word... Progress, wouldn't you say?

I rolled my eyes, though I couldn't deny the faint smile tugging at my lips. He was trying, and I supposed that counted for something.

Cassian: On a more somber note, how are the nightmares?

My fingers froze over the keyboard. The question came out of nowhere, and yet, it shouldn't have surprised me. He had been there the night before, watching me fall apart, hearing the things I tried so desperately to suppress.

Rosalie: I... they're fine. It's fine.

The reply felt weak, a shadow of the truth I wasn't ready to share. But of course, he saw right through it.

Cassian: Fine? Rosalie, you were tossing and turning all night. Even drunk, you couldn't escape them. Do you really think I didn't notice?

My chest tightened, the weight of his words pressing down on me. I hadn't realized how much of the night he'd been witness to, how exposed I'd been in my vulnerability.

Cassian: It hurt to watch you like that. You looked so... haunted. How often do you have them now?

Rosalie: Often enough.

I hesitated before adding another line.

Rosalie: But I don't really want to talk about it.

Cassian: Fair enough. You don't have to talk about it with me, but you should talk to someone.

The tormented part of my soul wanted to laugh out loud—who could I talk to? Damien Moreau was murdered in front of my eyes, and Cassian's insider detective, Markson covered it up. For a lack of anything better to do, I'd scoured the newspapers the few days after, and there was no mention of the man's death. Cassian had ensured he remained buried this time.

A second respond came just as quickly.

Cassian: But you know I'd listen if you did, right?

Rosalie: Yeah, I know.

The honesty of my response startled me. I did know. And that knowledge scared me almost as much as the nightmares themselves.

Cassian: Good. Now let's lighten the mood. You still sulking, or have you started smiling again?

Rosalie: I don't sulk.

Cassian: You absolutely do. It's adorable, but also mildly concerning.

Rosalie: Mildly? That's the best you can do?

Cassian: Fine, extremely concerning. Happy now?

I let out a short laugh, shaking my head at his ridiculousness. The absurdity of it was disarming, and for a moment, I forgot about the heaviness that had been hanging over me.

Rosalie: Do you always wear people down until they do what you want? That's not healthy.

Cassian: But effective. Look at that—first laugh of the day? You're welcome.

Rosalie: Second, actually. But don't let it go to your head.

Cassian: Too late.

The levity in our exchange felt strange, like stepping into sunlight after weeks of shadow. My grip on the phone tightened as I stared at his reply, a part of me reluctant to let the conversation drift back into serious territory.

Rosalie: You think you're funny, don't you?

Cassian: Funny, charming, resourceful. The list goes on.

Rosalie: Resourceful, huh? That's one way to describe meddling.

Cassian: And charming?

Rosalie: Let's not push it.

His reply came instantly.

Cassian: Charming as hell. Admit it.

I sighed, the faintest smile tugging at my lips.

Rosalie: If I do, will you stop pestering me?

Cassian: Not a chance.

The familiar rhythm of our banter eased some of the tension that had knotted itself in my chest. For the first time in weeks, I didn't feel like I was fighting to keep my head above water. But as much as the lightness soothed me, it didn't erase the deeper wounds still lingering between us.

Rosalie: This has been nice, but it doesn't change anything. An unexpected distracting from cleaning, but I still need time, Cassian, and I'm not sure I will ever return to Ivy & Bloom.

It was the first time I mentioned it out loud, beyond the hidden barriers of my mind. I'm not even sure I had admitted it to my self until now, as painful as it was. I didn't want to watch my family's legacy be a lie, supported by the mafia's dirty money. It wasn't why my mother built the shop, and it wasn't why I had stayed there for so long.

Cassian: You don't mean that.

Rosalie: I might, I do.

Cassian: Whatever you say, Rosalie, I do know you—and you would never walk away from something so deeply tied to your heart. Ivy & Bloom is a place where you can be you, pouring your heart and soul into it. If you're ready to turn your back on that, then maybe I don't know you as well as I thought.

I stared at the screen, his words striking a chord I wasn't prepared for. I wanted to argue, to push back against his presumption, but the truth in his statement rooted me in place. Ivy & Bloom *was* my soul—or at least, it used to be.

But could I truly go back, knowing everything it had been turned into? The ache in my chest grew heavier, and I closed my eyes, leaning back against the couch.

I didn't have an answer. Not yet.

CHAPTER EIGHT

The following evening, the weight in my chest felt marginally lighter, though the same couldn't be said for my lingering uncertainty. As the sun dipped below the horizon, casting the city in hues of amber and slate, I made the decision to venture out again.

This time, I didn't sneak out the back. When I opened the front door, Marcus and Sierra were already waiting, their post unwavering. Marcus raised a single brow, his dark, calculating eyes sweeping over me, while Sierra offered a brief nod of acknowledgment.

"I'm going out," I said simply, brushing past them.

"Where to?" Marcus asked, falling into step behind me as I descended the stairs.

"An art gallery."

Sierra's lips quirked into a faint smile as she exchanged a glance with Marcus, but neither of them pressed further. It was enough to know they would follow me, shadow-like, no matter where I went.

At the curb, I flagged a taxi. Sierra lingered by the door until I was seated, exchanging a few words with the driver before stepping back. Their presence, while intrusive, no longer felt oppressive—more like an unavoidable fact of life.

The cab ride was quiet, the muted hum of traffic filling

the space as I watched the city blur past the window. My destination was an art gallery I'd seen advertised on a poster a few blocks away from Ivy & Bloom. I wasn't sure what had drawn me to it—maybe the novelty, or perhaps the need to surround myself with something beautiful and untainted.

When the taxi pulled to a stop in front of the gallery, I stepped out, my breath hitching slightly at the sight of the building. The sleek, modern facade was striking, its glass walls glowing softly with warm light from within.

Inside, the atmosphere was hushed, almost reverent, the low murmur of voices mingling with the faint strains of classical music. The gallery was expansive but not overwhelming, its white walls adorned with an eclectic mix of paintings and sculptures that seemed to draw me in with an almost magnetic allure.

I wandered slowly, my footsteps muffled against the polished floors. Each piece seemed to speak its own story, vibrant and intricate in ways I hadn't expected. Some works were abstract, their meaning elusive yet oddly compelling; others were so detailed, so vivid, that they felt like windows into other worlds.

I paused in front of a large oil painting, its bold strokes and rich colors evoking a tempestuous sea under a stormy sky. My chest tightened as I studied it, the chaos and beauty of the piece resonating with something deep within me. I didn't know much about art—practically nothing, really—but standing here, I realized how foolish it was to have avoided places like this for so long.

It was serene, almost meditative. For the first time in a while, my mind felt quieter, the constant storm of thoughts dissipating into something more manageable.

As I moved to the next piece, a small smile tugged at my lips. I was beginning to understand why people loved galleries, why they were willing to immerse themselves in these spaces that felt suspended from the rush of the outside world. It was as though every piece here offered a reprieve, a chance to pause and reflect.

The sound of soft footsteps behind me barely registered

at first. I was too absorbed in a sculpture before me—a marble rendering of two figures locked in a silent, intimate dance. But as I turned toward the next piece, I noticed them: Marcus and Sierra.

They lingered near the entrance, as unobtrusive as body guards could possibly be, their presence a quiet assurance I hadn't asked for but didn't entirely resent. I sighed and shook my head slightly before continuing deeper into the gallery, weaving through the maze of exhibits with a growing sense of ease.

It wasn't until I rounded a corner, entering a dimly lit alcove showcasing a series of abstract landscapes, that my sense of peace faltered. There he was.

Cassian stood near the far wall, his tall frame draped in his usual dark attire, hands in his pockets as though he'd merely stumbled into the gallery by accident. But I knew better. His presence was deliberate, calculated—just like everything else about him.

I stopped in my tracks, crossing my arms as his gaze met mine.

"You really need to stop doing that," I said, the words escaping in a mix of irritation and resignation.

He tilted his head, his lips curving into a faint, almost playful smirk. "Doing what?"

"Showing up uninvited," I replied, though the heat creeping into my cheeks betrayed my annoyance wasn't as absolute as I wanted it to be.

Cassian took a step closer, his movements deliberate, each one radiating an authority I couldn't ignore. "I'll stop," he said quietly, his voice low enough that only I could hear, "if you tell me you never want to see me again—and mean it."

I blinked, his words hanging heavy in the air between us. There was no malice in his tone, no edge of challenge—only certainty, as if he already knew my answer.

"I—" I started, but the word caught in my throat as he took another step closer, his proximity suddenly overwhelming.

He leaned in, his breath warm against my ear as he

whispered, "But I'll know if you don't mean it, Rosalie."

The air between us thickened, electric with an intensity I didn't know how to navigate. My pulse quickened, a traitorous reaction that only seemed to embolden him.

I turned my head slightly, meeting his gaze. "If you keep this up, one might presume you've got stalker tendencies."

He smiled faintly, though his eyes held a fervent edge. "Is that what you call it? My therapist said it was an attachment disorder."

Before I could respond, the soft hum of gallery-goers filtered back into focus, grounding me enough to take a step back. I looked away, needing to reclaim some semblance of control over the situation.

"You see a therapist?" I muttered, trying to mask the way my voice wavered.

He didn't reply, but the weight of his gaze followed me as I moved to another painting. It was a tempestuous piece, its bold, chaotic strokes mirroring the swirling emotions Cassian always seemed to stir within me.

Even as I tried to ignore him, I could feel him lingering nearby, a magnetic presence I couldn't quite escape.

We moved through the gallery in near silence, the occasional murmur of other patrons and the soft, melodic strains of music filling the void between us. Cassian stayed close but not overbearing, letting me drift from piece to piece without comment or interference. He wasn't following so much as orbiting, his presence undeniable but unobtrusive.

I paused in front of a watercolor landscape, its gentle hues of green and gold evoking a serenity I hadn't felt in weeks. The edges of the image blurred into abstraction, as if the artist had deliberately left the work unfinished, inviting the viewer to complete it with their own imagination.

"It's peaceful," I said quietly, not expecting a response.

"It is," he replied, his voice soft, almost contemplative.

I glanced at him, surprised by the sincerity in his tone. Cassian wasn't usually one for reflection, or at least, he didn't show it often.

We continued walking, weaving through the maze of art, the silence between us no longer oppressive but oddly comfortable. I was grateful he didn't press me to speak, giving me the space I hadn't realized I needed. But eventually, the silence felt too heavy, too laden with unspoken words.

"How's the shop?" I asked, my voice breaking the quiet as I stopped in front of a sculpture—a sleek, obsidian figure that seemed to twist upward like smoke.

Cassian's gaze flicked to me, his expression neutral. "It's steady. Busier than usual, actually."

A pang of something bittersweet rippled through me. Ivy & Bloom had always been my sanctuary, my mother's legacy woven into every petal and stem. Now, it felt like a memory I couldn't bear to revisit. And it was doing better than ever, even in my absence.

"You should come by in the morning," he said, his voice devoid of pressure, as though he were merely suggesting something trivial.

I shook my head almost immediately, the reflexive motion surprising even me. "No," I said softly, and gave no further explanation.

Cassian nodded, his acceptance both surprising and strangely reassuring. "When you're ready," he said, his voice carrying a cogent weight that made it clear he wouldn't push further.

I studied him for a moment, the clean lines of his face illuminated by the soft gallery lighting. His calm demeanor was almost infuriating, as though he knew I'd come around eventually. And maybe I would. But not yet.

We stood there for a while longer, the silence settling over us again, though this time it felt less guarded. I turned back to the sculpture, tracing its jagged curves with my eyes, letting its abstract beauty distract me from the knot tightening in my chest.

Cassian shifted slightly, his posture relaxed but his gaze steady on me. "If you won't come to the shop," he began, his voice measured, "then at least join me for dinner tomorrow night."

I blinked, caught off guard by the suggestion. "Dinner?"

"Neutral ground," he clarified, his tone softer now, almost persuasive. "No agenda, no expectations. Just conversation."

I hesitated, my fingers brushing the edge of the sculpture beside me. The idea of sitting across from him, sharing a meal like everything was normal, felt both intriguing and daunting. I wasn't sure I could trust myself in that kind of setting—wasn't sure I could trust him either.

"Neutral ground?" I repeated, raising a brow. "And you're capable of that?"

A faint smile tugged at the corners of his lips, his eyes glinting with a flicker of amusement. "I am, believe it or not. I'll even let you choose the place."

That was unexpected. Cassian wasn't one to relinquish control, even in the smallest ways. It was disarming, and I hated how it made me pause, how it chipped away at my resistance just enough to consider it.

"I don't know," I said finally, my voice quieter.

"Think about it," he said, stepping closer, though his movements were deliberate, non-threatening. "It doesn't have to mean anything. Just... dinner. You and me."

I tilted my head, studying him. There was no demand in his expression, no trace of the sharp edge he so often wielded. He was just waiting, giving me the choice, and for a moment, it unsettled me more than any ultimatum could have.

"I'll think about it," I said at last, the words slipping out before I could stop them.

Cassian nodded, his gaze lingering on mine for a beat longer before shifting to the sculpture beside us. "Good. That's all I ask."

The ease in his response surprised me, but I didn't press it. I turned back to the artwork, letting the silence stretch between us as I tried to reconcile the knots of emotion twisting inside me.

Cassian was patient, his presence steady but unobtrusive as I moved to the next exhibit. He wasn't pushing, wasn't demanding. And yet, his suggestion lingered in the back of my mind, tempting in ways I wasn't ready to admit.

Dinner. Neutral ground. No agenda. Just conversation.

For someone like Cassian, it felt almost implausible. But maybe, just maybe, it could be real.

CHAPTER NINE

The restaurant was exactly what I'd imagined when I chose it: small, unpretentious, and comfortably tucked into a quiet corner of the city. Warm light spilled through the wide front windows, illuminating the chalkboard menu scrawled with daily specials in colorful cursive. Inside, mismatched wooden tables and chairs filled the cozy dining area, and the air carried the comforting aroma of fresh bread and herbs. It wasn't glamorous, but it was welcoming—a stark contrast to the sleek, high-end places Cassian usually frequented.

I spotted him the moment he arrived. It was impossible not to. His sharp features and commanding presence stood out starkly against the restaurant's casual ambiance. He looked as if he'd stepped out of a different world entirely, dressed in his usual tailored suit, every line and detail perfectly pressed. But even his refined air couldn't completely disguise the tension in his jaw as he scanned the room, clearly aware of how wildly out of place he appeared.

Before stepping inside, Cassian slipped off his suit jacket with a fluid motion and tossed it into the passenger seat of his car—a sleek black Aston Martin parked just outside, its gleaming exterior catching the last rays of the setting sun. He ran a hand through his dark hair, smoothing it back before finally walking through the door.

His eyes found me instantly, and for a moment, he hesitated, the faintest flicker of uncertainty crossing his face. But then he moved, weaving through the small tables with a confidence that belied his earlier discomfort.

"Rosalie," he said, his voice low and smooth as he reached my table.

I glanced up, noting the way the soft glow of the restaurant's lights seemed to soften the edges of his usual sharpness. "Cassian," I replied, gesturing to the chair across from me. "You came."

He did, his movements deliberate as he settled into the chair and surveyed his surroundings with a bemused expression. "You chose this place on purpose, didn't you?"

I smiled faintly, unable to suppress the satisfaction in my tone. "Of course I did. It's nice, isn't it?"

"Nice," he repeated, his lips curving into a wry smile. "Not quite the word I'd use, but I'll concede it's... charming."

"Charming," I echoed, leaning back in my chair. "That's a compliment coming from you."

He shook his head slightly, his gaze shifting back to me. "It's different," he admitted. "But you look comfortable here. And if that's what it takes to show you I am capable of forfeiting the reigns when it matters, so be it."

I raised a brow, surprised by his admission. "You mean you didn't come here to make a statement?"

"Not tonight," he said simply, his tone devoid of its usual sharpness.

For a moment, the hum of the restaurant filled the space between us. Servers moved deftly between tables, their trays laden with dishes that carried the tantalizing scents of roasted garlic and fresh basil. The atmosphere was lively yet intimate, a quiet background to the unspoken tension that lingered at our table.

We both glanced at the menus, the air between us settling into something quieter. The server arrived, a young woman with a friendly smile, and we placed our orders— simple dishes that suited the unpretentious charm of the restaurant.

As soon as she left, Cassian leaned back in his chair, studying me with an intensity that made it impossible to focus on anything else. His fingers tapped lightly against the edge of the table, a rhythm that seemed to match the pulse of the soft music playing in the background.

"What would it cost," he began, his voice measured, "to see you back at Ivy & Bloom?"

I blinked, the question catching me off guard. My fingers instinctively tightened around the glass of water in front of me as I tried to process his words.

"I thought you said there was no agenda." I said, forcing a lightness into my tone that I didn't quite feel. "You miss seeing me there?"

"I miss seeing you in your element," he clarified, his gaze unwavering. "The way you light up when you're surrounded by what you love. It's different now. Without you, it feels... hollow."

I exhaled slowly, my heart twisting at the sincerity in his words. It wasn't easy to hear, especially because a part of me missed it too—missed the shop, the flowers, the sense of purpose that had once driven me. But it wasn't that simple anymore.

"The shop is part of it," I admitted, my voice barely above a whisper. "But it's more about everything I've lost—the sense of control, of direction."

He frowned slightly, tilting his head as though urging me to continue.

I set the glass down, my fingers lingering on its edge. "Since the day you walked into Ivy & Bloom, I haven't felt like I've been in control. Of the shop. Of my destiny. My life."

The words spilled out, each one heavier than the last. "You turned my world upside down, Cassian. And maybe you didn't mean to—maybe some part of you thought you were helping—but it's been impossible to find my footing ever since."

His expression shifted, the confidence he usually wore like armor slipping just slightly. For a moment, he didn't respond, his lips pressing into a thin line as he leaned forward, resting his forearms on the table.

"I didn't realize," he said softly, his voice laced with a vulnerability I hadn't expected. "I thought I was protecting you. Helping you. But if I've taken that from you—if I've dimmed that light—I'm sorry, Rosalie."

I swallowed hard, my chest tightening at the rawness in his tone. Cassian Moreau didn't apologize often, and hearing him do it now felt like something I wasn't entirely prepared for.

"I don't think it's something you can fix," I admitted, my voice barely above a whisper. "Not with an apology. Not with promises. I need to figure out how to take back my life... my light."

He nodded slowly, his gaze never leaving mine. "I don't want to see you lose it," he said, the words carrying an earnestness that made my chest ache. "The fire, the determination—it's what drew me to you in the first place. I never intended to snuff it out, and that's exactly what I did, didn't I?"

The server returned then, setting our plates in front of us and breaking the moment. I glanced down at my dish, my appetite nowhere to be found despite the comforting aroma wafting up from the food.

Cassian picked up his fork but didn't touch his food, his eyes still fixed on me as though waiting for something. When I finally looked up, his expression had softened—not the sharp, calculating mask he wore so often, but something quieter, more contemplative.

"What would it take, hypothetically?" he asked, his voice even, measured.

I tilted my head, narrowing my eyes. "What would what take?"

"To see you back at Ivy & Bloom," he clarified. "Running it the way you want to. Making it yours again. What terms would make that possible? Think of it as a business deal, if you will."

I leaned back in my chair, crossing my arms. Part of me wanted to brush the question off, to tell him there was nothing he could say or do to fix it. But another part—the part that missed the shop, that missed *my* shop—couldn't let the question go unanswered.

"You really want to know?" I asked, my voice sharper than I intended.

He nodded, his gaze unwavering. "I wouldn't ask if I didn't."

I took a deep breath, letting the words form in my mind before speaking. "Full ownership," I said, the first term coming out stronger than I expected. "The shop is mine. Completely. No shared agreements, no oversight, no loopholes."

Cassian didn't flinch, though his lips pressed into a thin line.

"No illegitimate business is to be funneled through the shop—ever again," I continued, leaning forward slightly. "It's clean. It stays clean. If you want to play games with your empire, you leave Ivy & Bloom out of it."

He nodded, his expression unreadable but still attentive.

"Expansion—if I ever choose to expand—is at my pace. Not yours, not anyone else's. I decide when and how that happens."

"Fair," he said, his voice quiet but steady.

"Lena stays," I added after a pause. "But she doesn't touch the books anymore. Her expertise is useful, but I don't want her hands on anything financial."

Cassian raised a brow at that but didn't interrupt.

"And you," I finished, my tone firm, "don't meddle in Ivy & Bloom business. At all. If I take this back, it's on my terms—not yours."

He was silent for a moment, his fork resting idly against his plate. When he finally spoke, his voice carried a weight that made my chest tighten. "Those are your terms?"

"They are," I said, meeting his gaze with a steadiness I didn't quite feel.

He leaned back in his chair, his fingers drumming lightly against the edge of the table. "And if I agree to them?"

I hesitated, the question catching me off guard. "You'd

agree to that?"

Cassian tilted his head, studying me like he was dissecting each word, weighing their worth. "I'd agree," he said slowly, his voice thoughtful. "But I have my own terms."

I narrowed my eyes. "Terms? This isn't a negotiation, Cassian."

"With me, it always is," he replied, his lips curving faintly in that infuriatingly confident way that made me want to throw my fork at him. "If you want me to stay out of your business, I need assurances that you'll stay safe."

"Safe?" I repeated, leaning back in my chair. "I can take care of myself."

His brow lifted, unconvinced. "That's debatable, Rosalie. Especially given your proclivity for finding trouble."

I scowled, but he continued before I could fire back.

"First," he said, counting off on his fingers, "an elite security system installed in the building. State-of-the-art. Nothing less."

I opened my mouth to argue, but he held up a hand, cutting me off.

"Second, Marcus and Sierra remain as your security detail," he said firmly. "They're the best, and I trust them with your life. That doesn't change."

"Cassian—"

"Non-negotiable," he interrupted, his tone decisive.

I exhaled sharply, crossing my arms. "Fine. Anything else?"

He leaned forward slightly, his gaze sharpening. "You're never alone in the shop. Ever. Not during business hours, not after hours. There's too much risk."

I frowned, my mind racing as I processed his terms. They were logical, practical even, but they felt stifling, like invisible chains tightening around me. Yet the look in his eyes—the earnestness, the desperation to protect me—softened my resolve.

"Those are your terms?" I asked finally.

"They are," he said, his voice steady, though there was an intensity simmering beneath the surface that made my breath catch.

I hesitated for a long moment, my chest tightening with the weight of everything between us. Then, reluctantly, I extended my hand across the table. "Fine. Deal."

His lips quirked into the faintest smile as he reached out, his larger hand engulfing mine. The handshake was firm, deliberate, but as his fingers began to slip away, he held on just a fraction longer. His eyes found mine and it was impossible for me to look away.

"Move in with me," he said softly, the words so unexpected they left me momentarily speechless.

"What?" I managed, my voice barely above a whisper.

"Move in with me," he repeated, his tone resolute yet strangely gentle. His gaze didn't waver. If anything, it grew more intense, as though he was peeling back the layers he so carefully kept hidden. "The hole you've left in my life," he said, his voice low but carrying an undeniable weight. "I haven't slept—truly slept—since you walked away. Every night, I feel it, that absence. You."

The words struck something deep within me, a mix of longing and uncertainty twisting in my stomach.

"I thought I could handle it," he continued, his tone softening. "I thought giving you space would fix things. But it hasn't. I wake up reaching for you, only to remember you're not there. I broke the trust between us, and I will do everything in my power to never betray your trust again. And I can't keep pretending that doesn't tear me apart."

My breath hitched, my fingers curling into my lap. He wasn't pleading, wasn't begging—it wasn't his style. But there was a rawness in his voice that I couldn't ignore, an honesty that made it impossible to look away.

"Cassian..." I started, but the words failed me.

"You don't have to decide now," he said, leaning back slightly but keeping his eyes locked on mine. "But I needed you to know. Needed you to hear it from me."

I swallowed hard, the knot in my throat making it difficult to speak. My mind was racing, caught between the vulnerability in his confession and the walls I'd spent so long building to keep him at arm's length.

"This doesn't fix anything," I said finally, my voice trembling slightly. "You know that, right? Everything that's happened—it doesn't just go away because of... this."

"I know," he said simply, his voice steady. "But maybe it's a start—a step in the right direction."

The air between us felt heavier now, charged with the weight of his words. For the first time in a long while, Cassian Moreau didn't feel like the immovable force he so often projected. He felt real, raw, and entirely too close for comfort.

"You can't be serious—that not a step in the right direction, that's a fucking leap," I said at last, my voice louder now.

"I am very serious," he replied, his lips curving into the faintest of smiles. "I never would have asked otherwise, and you accepting or declining this, wont have an effect on the other terms. The shop is yours—I'll have the lawyer draw up the paperwork in the morning, but promise you'll think about it."

The server returned then, clearing away our plates and breaking the tension. But even as the conversation shifted to lighter topics, his words lingered, heavy and undeniable, echoing in the back of my mind.

CHAPTER TEN

The late-morning sun spilled across the city streets as I walked toward Ivy & Bloom, its golden light casting long shadows over the pavement. The air was crisp, carrying the faint promise of late spring, and with each step, my heart grew heavier. My chest felt tight, as though bracing for the sight that awaited me—the shop I'd called home for so many years, now irrevocably entwined with Cassian's world.

When I reached the storefront, I hesitated, my fingers tightening around the strap of my bag. The sign above the door, weathered but familiar, seemed to glimmer faintly in the light. With a deep breath, I pushed open the door, the familiar chime of the bell breaking the quiet.

I froze.

The shop was... perfect. Not in the clinical, meticulously efficient way Lena had imposed, but perfect in its own way—our way. The space was no longer stark and organized to an extreme. Instead, it was alive again, brimming with warmth and character. The stands were back, crowded with vases of lilies, roses, and hydrangeas that jostled for attention. Ivy trailed lazily along the shelves, and the air was thick with the scent of lavender and eucalyptus—a fragrant sanctuary that felt like home.

My eyes scanned the room, drinking in every detail. The

eclectic charm of mismatched vases on the counter. The slight lean of the shelf in the corner, weighed down by potted succulents and ceramic pots. Even the squeaky floorboard near the register, which I'd stepped on countless times, seemed to welcome me back. My chest tightened, not with apprehension, but with a swell of gratitude I hadn't expected.

And then, I saw him.

Cassian stood by the counter, a cup of coffee cradled in one hand and the other resting casually on the edge of a basket filled with freshly cut roses. He looked almost out of place among the chaos of the shop—his tailored suit a stark contrast to the cluttered, homey surroundings—but somehow, he also seemed to belong. His presence was commanding yet unobtrusive, like he was the thread quietly holding the room together.

"Morning, Rosalie," he said, his voice smooth, carrying that ever-present undercurrent of control. His eyes, sharp and discerning, softened as they met mine. "You're early."

"Couldn't sleep," I admitted, my voice quiet and gentle, an unspoken confession of another nightmare. I took a few hesitant steps forward, my gaze flicking to the basket beside him. "Didn't expect to find you here. Or this."

Cassian's lips curved into the faintest smile as he lifted a single rose from the basket. Its petals were just beginning to unfurl, a blush of pink softening the edges of its delicate blossom. He held it out to me, his movements unhurried.

"Beautiful, isn't it?" he murmured, his tone almost reverent as he studied the flower.

I took the rose carefully, my fingers brushing against his. "It is," I said softly, the faint fragrance wafting up as I brought it closer to my face. "But if you're planning on giving this to me, I should warn you—I'm not sure I can afford the price."

Cassian chuckled, a low sound that sent a shiver through me. "Consider it a gift," he said, leaning back slightly against the counter. "Though I'm sure I could come up with a fair price if you'd prefer."

The lightness in his tone was disarming, and I found

myself smiling despite the tension that had hung over me all morning. "I'll take the gift," I said, setting the rose gently on the counter. My gaze flicked to the neatly stacked documents beside his coffee. "So, this is it, then?"

He nodded, his expression sobering. "The pre-drafted agreement," he said, gesturing toward the papers. "Everything we discussed—your terms, my conditions. It's all here. My team worked through the night to get it done."

I swallowed hard, the weight of the moment settling over me. "And the shop?" I asked, my voice barely above a whisper.

"It's yours as soon as you sign," he said simply, his gray eyes steady and unwavering. "Under my protection, but yours to run as you see fit."

The word *protection* lingered in the air between us, heavy with implication. I didn't miss the subtle reminder of the dangerous balance we'd struck, nor the quiet promise that came with it.

I reached for the documents, my fingers brushing against the crisp edges of the paper. "You've been busy," I said, my voice tinged with something between gratitude and disbelief.

Cassian's smirk returned, softer this time. "You're worth it," he said simply.

The words settled over me like a blanket of warmth, their sincerity undeniable. For a moment, I allowed myself to believe him—to believe that, despite the tangled web of his world, he saw value in mine. And as I picked up the pen to sign my name, the rose resting beside me like a quiet promise, I realized that maybe—just maybe—I was ready to trust him.

I scanned the document in front of me, my fingers brushing over the crisp edges of the paper as I flipped through each page. My heart pounded, half-expecting to find some hidden clause, some trap waiting to spring the moment my pen touched the paper. But as my eyes moved over the neatly typed lines, my breath caught.

Every term I had laid out—every condition I thought Cassian would push back against—was there, meticulously outlined and agreed upon. The shop's autonomy. My authority over operations. Even a provision that explicitly removed Lena from having direct control of day-to-day decisions unless I requested her input. It was all there, written in black and white.

I glanced up at Cassian, my brow furrowing. "You didn't fight me on anything," I said, my voice tinged with disbelief. "Why?"

He leaned back against the counter, cradling his coffee cup with an ease that only heightened the intensity of his presence. "Because they were reasonable," he said simply. "I don't waste time arguing over things that make sense."

The answer was maddeningly straightforward, as though he hadn't just handed me everything I'd demanded on a silver platter. I searched his face for some hidden motive, some crack in his impenetrable calm, but found nothing. If there was a game at play, it was one I didn't yet understand.

Returning my focus to the documents, I flipped to the final page, my pen hovering over the line marked for my signature. "And the ledgers?" I asked, my voice quieter now. "I assume they're as clean as this agreement?"

Cassian's lips twitched, the faintest hint of amusement flickering across his face. "See for yourself."

I moved toward the office, the familiar hum of the shop grounding me as I opened the small desk drawer where the ledgers were usually kept. To my surprise, only one remained—the newer, streamlined book Lena had introduced. The older, chaotic ledger filled with haphazard notes and questionable entries was gone.

My fingers lingered on the single ledger, my mind racing. "Where's the second one?" I called out, turning back to Cassian.

He was still leaning against the counter, his expression unreadable. "Taken care of," he said simply, as though that explained everything.

"Taken care of how?" I pressed, stepping back into the room. The knot of suspicion in my chest tightened.

Cassian's gaze softened, though his tone remained firm.

"You said you wanted a fresh start for the shop. I assumed that included removing liabilities."

The words hung in the air between us, and though I wanted to push for more, I couldn't deny the relief that washed over me. The second ledger, with its tangled web of debts and errors, had been a weight I'd carried for far too long. Its absence felt like the first real breath of freedom in months.

Before I could say more, the sound of the back door opening drew my attention. Lena stepped into the shop, her polished heels clicking softly against the floor as she approached. Her usual air of aloofness was tempered by a genuine smile when she saw me, a flicker of warmth that caught me off guard.

"Rosalie," she said, her tone uncharacteristically bright. "You're back."

"I am," I replied, the tension in my shoulders easing slightly. "And the shop looks... incredible. Thank you."

Lena waved off the compliment, her smile softening into something more familiar—calculated but not unkind. "It wasn't just me," she said, her eyes flicking briefly to Cassian. "But I'm glad you approve. It feels good to have it thriving again."

Her words carried a weight I hadn't expected, and for a moment, I wondered if Lena had missed the shop as much as I had. But as she stepped closer, her gaze sharp and assessing, she added, "That said, there are a few things I'll need in order to continue contributing."

"Contributing?" I repeated, my brow furrowing. "You have your own stipulations?"

Lena smiled again, but this time there was an edge to it, a quiet assertion that left no room for misunderstanding. "Of course. If we're going to build something sustainable, I'll need certain assurances."

My stomach tightened, the words catching me off guard. Assurances? I glanced at Cassian, who remained silent, his expression carefully neutral as he sipped his coffee. It was clear he wasn't going to intervene—this was between Lena and me.

"What kind of assurances?" I asked, my tone cautious.

Lena tilted her head, her eyes sharp and calculating, yet her tone remained deceptively light. "Simple ones, really," she said, smoothing the lapel of her blazer. "If I'm to continue contributing to the business side of Ivy & Bloom, I'll need guarantees that my role remains indispensable—not equal, but appreciated."

"Appreciated?" I echoed, the word sticking in my throat. My grip on the rose tightened slightly as unease threaded through me. "Lena, I've appreciated you each and every day—expect for maybe when you were shredding my shop apart in the beginning, but I do appreciate you."

Lena's smile softened, a surprising warmth settling over her features. She stepped closer, her heels clicking softly against the wooden floor, and rested her hand lightly on the edge of the counter. Her gaze met mine—not sharp or calculating this time, but steady and earnest.

"I know you do, Rosalie," she said, her tone gentler now. "And I've appreciated every moment of working with you, even when we didn't exactly see eye to eye." A faint smile tugged at her lips, the hint of a shared memory lightening the tension. "But this isn't about acknowledgment or gratitude. It's about making sure Ivy & Bloom doesn't just survive—it thrives."

The knot in my stomach eased slightly, though confusion still lingered. "What are you saying, Lena?" I asked carefully. "What do you want?"

Lena lingered near the counter, fiddling with the edge of a ribbon tied around a vase of sunflowers. Her expression was thoughtful, as if carefully constructing what she wanted to say. Finally, she took a step closer, her polished demeanor softening just enough to seem approachable.

"I've been wanting to bring this up for a few weeks now, but the timing didn't seem right," she began, her voice carrying a deliberate calmness that instantly put me on guard.

I leaned against the counter, the rose still in my hand, and gestured for her to continue.

"You've probably noticed Bateman & Sons next door,"

she said, glancing toward the window as though she could see the antique shop through the ivy-covered glass. "They're closing. The owner is retiring and putting the space up for sale."

My brow furrowed. "Ivy & Bloom already has enough going on without me worrying about what's happening next door."

Lena's lips quirked in a small, knowing smile. "I'm not suggesting you worry about it, Rosalie. I'm suggesting you buy it."

The words hit me like a jolt. "Buy it?" I repeated, shaking my head. "Lena, I just got this shop back under control. Now you want me to double the space, double the responsibilities—"

"Not double," she interrupted, raising a hand as if to calm me. "Expand. Imagine what we could do with that space if we knocked the wall down and connected the two shops. You'd keep the charm of Ivy & Bloom, but with Bateman & Sons, you'd have room to grow. A larger showroom. Dedicated spaces for workshops and event planning. Even a private office for me to handle the bigger accounts."

I stared at her, utterly bewildered. "A private office? Bigger accounts? Lena, where is this coming from?"

She folded her arms, her gaze steady but tinged with a rare vulnerability. "Rosalie, you've seen it yourself. The kind of clients we've been catering to lately—they're not just looking for bouquets or simple centerpieces. They want grand displays. High-end events with intricate designs. Weddings, galas, corporate launches. These are people willing to pay top dollar for something extraordinary, and Ivy & Bloom is becoming known for that."

"And you think the solution is... knocking down walls?" I asked, still trying to wrap my head around the enormity of what she was suggesting.

"Yes," Lena said, without hesitation. "Think about it. We could turn this into a boutique destination. A space where we create more than just flowers—we create experiences. You could continue doing what you love, focusing on the design and the customers, while I handle the logistics, the contracts, the—"

"Paperwork," I said flatly, cutting her off.

She didn't miss a beat. "Yes, the paperwork. And the client relations. And the larger-scale planning that's becoming a bigger part of our business. We'd both be doing what we're good at, but with the space and resources to actually thrive."

I looked at her for a long moment, her words swirling in my mind. It was a lot—too much. The thought of breaking down the wall between Ivy & Bloom and Bateman & Sons, of transforming my mother's cozy flower shop into a sprawling operation, felt overwhelming. And yet, there was a flicker of possibility in what Lena was saying. A glimmer of something that could be beautiful, if only I had the courage to see it through.

"You make it sound so easy," I said quietly, looking down at the rose in my hand. Its petals were soft and just beginning to unfurl, as if opening to the world for the first time.

"It won't be easy," Lena admitted, her voice softening. "But nothing worth building ever is. Rosalie, I know this shop means everything to you—it's your legacy, your family's story. I don't want to change that. I want to help it grow. To give it the foundation it needs to become something even greater."

I looked up at her, searching her face for any sign of insincerity, but there was none. Lena was ambitious, yes, but there was a genuine care in her tone that I hadn't expected.

"And the office?" I asked, my voice tinged with skepticism. "That's non-negotiable?"

She smiled, the warmth returning to her expression. "I'll need somewhere to take calls and meet with clients who expect discretion and professionalism. Let's be honest— having a dedicated space will make us look more polished. And it'll keep me out of your hair when you're busy with your own work."

I let out a soft laugh despite myself. "That's an appealing

argument."

"I thought so too," Lena said, her smile widening. "Because wearing three inch stilettos all day long demands perfection—and a place to kick my feet up when no one is looking." She laughed, a unusual break in Lena's stoic, professional demeanor. "You've done an incredible job bringing this place back to life, Rosalie. Now let's take it one step further."

Her words hung in the air, full of both promise and challenge. I looked toward the wall that separated Ivy & Bloom from Bateman & Sons, the possibilities beginning to take shape in my mind. It was a leap, a risk, and it terrified me. But it also stirred something deeper—a yearning to create something my mother would be proud of, something that could stand the test of time.

"Let's do it," I said finally, meeting Lena's gaze. "It's a wonderful idea, and you're right, so, let's do it."

"Great!," she said excitedly, her tone light but resolute. "I'll reach out to the realtor and get things rolling in the right direction. And I'll start working the color scheme for my new office."

I shook my head, a small smile pulling at my lips despite myself. "Don't push your luck, Lena."

Her laugh echoed softly as she turned to check on the customers in the corner, leaving me alone with my thoughts. I glanced back at the rose in my hand, its delicate blossom a quiet reminder that growth—real growth—required courage. And for the first time in a long while, I wondered if I had enough of it to take the next step.

As Lena walked away to tend to the customers, I stood there, picking up the rose from the counter again, the weight of her ideas bringing with it a newfound hope.

The sound of Cassian setting his coffee cup down pulled me back. He stepped closer, hands casually in his pockets, his steady gaze locking onto mine. "You're going to think yourself into a corner over that flower," he said lightly, nodding toward the rose in my hand.

I let out a small laugh, glancing down at it. "Maybe. It's just... a lot of change in the last few days."

"Change doesn't have to erase the past, Rosalie," he said softly. "Sometimes it honors it."

The words settled in my chest, grounding me. He glanced toward the door, a faint smile playing on his lips. "Let's take a walk," he said. "You look like you could use one."

I hesitated, the weight of everything still heavy, but the crisp air outside called to me. "Alright," I said, placing the rose back in its basket.

He held the door open, and I stepped out into the cool breeze. Cassian joined me, his presence quiet but steady as we fell into step. For now, the legal documents could wait.

CHAPTER ELEVEN

The city stretched out before us, bathed in the soft, golden hues of late afternoon. The streets hummed with life—a mix of bustling pedestrians, honking cars, and the occasional distant melody of a street performer's saxophone. The mild spring air carried the scent of blooming flowers from sidewalk planters and the faint aroma of fresh bread from a nearby bakery. It was the kind of day that felt suspended in time, where everything seemed just a little softer, a little more bearable.

Cassian walked beside me, his stride measured, his presence electrifying. Behind us, I could hear the faint footsteps of Sierra and Marcus, ever-watchful, maintaining a respectful distance as though they were invisible. I glanced at Cassian from the corner of my eye, his sharp features softened by the golden light, though his expression remained contemplative. He had been uncharacteristically quiet since we'd left the shop, and it left me waiting for whatever thought he was clearly weighing.

We turned down a quieter street lined with brownstones, their iron railings adorned with budding ivy and trailing wisteria. Window boxes overflowed with bright daffodils, tulips in soft pastels, and vibrant hyacinths, their fresh blooms infusing the area with a charm that felt alive and renewing. A dog barked in the distance, and a cyclist whizzed by, the faint hum of his tires blending seamlessly into the rhythm of the city.

Cassian broke the silence first, his voice low and deliberate. "Rosalie, there's something I've been meaning to talk to you about."

I slowed my pace slightly, looking up at him. "That sounds ominous."

"It's not," he assured me, though the faint crease in his brow suggested otherwise. "I've been thinking about what you've been through—what we've all been through—and... I think it might help if you talked to someone."

I stopped, blinking at him. "Talked to someone?" I repeated, my tone cautious.

"A professional," he clarified, pulling a small, cream-colored business card from the inside pocket of his jacket. He held it out to me, his fingers brushing mine as I hesitated to take it. "Dr. Eleanor Whitaker. She's... exceptional at what she does."

My eyes flicked to the card. The name was embossed in clean, serif lettering, understated and professional. I could almost hear my heartbeat in the quiet pause that followed.

"I don't need therapy, Cassian," I said, my voice coming out softer than I'd intended, though it carried an edge of resistance.

"I'm not saying you do, but maybe it will help to talk to someone outside of my world... She knows who I am, but you'd be protected by confidentiality," he said gently. "Perhaps she can help you navigate everything that's happened. Damien's death. The shop. Even me." He said the last part with a faint, self-aware smirk that almost made me laugh.

Almost.

I looked away, focusing instead on a cluster of pigeons pecking at crumbs near the edge of the sidewalk. The thought of unpacking all of this with a stranger felt wrong, like opening a box I wasn't sure I'd be able to close again. "I don't know, Cassian," I said after a moment, my voice hesitant. "It feels... unnecessary."

"It's not," he said firmly, stepping closer, his presence radiating warmth despite the crisp chill in the air. "You've been carrying a lot, Rosalie. More than anyone should have to. Talking to someone doesn't make you weak; it just makes you human—and maybe, it can help you come to terms with everything that has happened."

"Okay," I said, staring at the card. "I'll try."

Cassian nodded, as though he'd expected that answer, and the faintest trace of relief flickered across his face. "That's all I ask."

We resumed walking, the silence between us lighter now, though the weight of his suggestion lingered in my chest. The brownstones gave way to a small park, where children's laughter filled the air, and the trees swayed gently in the breeze, their leaves catching the light like fragments of amber. It was beautiful, serene, yet my mind remained tethered to the card in my pocket and the questions it represented.

We walked in companionable silence for a few moments, the crunch of our footsteps on the pavement blending with the distant hum of the city. The park stretched out before us, vibrant with springtime energy. Cherry blossoms in full bloom framed the walking paths, their pale pink petals fluttering gently in the breeze like whispers of renewal. Clusters of bright daffodils and tulips swayed at the base of ancient oaks, their presence cheerful against the deep green of freshly sprouted grass.

I caught Cassian glancing at me from the corner of his eye, his expression unusually soft. It was rare to see him this unguarded, and for a fleeting moment, I felt the pull of safety in his presence—a sharp contrast to the turmoil in my chest.

But then his phone buzzed, shattering the peace.

Cassian pulled it from his pocket with a fluid motion, his brows knitting together as he glanced at the screen. Without a word, he answered, his tone immediately shifting into something colder, sharper.

"This better be important," he said, his voice low, clipped.

I slowed my steps, giving him a bit of space as his tone darkened with each passing second. His answers were terse, his usual commanding calm fraying at the edges. I couldn't make out the words from the other end, but whatever he was hearing was serious.

"When?" he demanded, his pace quickening slightly as if to distance himself from me. "How bad is it?" A pause. "No. I'll handle it. Keep him where he is until I get there."

He ended the call abruptly, slipping the phone back into his pocket. His jaw was tight, his eyes stormy with a tension I hadn't seen in a while. Cassian rarely let his emotions bleed through like this, and it unsettled me.

"Cassian?" I asked, my voice cautious. "What's going on?"

He slowed just enough to meet my gaze, but the steel in his expression didn't soften. "Nothing, just something that needs my attention," he said firmly, his tone shutting the door before I could even reach for the handle.

"Doesn't sound like nothing," I pressed, frowning. "Who was that about?"

He stopped walking entirely, turning to face me fully. His hands found his pockets, his stance guarded yet calm. "Rosalie," he said evenly, "I pushed you too much last time, I won't make that same mistake again."

His words hurt, even though I knew he was trying to protect me. I could feel the wall between us slowly climbing back up, its presence suffocating in its simplicity. "Alright."

His lips parted as if to say something, but then his phone buzzed again. He glanced at it, cursed under his breath, and waved toward Marcus and Sierra. Within moments, a sleek black SUV appeared at the curb, the door already open, waiting.

"I have to go," Cassian said, his tone clipped. "It's urgent."

"I understand." I said reluctantly, but he was already stepping toward the car.

He paused at the open door, glancing back at me. For a fleeting second, his expression softened, the tension in his features giving way to something more vulnerable. "We'll talk later," he said, his voice almost gentle. "Promise me you'll think about what we discussed."

I nodded, unsure whether the ache in my chest was frustration or something else entirely. "I will."

And then he was gone, the SUV pulling away with Marcus and Sierra stepping back to my side. The city buzzed on around me, indifferent to the storm I felt brewing just beneath my skin. Whatever had pulled him away was more than urgent—it was something he didn't trust me to handle. And that hurt more than I cared to admit.

But for now, I remained standing there, caught between the soft petals of spring and the cold distance Cassian had just left in his wake.

I took a deep breath, staring at the card in my hand as though the embossed letters could somehow answer the questions swirling in my mind. The hesitation clawed at me, but Cassian's words lingered, urging me forward. I dialed the number before I could change my mind, pressing the phone to my ear as the line rang.

"Dr. Eleanor Whitaker's office, this is Avery. How may I help you?" The receptionist's voice was soft, inviting, with a tone that immediately eased some of the tension in my chest.

"Hi," I began, my voice tentative. "I'd like to schedule an appointment."

"Of course," she said warmly, her tone unwaveringly pleasant. "And may I ask who referred you?"

"Cassian Moreau," I replied, glancing absently at the pigeons pecking near the sidewalk as I spoke.

"Oh, yes!" Amy said, her voice brightening. "Dr. Whitaker mentioned you might call. We've set aside time for you later this week if you're available."

Her response surprised me, a mix of relief and unease washing over me. Of course, Cassian would have told her. "I'm available," I said, leaning into the familiarity of decisiveness. "What time?"

"Friday at 2 p.m. Does that work for you?"

"Yes, that works," I replied quickly, some of the tension in my voice fading.

"Wonderful," Amy said, her tone exuding encouragement. "Dr. Whitaker specializes in creating a welcoming, comfortable space. She's looking forward to meeting you, Rosalie. I'll send a confirmation text with the office details right away. If you have any questions before Friday, feel free to call."

"Thank you," I said softly, my fingers curling slightly around the phone. "I appreciate it."

"We're happy to help," Amy replied, the sincerity in her voice like a soothing balm. "We'll see you Friday."

I ended the call, exhaling slowly as I slipped the phone and card back into my pocket. The warm tone of the conversation had taken the edge off my apprehension, but the decision still felt significant—like a tether pulling me toward something I wasn't sure I was ready to face.

"Everything good?" Sierra asked, her voice gentle but attentive.

I nodded, brushing my hair behind my ear as I glanced toward her and Marcus. "Yeah," I said quietly. "It's all good."

They didn't press further, giving me space as I started walking again. The city felt lighter somehow, the late-April air carrying the delicate fragrance of lilacs from a nearby garden. Children's laughter rang out from the park across the street, mingling with the soft rustle of new leaves overhead. For the first time in a while, I felt as though I'd taken a step forward—small, but forward nonetheless.

CHAPTER TWELVE

Later that night, I sat cross-legged on my bed, staring at the contract spread across my lap. The words blurred slightly under the dim light of my bedside lamp, but I forced myself to focus. This was too important to let slip through the cracks, and I couldn't afford any surprises.

My pen hovered over a clause titled Operational Oversight and Consultation, the words meticulous but undeniably slippery: *"The primary owner reserves the right to review operational decisions deemed detrimental to the shop's performance."*

Detrimental to whom?

The question burned at the back of my mind, and I could feel a flicker of irritation spark to life. I scribbled a note in the margin: *Define 'detrimental'—too vague. Cassian's idea of harm and mine aren't the same.*

I moved on, but another line under Expansion Plans and Business Growth made my stomach tighten. It read: *"All strategic partnerships must align with overarching business goals and retain review for strategic congruence."*

Strategic congruence? Really?

I snorted softly, circling the phrase with deliberate strokes of my pen. It was Cassian's charm distilled into legal language: polite, polished, and maddeningly opaque.

I underlined the clause twice, adding a sharp note beside it: *No loopholes—this is my shop.*

Each line I read felt like peeling back another layer of Cassian's influence, subtle and pervasive. It wasn't overt control—he wasn't careless enough for that—but there was enough ambiguity to keep his fingers in the pie if he wanted to.

And that was the problem. I wasn't sure I trusted him to let go. Not fully.

I leaned back against the headboard, letting the pen fall to my side as I stared at the contract. It was beautifully written, every line carefully crafted, and it left no overt reason to call foul. But the nuances made my chest tighten. Was this his way of holding on to a piece of Ivy & Bloom? Or was I reading too much into it?

I rubbed a hand over my face, trying to shake off the creeping exhaustion. The shop meant everything to me, and the thought of surrendering even an ounce of control left a bitter taste in my mouth. If I signed this, it would be on my terms—no compromises.

Pulling the contract closer, I circled a few more areas that bothered me, jotting down quick notes: *"Vague." "Clarify." "Discuss with Cassian."*

I stopped for a moment, my pen hovering in the air, before writing at the bottom of the page: *Trust?*

It wasn't just the contract I was questioning. It was him. His world, his promises, his capacity to let me truly take back what was mine. Could I trust him to mean every word he'd said, to step back and let me breathe? Or was I stepping into another snare, more polished and carefully hidden than the last?

The thought tightened something in my chest, and I set the pen down with a sharp sigh. Picking up my phone, I scrolled to Cassian's name. My thumb hovered over it, my mind flicking through every conversation we'd had, every unspoken question still hanging between us.

Not tonight.

I placed the phone face down on the nightstand, shifting my focus back to the contract. If Cassian thought I'd sign this blindly, he had another thing coming. Tomorrow, we were going to have a very thorough discussion about every single clause. And if he thought he could charm his way around my questions, he didn't know me as well as he thought he did.

I straightened the stack of papers, setting them aside before sliding under the covers. My mind was still spinning as I stared at the ceiling, the faint hum of the city outside filtering through my window. Reaching for my headphones, the music flooded my ears as I lay back against the pillows, letting the deep, soulful rhythm of "Jericho" by Iniko wash over me. It didn't quiet my thoughts entirely, but it gave them something to anchor to, a cadence that kept the swirling doubts at bay. My hand absently traced patterns on the comforter while my other fingers tapped lightly to the beat.

It didn't last.

The sudden movement at the doorway sent a jolt through me. I gasped, yanking out one earbud and sitting up, my heart pounding. Cassian stood there, leaning against the frame with a bemused expression that only infuriated me further.

"Do you ever knock?" I demanded, trying to mask my shock with indignation. "Locks on doors are supposed to keep people out."

"Good thing I own the building," he retorted smoothly, his smirk deepening. He pushed off the frame and sauntered into the room, his eyes sweeping over the scattered papers on the bed before landing on me.

I glared at him, clutching the headphones in my hand like a shield. "That doesn't give you the right to just barge in."

Cassian tilted his head, his gaze lingering on me with an intensity that was both unnerving and impossible to ignore. "Adorable," he murmured, almost to himself.

"What?" I snapped, caught off guard.

"The way you bite your lip when you're concentrating. It's... adorable." He leaned against the edge of the dresser, his casual stance a stark contrast to the electric charge in the air.

Heat crept up my neck, and I scrambled to find a retort. "Shouldn't you be busy running your empire or intimidating someone?"

"I am," he said, his smirk returning. "You just don't realize it yet."

His words were a challenge, and the way he studied me—like I was a puzzle he was intent on solving—set my nerves on edge. I crossed my arms, determined not to let him see how much his presence unsettled me.

"Is that so?" I chuckled under my breath, "Are you going to intimidate me into signing this contract with obscure loopholes laced throughout?"

He seemed genuinely surprised, but didn't answer at first. "I can't say I know what you're referring to specifically."

Cassian tilted his head, his gray eyes glittering with amusement. "Loopholes? Sounds like you've been busy." He crossed his arms, mirroring my stance, though the effect was entirely different. Where I hoped to project defiance, he exuded confidence, like he was enjoying this too much.

I narrowed my eyes, grabbing the contract from the nightstand and brandishing it like a weapon. "Don't play dumb with me, Cassian. 'Operational Oversight'? 'Strategic Congruence'? Do you think I don't see what those terms really mean?"

He watched me, utterly unruffled, and something about his silence set my pulse racing. When he finally spoke, his voice was low, almost a purr. "You're upset about language meant to protect my investment? Terms designed to protect you. Tell me, Rosalie, is that what's really bothering you?"

"Don't twist this," I said smoothly, moving from the bed to put some distance between us. He took a step forward, while I took a step backward. "You're trying to keep control of something you claim you're handing over. If I'm supposed to trust you, then prove it. Make the terms as clear as day."

His smirk deepened, and he pushed off the dresser, closing the space between us. "And if I did, would you trust me then?"

My breath hitched as he drew closer, and I took an instinctive step back, only to find the bed against the backs of my knees. "That's not the point."

"Isn't it?" His voice dropped, intimate and dangerous, as he leaned in. "You think this is about power, Rosalie. About me controlling you. But what if I told you it's about something else entirely?"

I opened my mouth to argue, but no words came out. The air between us seemed to hum, charged with an energy I couldn't name. His eyes flicked down to the contract still clutched in my hand, then back to my face, lingering on my parted lips.

"You have questions about the contract," he murmured, his gaze never leaving mine. "Ask them."

For a second, I forgot how to breathe. "Why," I managed, though my voice was a whisper, "are the terms so vague? Why leave room for interpretation?"

He reached up slowly, brushing a stray strand of hair behind my ear. The touch was featherlight, yet it burned through me like a spark catching dry kindling. "Because, Rosalie," he said softly, "you and I both know that control isn't about what's written on paper. It's about leverage. And right now, I think we both know where the leverage lies."

I swallowed hard, my heart hammering against my ribs. "You're infuriating," I whispered, hating the tremor in my voice.

He chuckled, low and rough. "And you're intoxicating."

Before I could react, he shifted, his hands bracketing either side of me on the bedframe. The contract slipped from my fingers, forgotten, as he leaned in, close enough that I could feel the heat radiating from his body. The scent of him—spice and something darker, richer—clouded my thoughts, leaving me dizzy.

"Cassian..." My voice was barely audible, a plea or a warning—I couldn't tell which.

"Am I being transparent now?," he murmured, his lips so close to mine I could feel his breath. His eyes bore into mine, dark and endless, drawing me in like a tide. "You're trying so hard to fight me. But tell me, Rosalie, is it really the contract you're resisting? Or something else?"

I couldn't think, couldn't speak. His presence consumed me, every nerve in my body attuned to the smallest shift in his posture, the slightest brush of his breath. He tilted his head, and for a moment, I thought he might kiss me. My heart leapt into my throat.

Cassian didn't move away. Instead, he lingered, his dark gray eyes locked onto mine, his breath warming my skin. Slowly, deliberately, he leaned back just enough to create space between us. For a fleeting second, I thought he might step away entirely, but instead, his hands moved to the knot of his tie.

The silk slid free with a practiced ease, the sound of the fabric against itself startlingly loud in the charged silence. He draped it over the chair beside the dresser, his movements unhurried but purposeful. Next, his hands went to the buttons of his burgundy jacket. One by one, they came undone until he shrugged it off, letting it fall in a soft heap onto the nearby chair.

My breath hitched as his gaze returned to me, molten and unyielding. He rolled his sleeves with precision, baring strong forearms corded with muscle and dusted with faint scars. The deliberate motions made it impossible to look away, and though I wanted to demand what he thought he was doing, the words refused to form.

"Still resisting, Rosalie?" he asked softly, his voice a low rasp that sent a shiver through me.

I tried to summon an answer, but all I managed was a stuttering exhale. His lips twitched, and before I could regain my bearings, he leaned down, his hands brushing my shoulders as he guided me back onto the bed.

"Cassian..." My protest was weak, my voice shaking as I gripped the edge of the comforter like a lifeline.

"Yes?" he murmured, the word full of feigned innocence as he settled one knee on the bed. Then the other.

He hovered over me, his hands bracketing my hips as he leaned closer. The mattress dipped under his weight, locking me into the space between his arms. His body radiated heat, and I was acutely aware of every breath, every inch of space—or lack thereof—between us.

"You keep pushing me," he said, his voice low and even, "but I think we both know where this is headed."

My pulse thundered, and I forced myself to look away, my gaze darting to the nightstand, the ceiling—anywhere but his face. But he wasn't having it. His hand cupped my jaw, gently but firmly guiding my gaze back to his.

"Don't look away from me, Rosalie." The command in his tone was impossible to ignore, and I hated how my body responded instinctively, my head turning as if compelled.

His thumb brushed the edge of my jaw, his touch a stark contrast to the steel in his voice. "You're fighting me so hard," he murmured, his lips curving into the faintest of smiles. "But do you even know why?"

"Because you—" I started, but the words faltered as he shifted his weight, straddling me fully. The action pinned me beneath him, his thighs bracketing mine with an intimacy that left no room for escape.

"Because I what?" he prompted, his voice soft but insistent.

I couldn't answer. Not when his presence consumed me so completely, not when every thought felt drowned beneath the crashing wave of him.

"Say it, Rosalie," he urged, his gaze never leaving mine. "Tell me what you're really afraid of."

I pressed my lips together, determined not to let him win, but the defiance was short-lived. His hands found mine, prying them away from the comforter and pinning them above my head with one smooth motion. His grip was firm but careful, his strength unmistakable.

"You don't hate this," he said, his voice a whisper against my lips. "You hate that I know you don't."

I couldn't breathe, couldn't think, my mind spinning as I stared up at him. His face was so close, his expression an intricate mix of desire and control that left me utterly undone.

"Tell me to stop," he said, his tone softening slightly, though his intensity remained. "Tell me, and I will."

I opened my mouth, but no sound came out. My heart

pounded erratically, and the silence stretched between us like a taut wire, ready to snap.

He leaned in, his breath mingling with mine as his lips hovered just out of reach. "That's what I thought," he murmured.

For a moment, time seemed to freeze. The room faded away, leaving only the weight of his presence, the heat of his body, and the steady, unyielding hold of his gaze. It wasn't anger or dominance or even lust that filled his expression—it was something deeper, something I didn't dare name.

And then, as if drawn by some unseen force, our foreheads touched, the tension crackling between us. Neither of us moved, neither of us spoke. The silence was louder than words, and the look in his eyes seared itself into my memory, indelible and ineffable.

CHAPTER THIRTEEN

Cassian's hand tightened around my wrists, pinning them effortlessly above my head. The intensity in his eyes pinned me just as effectively, leaving me breathless under the weight of his gaze.

"Cassian," I murmured, though I wasn't sure if I intended it as a protest or a plea.

"Hush," he said softly, his voice dark and smooth, like velvet brushing against steel. His free hand trailed down the side of my neck, his fingertips grazing the bare skin of my collarbone. "You're always so quick to argue, Rosalie. Always so quick to fight me."

"I'm not—" I started, but the words died on my lips as his fingers slipped under the hem of my shirt.

"Shhh," he repeated, the corner of his mouth lifting into a smirk that sent heat flooding through me. "You don't need to say anything. Just... be still."

The fabric of my shirt rose as he dragged it up, his touch slow and deliberate, exposing my stomach and ribs. He paused just beneath my bra, his eyes meeting mine with a challenge that made my pulse race.

"Tell me to stop," he said, his voice low and teasing. "Say the word, and I'll let you go."

I swallowed hard, the words tangled in my throat. My

heart thundered against my ribs as his fingers resumed their slow exploration, pulling the shirt over my head and discarding it to the side. The cool air brushed against my skin, but it was nothing compared to the heat radiating from him.

"Still quiet," he murmured, his lips quirking as his gaze traveled over me. "Has the cat got your tongue, Rosalie?"

Cassian's eyes glittered with amusement as he leaned closer, his hands bracketing my hips. The weight of his gaze felt like a touch all on its own, igniting every nerve in my body. My breath hitched as his fingers ghosted over the waistband of my jeans, his movements deliberate, slow enough to drive me mad.

"I expected more of a fight," he teased, his voice a low rumble. "You're usually so fiery."

"Don't flatter yourself," I managed, though the tremor in my voice betrayed me. "I'm just... processing."

"Processing," he repeated, his lips curving into a wicked smile. "Is that what you're calling it?"

Before I could respond, his fingers hooked into the denim, tugging it down over my hips. The fabric dragged against my skin in an excruciatingly slow descent, pooling at my ankles. The vulnerability of being exposed, of being completely at his mercy, sent a flush spreading across my chest and neck.

Cassian tilted his head, studying me like I was a puzzle he was determined to solve. "You're beautiful like this, you know," he said softly, his voice carrying an edge of something I couldn't quite name. "Bare. Unfiltered. Mine."

My breath caught at the possessiveness in his tone, and I instinctively tried to shift beneath him, to regain even a semblance of control. But his hands pinned me in place, firm yet careful, like he was reminding me just how little power I had in this moment.

"Yours?" I breathed, my voice barely above a whisper. "You still so sure?"

His eyes darkened, a predatory glint flickering in their depths. "Positive. And I intend to ensure you never forget it, Rosalie. Not for one fucking moment."

His words sent a shiver down my spine, equal parts fear and exhilaration. I wanted to argue, to push back against his assumption, but the heat of his body and the intensity of his gaze robbed me of coherent thought.

Cassian leaned in closer, his lips brushing against my ear. "You can deny it all you want, but your body doesn't lie. I can feel your pulse racing, see the flush on your skin. You want this as much as I do."

His hand trailed down my side, fingers skimming over my ribs, my waist, my hip. Each touch left a trail of fire in its wake, igniting sensations I'd never experienced before. I bit my lip, trying to stifle the moan threatening to escape.

"Don't hold back," he murmured, his breath hot against my neck. "I want to hear every sound, every gasp, every plea. Let me hear you, Rosalie. I want to hear you beg."

His words were a siren song, tempting me to surrender. I closed my eyes, my resolve crumbling with each passing second. When I opened them again, Cassian was watching me, his gaze a mix of desire and something deeper, more profound.

"Tell me you want this," he said, his voice low and commanding. "Say it, Rosalie."

I swallowed hard, my heart pounding so loudly I was sure he could hear it. "I... I want this," I whispered, the admission both terrifying and liberating. "I want you."

A slow, triumphant smile spread across his face. "Good girl," he purred, and before I could process the thrill those words sent through me, his lips crashed against mine in a searing kiss.

The world fell away, leaving only the heat of his mouth, the pressure of his body against mine, and the intoxicating sense of surrender. As Cassian deepened the kiss, his hands roaming my body with increasing urgency, I knew there was no turning back. Whatever happened next, I was irrevocably his.

Cassian's kiss was consuming, his lips moving against mine with a fierce intensity that left me breathless. His hands roamed my body, leaving trails of fire in their wake. I arched into his touch, desperate for more contact.

He broke the kiss, his breath hot against my neck as he trailed his lips down to my collarbone. "So fucking responsive, look how wet you are" he murmured approvingly as one hand grazed the wetness between my legs. His teeth grazed my skin, eliciting a gasp from me.

Suddenly, he pulled back, his eyes dark with desire as they raked over my nearly naked form. "Turn over," he commanded softly.

My heart raced as I complied, rolling onto my stomach. I felt exposed, vulnerable, yet thrillingly alive under his gaze. The mattress shifted as Cassian moved, and I sensed him hovering over me.

His hands skimmed down my back, fingers tracing the curve of my spine. I shivered at the feather-light touch.

With deft fingers, he unhooked my bra, sliding the straps down my arms. As he tossed it aside, I felt the heat of his body as he leaned over me again.

His lips brushed the nape of my neck, then trailed down between my shoulder blades. Each kiss sent sparks of pleasure coursing through me. I gripped the sheets, trying to ground myself against the onslaught of sensation.

Cassian's hands kneaded my lower back, working out tension I didn't even know I was holding. As his fingers dipped lower, brushing the waistband of my panties, I held my breath in anticipation.

"Relax," he murmured against my skin. "I've got you."

His words, combined with his touch, melted away my remaining reservations. I surrendered myself fully to his ministrations, letting out a soft moan as his hands continued their exploration.

Cassian took his time, alternating between gentle caresses and firmer touches that had me squirming beneath him. Just when I thought I couldn't take anymore, he'd back off, leaving me teetering on the edge of pleasure.

"Cassian," I whimpered, frustration coloring my voice.

He chuckled, the sound sending vibrations through my body. "Patience, Rosalie. I won't leave you wanting forever."

I heard the rustle of fabric, followed by the soft thud of clothing hitting the floor. The mattress dipped as Cassian shifted, and I felt the warmth of his now-naked body press against me.

His hand slid down to cup my ass, squeezing gently. "I have something for you," he whispered, his voice thick with promise.

I turned my head, trying to catch a glimpse of what he meant. I heard the soft click of a cap opening, followed by the cool sensation of lubricant being applied. My breath caught as I realized what was coming.

Cassian's fingers circled my entrance teasingly. He chuckled as my body tensed. "Relax," he murmured again, his free hand stroking soothingly down my back.

I took a deep breath, willing my body to loosen. Slowly, carefully, he began to work the tip of a small, metal plug inside me. The initial sensation was cold and firm, heavy and filling. The stretch was unfamiliar but not unpleasant. I gasped softly as it slid fully into place, my body greedily taking it in.

"Good girl," Cassian praised, his voice husky. "How does that feel?"

"Full," I breathed. "Different, but...good."

"One day I'm going to take this virgin ass of yours," he hummed approvingly, his hands caressing my hips and thighs. "It'll only get better," he promised.

Cassian guided me onto my back once more, his eyes dark with desire as they raked over my body. The plug shifted inside me as I moved, sending little sparks of pleasure through my core.

His fingers trailed up my inner thigh, teasing but never quite reaching where I desperately wanted him. I squirmed, silently begging for more.

"You just can't stay still, can you?" he murmured, a smirk playing at his lips. "We'll have to do something about that... now, won't we?" He grabbed ahold of my wrists, bringing them above my head once more. "Don't move them, Rosalie. If you do, I'll make you wait that much longer for release."

His thumb brushed over my clit, and I gasped at the jolt of sensation. He repeated the motion, building a slow, maddening rhythm that had me arching off the bed.

Just as the pleasure began to crest, he pulled away. I whimpered at the loss, my hips chasing his touch.

"Not yet," Cassian said firmly. "I want you right on the edge."

He continued this exquisite torture, bringing me to the brink over and over, only to deny me release. The plug inside me amplified every sensation, leaving me trembling and desperate.

"Please," I finally gasped, beyond pride or hesitation. "Please, Cassian, I need..."

"What do you need?" he asked, his voice low and commanding. "Tell me."

"You," I breathed. "I need you. Please."

A slow, satisfied smile spread across his face. "That's what I wanted to hear."

CHAPTER FOURTEEN

Cassian freed himself from his pants, his hand wrapping firmly around his impressive length. His slow, deliberate strokes were mesmerizing, a tantalizing display of control that only heightened the ache building inside me.

His eyes gleamed with a predatory satisfaction as he settled himself between my trembling thighs, his body a warm, solid weight above me. The blunt head of his cock pressed insistently against my entrance, teasing me with the promise of fullness. It was almost surreal—his size, his presence. No matter how many times this happened, the sheer magnitude of him left me breathless.

"Ready?" he murmured, his voice thick with restrained desire. The timbre of it sent shivers down my spine. "I've waited weeks for this moment, and I won't be quick about it."

I nodded, unable to summon words, my anticipation tightening every nerve in my body. Slowly, excruciatingly slowly, he began to push inside. The initial stretch was staggering, bordering on painful, but the discomfort gave way to an intoxicating, all-consuming pleasure.

The plug in my ass amplified everything, making me feel impossibly full. The dual sensations sent my senses spiraling, my body trembling beneath him.

"Rosalie," Cassian groaned as he bottomed out, his impressive length sheathed completely within me. "So tight," he growled, his hands gripping my hips with an almost reverent fervor. "So perfect."

He began to move, setting a languid pace that had me gasping with each thrust. The dual stimulation from his cock and the plug was overwhelming, pushing me rapidly towards the edge he'd been denying me.

He began to move, his pace languid and deliberate, every thrust igniting a new wave of ecstasy that had me gasping. The fullness, the friction—it was overwhelming, my body responding to him with an urgency that bordered on desperation.

"Cassian," I whimpered, my voice breaking as my hands fisted the sheets above my head. "Please... it's so much."

He leaned down, capturing my lips in a searing kiss, his tongue delving deep as his thrusts quickened. "Then come for me," he commanded against my mouth, his voice both a demand and a promise. "Let me feel you fall apart. But know this, Rosalie—it won't be the last time tonight."

His words were my undoing. With a cry of ecstasy, I came undone beneath him, my body clenching around him as waves of pleasure crashed over me. Cassian groaned, his thrusts becoming erratic as he chased his own release.

The overstimulation left me trembling, but Cassian's relentless pace only pushed me higher. The initial orgasm had only heightened my sensitivity, and I felt another climax building, sharp and insistent. The plug shifted with each movement, sending shockwaves of pleasure radiating through me.

"That's it," he growled, his voice rough and ragged. "I can feel you tightening around me. You're going to come again, aren't you?"

I could only nod, a strangled moan escaping my lips as Cassian's hand snaked between us. His thumb found my clit with unerring accuracy, circling it mercilessly. The added stimulation was maddening, pushing me dangerously close to the edge.

"Come for me," he ordered, his eyes blazing with

intensity as they bore into mine. "Now, Rosalie."

The sheer dominance in his tone, coupled with the relentless sensations, undid me. My second orgasm tore through me, my cry muffled against his shoulder as I convulsed around him.

"Fuck," Cassian groaned, his rhythm faltering as he buried himself deep inside me. His release was hot and overwhelming, leaving me breathless beneath him.

He collapsed against me, his weight a comforting anchor as we both struggled to catch our breath. His fingers traced lazy patterns along my skin, grounding me in the aftermath of what felt like a storm.

"You're exquisite," he murmured, lifting his head to meet my gaze. His smirk was wicked, his gray eyes glinting with unspent energy. "And this, Rosalie, is just the beginning," he murmured, his eyes glinting with promise. "I hope you're ready for a long night, Rosalie. I'm nowhere near done with you yet."

I shivered at his words, torn between exhaustion and the electric anticipation coursing through me. Slowly, he withdrew, leaving me achingly empty, only to roll me onto my stomach.

His lips trailed down my spine, each kiss soft and reverent. "Every inch of you deserves to be worshipped," he murmured, his hands massaging the tension from my back.

His hands kneaded my lower back, working out the tension from our previous activities. I melted into his touch, sighing contentedly.

"That plug looks perfect nestled between your cheeks," Cassian said, his voice low and appreciative. His finger traced around the base, sending shivers through me. The bluntness of his observation ignited a fire deep within me, and his finger traced around the base with maddening precision, each pass sending jolts of pleasure spiraling through my core.

"How does it feel?" he asked, his tone laced with curiosity and desire.

"Good," I breathed, the word trembling from my lips. "Despite it being so taboo, it feels... heavenly."

His lips quirked in approval as he hummed softly. "We'll work up to something bigger, in time. For now, let yourself savor the sensation."

His hands moved lower, gliding over my thighs and calves with a touch so tender it bordered on worshipful. The contrast to the intensity of our earlier coupling left me disarmed, as if I were suspended between being cherished and consumed.

Gradually, his touch shifted, becoming more deliberate, his fingers sliding up the insides of my thighs. My legs parted instinctively, granting him silent permission, my body betraying my mounting anticipation.

Cassian chuckled, the sound rich and dark as his fingers hovered just shy of where I needed them most. "So eager," he teased, his eyes gleaming with a devilish glint. "I love how insatiable you are. Hungry, are you?"

His fingers ghosted over my folds, slick and sensitive, gathering the evidence of our shared release. My breath hitched as he slowly pushed two fingers inside me, curling them with unerring precision to graze that spot that made my vision blur.

"Still so tight," he murmured, his voice carrying a note of awe that sent a shiver racing up my spine. "Let's see how many times I can make you fall apart tonight."

His movements were artful, stroking and teasing with an expertise that left me trembling beneath him. The dual sensations of his fingers inside me and the plug nestled in my ass created a heady combination, a relentless onslaught of pleasure that had me writhing in moments.

"That's it," he murmured, his tone coaxing yet firm. "Let yourself go. I want to feel you come apart on my fingers."

I gasped, my body arching into his touch as his pace quickened, only for him to halt abruptly. My hips jerked involuntarily, seeking the friction he denied, a whimper escaping my lips.

"Hands above your head, Rosalie," he commanded, his voice dark and unyielding. "This is your only warning."

Instinctively, I obeyed, my trembling arms returning to their place above my head as he resumed his tantalizing thrusts. His free hand slid down, kneading the curve of my ass, occasionally brushing against the base of the plug. Each subtle shift sent sparks of sensation rippling through me, the pressure mounting with dizzying intensity.

His free hand kneaded my ass cheek, occasionally brushing against the base of the plug and sending jolts of pleasure through me. The pressure built steadily, my breath coming in short gasps as I climbed towards another peak.

Just as I teetered on the precipice, Cassian withdrew his fingers, leaving me gasping and disoriented.

"Not yet," he said, his tone dripping with authority and amusement. "I'm not done with you."

I felt the mattress shift beneath me as his strong hands guided me onto my knees. My body trembled with need, every fiber of my being attuned to him.

His hand trailed down my spine in a slow, deliberate caress, his touch igniting a fire in its wake. When he reached the base of the plug, he paused, his thumb circling it with teasing precision.

"I think it's time we put this to good use," he murmured, his voice a sinful promise.

He began to work the plug in and out, each movement slow and deliberate, the sensations sending shockwaves of pleasure radiating through me. My fingers curled into the sheets, desperate for an anchor as he unraveled me piece by piece.

"How does that feel?" he asked, his breath warm against my ear, the huskiness of his voice making my toes curl.

"So good," I gasped, the words barely coherent.

He hummed approvingly, increasing the pace slightly. "You take it so well," he praised. "One day, you'll take my cock just as beautifully."

The thought sent a shiver of excitement through me, mingled with a touch of apprehension. Cassian was well-endowed, and the idea of taking him there was both thrilling and daunting.

As if reading my thoughts, Cassian leaned over me, his chest pressing against my back. "Don't worry," he murmured in my ear. "When the time comes, I'll make sure you're ready. I'll stretch you slowly, carefully, until you're begging for more."

His words, combined with the continued stimulation from the plug, had me teetering on the edge once more. "Cassian," I whimpered. "Please..."

"Please what?" he asked, a smirk evident in his voice. "Tell me what you need, Rosalie."

"I need to come," I breathed. "Please, let me come."

Cassian's free hand snaked around to my front, his fingers finding my clit with unerring accuracy. "Then come for me," he commanded, applying firm, circular pressure.

The dual stimulation was too much. With a cry of ecstasy, I shattered, my body convulsing with the force of my orgasm. Cassian worked me through it, his fingers relentless as he drew out every last tremor of pleasure. I moaned so loud I was sure the neighbors could hear, but I didn't care. It felt so damn good, so wrong—sin, desire, insatiable lust. And I wanted more.

As the aftershocks subsided, I collapsed onto the bed, my limbs feeling like jelly. Cassian followed me down, his body a warm, comforting weight against my back. He placed gentle kisses along my shoulder and neck, murmuring words of praise.

"Now," he said, his tone playful yet smug, "what was it about the contract you wanted to discuss? Or is this a bad time?"

Exhausted, sticky, and overwhelmed, I turned my head just enough to glare at him. "Fuck you, Moreau."

He winked, his smirk downright devilish. "You just did."

CHAPTER FIFTEEN

The next morning, I woke with a groan, every muscle in my body aching in a way that felt both punishing and satisfying. The soreness was a testament to the previous night—a relentless symphony of pleasure and exhaustion orchestrated by Cassian. My limbs felt heavy, as though they were made of lead, and even the thought of moving seemed insurmountable.

The sunlight streaming through the window was soft, diffused by the pale curtains that swayed faintly in the morning breeze. I stretched tentatively, wincing as the ache in my thighs and back reminded me of how thoroughly spent I was. My fingers brushed against the empty sheets beside me, cool to the touch.

Cassian was gone.

The realization stung more than I wanted to admit. No note, no whispered goodbye—just the lingering scent of him on the pillows and the faint imprint of his weight on the mattress. My chest tightened as I stared at the ceiling, frustration and a sliver of hurt warring within me. He always left like this, slipping away as though vanishing was an art form he'd perfected.

I pushed myself upright with a groan, reaching for the glass of water he'd thoughtfully left on the nightstand. The cold liquid soothed my parched throat, and I leaned back against the headboard, willing myself to shake off the mix of emotions swirling inside me.

Just as I was gathering the strength to rise, my phone buzzed on the nightstand. I grabbed it, my pulse quickening when I saw his name light up the screen.

Cassian: Come outside.

No explanation, no elaboration, just a command. Typical.

Despite my irritation, I swung my legs over the side of the bed and padded to the bathroom. A quick glance in the mirror revealed tousled hair and faint shadows beneath my eyes—a far cry from presentable. I ran a brush through my hair, freshened up as best I could, and slipped into a pair of jeans and a soft sweater before heading downstairs.

When I stepped outside, the sight waiting for me stole the breath from my lungs. Cassian leaned casually against the sleek, glistening frame of an Audi RS e-tron GT—a car I remembered vividly from the beginning of our tumultuous connection. The car's glossy black exterior reflected the morning sunlight, its elegance an extension of him.

He straightened as I approached, his gray eyes unreadable but piercing, as always. He was dressed simply today—rugged boots, dark jeans that fit him far too well, a short-sleeve black shirt that revealed his sculpted forearms, and a lightweight windbreaker that fluttered faintly in the breeze. The casualness of his outfit somehow didn't detract from his presence. If anything, it amplified his effortless command of the space around him, as though he could make even the simplest ensemble look like armor.

"You're awake," he said, his tone low and smooth, a hint of amusement dancing on his lips.

"Barely," I muttered, crossing my arms as I stopped a few feet away. "You could've at least left a note."

His smirk widened, unapologetic, the curve of his lips a deliberate provocation. He leaned slightly against the car, crossing his arms loosely over his chest. His head tilted as his gray eyes swept over me, amusement flickering in their depths. "What would it have said?" he mused, his voice a teasing drawl. "'Thanks for last night, see you in the morning'?"

I rolled my eyes, even as I felt the heat creeping up my neck and pooling in my cheeks. My arms folded tightly across my chest, a poor attempt to shield myself from his unrelenting gaze. "Why am I here, Cassian?" I asked, trying to inject some sharpness into my tone, though it sounded weaker than I'd hoped.

"Because I'm taking you away from the day," he said simply, uncrossing his arms with a fluid motion. He pushed off the car with an easy grace, his boots scraping softly against the pavement. His hand moved to the passenger door, and with a swift flourish, he pulled it open, gesturing inside with a subtle nod of his head.

I blinked, caught off guard, my feet hesitating where I stood. "You're what?"

His lips twitched, the faintest hint of a smirk reappearing as he stepped back just enough to let the open door speak for itself. His posture remained relaxed, but there was an unyielding set to his jaw. "Get in, Rosalie," he said, his voice dropping into that low, commanding timbre that always made it clear there was no room for argument.

I took a half step forward before stopping again, casting him a wary glance. "What about the shop?" My question sounded more like a token protest than a genuine challenge, especially as my body seemed to move of its own accord, gravitating toward the open door.

Cassian's gaze softened, but only slightly, as he leaned one arm casually against the car roof. "You've been gone for weeks—one more day won't hurt it Lena has everything under control," he replied, his tone smooth and steady. His fingers drummed briefly against the car before he added, "so stop trying to find an excuse to fight this."

His voice dipped, the lightness giving way to something darker, though the shift was so subtle it might have gone unnoticed if I hadn't been watching him so closely. His eyes narrowed slightly, a flicker of something sharp and calculating passing through them before he straightened and stepped back, waiting for me to comply.

I hesitated for a beat longer, torn between the tug of curiosity and the instinct to assert control over a situation I knew I couldn't win. Cassian's eyes remained locked on mine, steady and unyielding, his presence radiating the kind of authority that left little room for debate. Finally, I exhaled softly and slid into the passenger seat.

The cool leather cradled me as I settled in, my hands resting awkwardly on my thighs. Before I could reach for the seatbelt, Cassian leaned in, his proximity stealing the air from my lungs. His scent—woodsy with a hint of spice—enveloped me as he grasped the seatbelt, pulling it across my body with practiced ease.

The motion was simple, utilitarian, but his fingers brushed lightly against my collarbone as he clicked the buckle into place, sending an unexpected jolt of warmth through me. My lips parted in surprise, but before I could speak, his hand lingered, his fingers grazing the edge of the belt where it crossed my chest.

"You always hesitate," he murmured, his voice low and intimate, as though we were the only two people in the world. His gaze dipped to my lips for a fraction of a second before meeting my eyes again.

"I—" The word caught in my throat as he leaned in further, his mouth capturing mine in a kiss that was both commanding and tender. The press of his lips against mine sent a rush of heat through my veins, erasing any lingering protest.

The kiss was brief, a stolen moment that left me breathless. When he pulled back, his lips curved into a satisfied smirk. "Now you're ready," he said, his voice laced with quiet amusement.

I stared at him, still reeling, as he stepped back and rounded the car with an easy confidence that seemed to define him. He slid into the driver's seat, his movements smooth and assured, and turned to glance at me as the car hummed to life.

"Where are we going?" I asked, my voice softer now, tinged with both curiosity and caution.

Cassian's smirk deepened as he shifted into gear, the car

rolling forward with effortless precision. "It's a surprise," he said simply, his tone offering no hint of what lay ahead.

I turned to look out the window, watching the familiar city streets blur into a backdrop of motion. The morning sunlight cast long shadows across the pavement, but my focus remained on the man beside me, his hands gripping the wheel with quiet strength.

A surprise. With Cassian, that could mean anything and that was equal parts exciting, equal parts terrifying.

The hum of the engine filled the air, a steady undertone to the silence between us. Cassian drove with the same focus and precision he seemed to bring to everything he did. His hand rested lightly on the wheel, his fingers drumming against the leather in a subtle, almost absent rhythm. I watched him from the corner of my eye, the sunlight catching the sharp angles of his face as the city skyline gave way to sprawling green hills.

As we left the confines of the city, the scenery transformed. The edge of the city unfolded into a patchwork of elegant houses, each one more striking than the last. Manicured lawns, sprawling verandas, and oversized windows glinted in the morning light. The countryside seemed to breathe, its rolling hills dotted with wildflowers and vibrant green fields that stretched endlessly. The sight was a stark contrast to the gray, bustling streets we'd left behind.

"This is beautiful," I murmured, unable to keep the awe from my voice.

Cassian glanced at me, his lips curving into a faint smile. "It has its moments."

He didn't elaborate, his attention returning to the road as we passed another picturesque house. This one stood back from the road, its ivy-covered stone walls exuding timeless charm. For a moment, I let myself imagine what it would be like to live in such a place—peaceful, quiet, and far removed from the chaos that seemed to follow Cassian wherever he went.

We drove for another twenty minutes before Cassian turned down a narrow, winding road framed by towering trees. The dappled sunlight filtered through the canopy, casting shifting patterns on the ground. Finally, the car slowed as we approached a gravel driveway leading to a secluded house perched on the edge of a wide, sparkling lake.

The house was stunning in its simplicity—a blend of rustic charm and modern design, with large windows that reflected the surrounding water and trees. The lake stretched out like a mirror, its surface rippling faintly in the breeze.

Cassian parked the car and stepped out, the crunch of gravel beneath his boots breaking the stillness. I followed, my breath catching as I took in the tranquil beauty of the place.

"This is one of your favorite places?" I asked, my voice soft.

He nodded, his gaze distant as he looked out over the lake. "It's where I come when I need to think—or when I need to remember."

"Remember what?" I ventured, stepping closer.

Cassian's shoulders stiffened, but he didn't move away.

"My father," he said finally, his voice devoid of its usual confidence. His shoulders, usually squared with effortless dominance, now sagged ever so slightly, as though the weight of the memory pressed down on him. His hand slipped from his pocket, hanging loosely at his side before curling into a faint fist. "This was one of his properties. He'd bring me and my siblings here when we were kids."

I stayed quiet, watching the way his jaw tightened and then released, his gaze locked on the lake as though it held the answers to something he couldn't articulate. The usual sharpness in his features seemed dulled, softened by an emotion I couldn't quite place—was it pain, regret, or something deeper?

Cassian took a slow, deliberate breath, his chest rising and falling in a rhythm that felt controlled, almost practiced, as if the mere act of speaking about his father required preparation. "Damien wasn't the kind of father who believed in kindness or patience," he said, his voice hardening like stone. His hands shifted to his hips, his fingers gripping the material of his windbreaker tightly, his knuckles pale. "To him, weakness was a disease—something to be rooted out before it could infect everything else."

He paused, exhaling sharply through his nose, and tilted his head slightly, his gaze still fixed on the water. I caught the faintest tremor in his fingers before he clenched them into fists again, steadying himself. "If you showed fear, hesitation, or vulnerability..." His voice dropped, and for a moment, I thought he wouldn't finish the sentence. "He'd make sure you regretted it."

I swallowed hard, the weight of his words sinking in like a lead anchor in my chest. My stomach twisted, imagining a younger Cassian facing that kind of relentless scrutiny, the bruises it must have left behind—physical or otherwise. "That sounds... horrible," I said softly, my voice barely above a whisper.

He turned slightly, his eyes finally flicking to mine. They were dark and stormy, unreadable, though the tension in his jaw and the tight line of his lips revealed more than he intended. "It was," he admitted, his voice quiet but unwavering. His hand moved to rake through his hair, the movement sharp and agitated before it fell back to his side. "But it was also effective. He didn't care about being loved or admired—only respected. Only feared."

The wind stirred around us, rustling the leaves, but neither of us moved. The air felt heavy, charged with the unspoken emotions lingering between us.

Cassian's gaze lingered on mine for a moment before he turned back toward the lake, his shoulders visibly stiffening. "He believed that softness was a liability, that it made you weak," he said, his voice low and controlled, like a dam holding back something far more volatile. His fingers flexed and released at his sides, as though the memory of his father's lessons was still imprinted on his skin. "And he made damn sure I understood that lesson."

His words hung in the air, heavy and bitter, and I felt an ache settle deep in my chest. Without thinking, I took a step closer, my hand brushing lightly against his arm. The tension in his body seemed to waver for the briefest moment, but his gaze remained fixed on the horizon, unwavering, as though looking at me would shatter the fragile veneer of control he'd constructed.

I didn't say anything more; I didn't need to. The way his fingers curled tightly, the sharp line of his profile, and the subtle rise and fall of his breathing told me everything his words didn't. This was a wound he carried silently, a part of himself he didn't often share. And as much as it hurt to hear, I could tell it hurt him more to say it aloud.

"That's why I don't think I'd ever be a good father," Cassian said quietly, his voice barely louder than the soft lapping of the lake against the shore. He shifted his weight from one foot to the other, his posture rigid, as though the admission itself threatened to topple him. His gaze remained locked on the water, his hands retreating into the pockets of his windbreaker like shields against the vulnerability he was allowing himself to expose. "I don't know how to be anything other than what he taught me. Brutal. Unforgiving. Always in control."

The rawness in his tone left me momentarily speechless. This wasn't the composed, calculating Cassian I'd come to know—this was a man stripped bare, his armor cracked to reveal the scars beneath. His jaw tightened, and I could see the faint movement as he swallowed hard, his profile sharp against the shimmering lake.

"That's not true," I said finally, my voice steady despite the storm of emotions churning inside me. My fingers curled reflexively at my sides, aching to reach for him. "You're not him, Cassian. You're more than the lessons he tried to teach you."

He let out a bitter laugh, shaking his head with a quick, almost jerky motion. "You don't know that, Rosalie," he said, his voice tinged with a frustration that felt as much directed at himself as at me. His hand lifted briefly, running through his hair before dropping back to his side, the movement restless. "I think there is a part of you that realizes just how much like him I really am. The brutality

I am capable of—you've said it yourself... I scare you. That's not a good father."

I stepped closer, closing the small distance between us. My hand reached out, tentative but deliberate, my fingers brushing lightly against his arm. His muscles were taut beneath my touch, but the faintest exhale slipped past his lips, and the tension softened ever so slightly, like a bowstring loosening.

"You're not your father," I said firmly, my voice quiet but resolute. My fingers slid lower, resting against the crook of his elbow. "You're capable of so much more than he ever was. And just the fact that you're even questioning this—that you're afraid of being like him—proves it."

Cassian's head tilted slightly, his gaze dropping to where my hand rested before he turned to look at me fully. His gray eyes, usually so guarded, were shadowed but searching, as though he was trying to find the truth in my words. The wind picked up, rustling the leaves above us, but neither of us moved.

"Maybe," he said at last, the word escaping with a quiet exhalation, though his tone carried a note of doubt that lingered in the air. He glanced back at the lake, the set of his shoulders still heavy with the weight of the past. "But it doesn't change the past."

"No," I agreed softly, my hand sliding down to take his. His fingers were cool, hesitant as they curled around mine, but the gesture felt monumental, a thread of connection pulled tight between us. "But it doesn't define your future, either."

For a moment, we stood in silence, the world around us narrowing to the space we shared. Cassian's grip tightened slightly, his thumb brushing once against my knuckles, a subtle motion that spoke louder than words. When his gaze returned to mine, there was something different in his expression—a faint smile that touched his lips, not the smug or calculated grin I'd come to expect, but something softer. Something real.

"Come on," he said, his voice lighter now, though the echoes of his past still lingered in his tone. "There's more to see."

He turned, tugging me gently forward as we walked toward the edge of the lake. The crunch of gravel beneath our feet mingled with the rhythmic sound of the water lapping against the shore. Cassian's steps were measured, deliberate, his hand never releasing mine as though anchoring both of us to the present.

I glanced up at him, the lines of his profile softened in the golden light filtering through the trees. Though the weight of his past still clung to him, like shadows cast by the fading sun, there was something else, too—a quiet understanding, fragile yet unbreakable, tethering us in a way that felt profoundly unspoken but deeply understood.

CHAPTER SIXTEEN

The crisp scent of pine and earth filled the air as Cassian shut the trunk with a solid thud. He slung a sleek black bag over his shoulder, its weight shifting the fabric of his windbreaker. His movements were unhurried, deliberate, as if this morning—this moment—was untouched by the relentless urgency that usually followed him.

"Come on," he said, tilting his head toward a narrow trailhead nestled between two towering oaks. The path was framed by lush greenery, its entrance marked by a simple wooden post with a faded sign reading *Lakeview Trail*.

I glanced at him, arching a brow. "We're hiking?"

"Observant as ever," he quipped, his smirk faint but unmistakable. "There's a trail behind the house. I figured it's time you got a proper introduction to it."

I hesitated, eyeing the uneven ground and the overgrown edges of the path. "In these?" I motioned to my sneakers, which, while comfortable, were hardly designed for trekking through wilderness.

Cassian's eyes sparkled with amusement, the corners of his mouth twitching upward. "Don't worry," he said, his voice carrying that maddeningly calm assurance. "I've come prepared."

Before I could press him, he started toward the trail, his

long strides eating up the distance. I followed, quickening my pace to keep up. The sound of gravel crunching beneath our feet mingled with the rustle of leaves overhead, the sunlight dappling the ground in golden patches.

The trail wound gently upward, the incline steep enough to make me breathe a little harder but not so much that it was uncomfortable. The scenery was breathtaking— towering trees stretching toward the sky, their canopies creating a quilt of green above us. Every now and then, the trail opened up to reveal glimpses of the lake glimmering below, its surface rippling softly in the breeze.

"This is beautiful," I admitted, the tension in my shoulders easing with each step.

Cassian glanced back at me, his expression softened by something almost like contentment. "It's one of my favorite places. Quiet. Secluded. Not much to disrupt the view."

"Disrupt the view," I repeated, a faint smile tugging at my lips. "You sound like a tour guide."

He chuckled, low and deep, the sound blending seamlessly with the natural quiet around us. "Maybe I missed my calling."

We continued along the trail, the bag on his shoulder swaying with his movements. Despite the uneven terrain, Cassian navigated it with an ease that hinted at familiarity, his boots crunching steadily against the dirt and loose stones.

After a few minutes, the trail widened into a small clearing shaded by a cluster of birch trees. Cassian stopped, setting the bag down at the base of one of the trunks. He crouched, unzipping it with practiced efficiency, and pulled out a pair of hiking boots—sleek, sturdy, and unmistakably new.

"What's this?" I asked, stepping closer.

"These," he said, holding the boots up, "are for you."

I blinked, taken aback. "You bought me boots?"

He straightened, the faintest glint of satisfaction in his eyes as he held them out. "You didn't think I'd let you hike in those flimsy sneakers, did you?"

"They're not flimsy," I argued half-heartedly, though my

gaze was already drifting to the boots.

Cassian ignored the protest, one corner of his mouth lifting in a smug smile. "Try them on. They're your size."

I stared at him, caught between annoyance and something warmer that I wasn't ready to name. "You don't know my size."

His brow arched, his smirk deepening. "So sure about that? Remember that file I had made on you all those months ago—my men were very thorough. Down to your pantie size."

I bit back a retort, taking the boots from his hands. "I'm tell you—stalker vibes." They were the perfect size—of course, they were. Cassian never did anything halfway, and somehow, that thought was both infuriating and endearing.

As I sat on a nearby log to try them on, Cassian stood nearby, his gaze drifting to the trail ahead. For a moment, I let myself watch him, the sunlight catching in his hair, the set of his shoulders relaxed in a way I rarely saw.

We continued up the trail, the crunch of boots against the earth blending with the occasional call of a bird or the rustling of leaves in the wind. The air was cool but refreshing, the kind that seemed to clear your head just by breathing it in. Cassian walked ahead of me for a while before slowing his pace so we were side by side.

"I come here when I need to disconnect," he said suddenly, his voice breaking the natural rhythm of the forest.

"Disconnect?" I asked, glancing at him.

He nodded, his gaze fixed on the trail ahead. "Sometimes I need to shut it all out. The calls, the messages, the constant demands—it doesn't stop. But here?" He gestured to the trees around us, their towering forms casting dappled shadows over the path. "It's quiet. The cell service is horrible, so no one can bother me unless I want them to."

I smirked, glancing at him out of the corner of my eye. "Sounds like the perfect place to bury a body."

Cassian stopped mid-step, turning to look at me with an arched brow.

I held up a hand, cringing slightly. "Okay, that was a really messed-up joke. I didn't mean—"

He chuckled, low and quiet, his lips curving into a faint smirk. "Remind me not to let you pick the next location."

I laughed softly, the sound fading into the forest air like an echo that didn't quite belong. But as the humor slipped away, a heaviness settled over me, creeping in like a shadow I hadn't anticipated. My steps faltered, my feet dragging slightly against the dirt trail. I looked down, unable to meet Cassian's gaze just yet, as though saying the words aloud would make the weight of them unbearable.

Cassian noticed immediately. His pace slowed, his body turning ever so slightly toward me as we walked. His gaze sharpened, his gray eyes narrowing with quiet intensity as he studied me, his jaw tensing. He didn't say anything, but his posture shifted, his hands brushing against his sides as though unsure whether to reach for me or hold back.

"It's not just a joke," I admitted, my voice softer now, the usual strength behind it ebbing away. My arms folded across my chest, a subconscious attempt to shield myself from the vulnerability I was exposing. "I've been... struggling with all of this. Your world, I mean." I gestured faintly, my hand hanging limply at my side before I let it drop again. "Drugs, guns, murders—it's cutthroat. Brutal."

Cassian's jaw tightened further, his lips pressing into a hard line. He exhaled slowly through his nose, his gaze sliding away from me to focus on the trail ahead. His steps became deliberate, measured, as though the weight of my words had seeped into him too.

The silence between us stretched, heavy and unrelenting, until I couldn't hold it anymore. "I didn't realize how much it would get to me," I continued, the words spilling out faster now, tumbling over themselves like an unraveling thread. "I mean, I knew—sort of—but being close to it, seeing it... It's just so much."

I stopped walking, my body shifting awkwardly as I turned to face the woods beside the trail. My hand came up to brush my hair back, my fingers catching in the strands before falling uselessly to my side. "Sometimes, I don't know if I can reconcile it," I admitted, shaking my head. My voice wavered, though I tried to steady it. "The person I see when we're together and the person you have to be to survive out there—it's like two different people."

Cassian stopped a few paces ahead, the dirt crunching faintly under his boots. His shoulders, broad and usually so steady, seemed to slump for a moment before he turned slowly to face me. His movements were deliberate, almost heavy, as though every step carried the weight of what I'd said.

He stood there for a long beat, his hands flexing and then curling into fists at his sides. His gray eyes found mine, but they were darker now, clouded with something I couldn't quite place. A flicker of conflict crossed his face—a tightening around his mouth, a faint crease between his brows—before he spoke.

"You're right," he said finally, his tone low but steady, like a current pulling you under. "It's not for the faint of heart. My world doesn't give second chances. It's ruthless because it has to be."

His words settled between us, stark and unflinching. He dragged a hand through his hair, his fingers pausing at the nape of his neck before falling back to his side. The tension in his posture softened slightly, though his shoulders remained taut, as if the admission itself cost him something.

"But I was wrong to push you into it," he admitted, his voice quieter now. His gaze dropped briefly to the ground before lifting again to meet mine, his expression heavy with regret. "I thought I could bring you in and keep you close, but I didn't think about what it would cost you."

He exhaled sharply, his hand brushing over his mouth before falling to his side again. "And I'm sorry for that," he added, the words barely audible but carrying a weight that made my chest tighten.

His eyes held mine, the usual guardedness slipping just enough for me to see the truth beneath them—his conflict, his guilt, and something softer that he rarely let surface.

He didn't move, didn't look away, his stillness speaking louder than anything else.

He ran a hand through his hair again, glancing at the ground for a moment before meeting my gaze again. "I've been trying to protect you from it, to shelter you from the worst parts. I can't undo what's already happened, but I can keep you from seeing more of it than you need to."

"You would do that for me? Why?" I asked softly, my chest tightening as I searched his face.

Cassian's lips pressed into a thin line, his gaze unwavering. "Because you deserve better than what my world can offer you. And I selfishly don't want to lose you to it."

The vulnerability in his words left me momentarily speechless. For all his bravado, all his sharp edges, there was something deeply human beneath it—something raw and unguarded that he rarely let anyone see.

I reached out, my hand brushing lightly against his arm. "I'm not going anywhere," I said quietly, my voice firm despite the uncertainty still gnawing at me. "But I need to figure out how to live with this, Cassian. How to live with you."

His lips twitched into the faintest of smiles, though it didn't quite reach his eyes. "We'll figure it out," he said. "Together."

For a moment, neither of us moved, the quiet of the forest wrapping around us like a cocoon. Then, with a subtle nod, he turned and continued up the trail.

As we walked, the tension in my chest began to ease, replaced by the faint stirrings of something else—hope. Maybe we could figure this out, one step at a time.

When we reached another clearing, Cassian stopped and reached into the bag slung over his shoulder, pulling out a water bottle and handing it to me. I took it with a murmured thanks, watching as he rummaged through the bag again.

Then, with a triumphant grin, he pulled out another item and held it up—the Queen chess piece that I'd given him the day I walked away.

I smiled, my heart leaping just a little.

I stared at them, a mix of exasperation and warmth flooding through me. "You really don't miss a detail, do you?"

His smirk deepened as he held the intricately carved piece out to me. "Never."

I rolled my eyes but took the piece, a small smile tugging at the corners of my lips. For all the chaos and uncertainty his world brought, moments like this reminded me why I stayed.

CHAPTER SEVENTEEN

The forest began to thin as we made our way back toward the car, the sunlight breaking through the canopy in golden streaks that dappled the dirt trail. The hike had left my legs pleasantly tired, but my mind felt lighter, less tangled, after the morning. Cassian walked ahead, his shoulders relaxed, the bag still slung over his back.

As we rounded the last bend, the sleek black Audi came into view—and so did the figure leaning casually against it.

Cassian's posture stiffened instantly, his steps slowing as he clocked the stranger. Without a word, he reached back, his hand brushing the gun tucked in the waistband of his jeans. He didn't draw it, not yet, but his fingers lingered there, ready.

"Stay behind me," he said quietly, his tone low and clipped.

I froze for a second, caught off guard by the sudden shift in his demeanor, before falling into step behind him. My heart began to thrum faster, the relaxed calm of the hike evaporating in an instant.

The figure turned as we approached, his movements slow and deliberate, revealing the familiar face of Detective Markson. His gaze swept the woods before settling on Cassian, his mouth pulling into a tight, professional line.

Cassian's shoulders didn't relax, though his hand moved slightly away from the gun. "Markson," he said flatly, his voice carrying a hint of annoyance. "You know, most people call first."

Markson straightened, brushing a speck of dust off his jacket. "I did," he replied evenly, his tone betraying none of the tension in the air. "When I couldn't get ahold of you, I ran your plates and found you here."

Cassian's jaw tightened, his hand flexing at his side. "Resourceful, aren't you? Must be nice having the city's databases at your fingertips—I knew there was a reason to keep you around," he said, his tone carrying a razor-sharp edge wrapped in feigned admiration.

Markson gave a faint shrug, his gaze flicking past Cassian to me. "I needed to talk to you," he said, though his eyes lingered on me for a moment before returning to Cassian.

Cassian shifted subtly, his body angling just enough to block Markson's view of me. "I'm assuming it's important if you went through the trouble."

"Very," Markson replied, his voice steady but his expression unreadable.

The air between them crackled with unspoken tension, the kind that spoke of history and grudging familiarity. I stepped closer to Cassian, my fingers brushing against his arm. His muscles were taut, coiled with a readiness that hadn't quite eased.

"What's this about?" Cassian asked, his tone sharp but measured.

Markson's gaze didn't waver, his hands slipping casually into his jacket pockets. "Why don't we talk somewhere a little less exposed?" he suggested, his eyes darting briefly to the house behind us.

Cassian's jaw tensed at Markson's suggestion, his gray eyes narrowing slightly. For a moment, I thought he might refuse outright, but instead, he exhaled slowly, the movement deliberate. "Fine," he said finally, his voice carrying the weight of reluctant agreement.

Cassian turned toward the house, with Detective

Markson and I following behind. He had a distinct limp in his leg, a reminder of that night when Victor shot him—and me.

"Miss Quinn," he said as a way of acknowledging me. "I see you never took my advice." ...to stay away from Cassian Moreau.

"I tried," I confessed, "but he has a way of drawing people in."

"Ain't that true."

When we reached the house, Cassian pulled the key fob from his wallet with a practiced motion, the small device glinting in the sunlight as he pressed it. The lock on the house clicked audibly, and he gestured for Markson to follow.

"Rosalie," Cassian said without looking at me, his voice soft but firm. "Stay close."

I nodded, trailing behind them as we entered the house. The cool air inside was a stark contrast to the warmth of the woods, and the faint scent of cedar lingered in the space. Cassian led us into the main living area, a wide, open room with high ceilings and floor-to-ceiling windows that offered an unobstructed view of the lake.

Markson glanced around briefly, his expression unreadable, before settling his gaze back on Cassian. "Nice place," he said casually, though there was a flicker of something in his eyes—appreciation or envy, maybe both.

Cassian ignored the comment, crossing his arms as he leaned against the edge of the long wooden dining table. "You went to a lot of trouble to find me, Markson. Start talking."

Markson's posture shifted slightly, his shoulders squaring as he stepped closer. "We've got a lead on the drugs showing up at Salvatori's club," he began, his tone measured. "The stuff is potent—highly addictive, easy to conceal, and deadly in the wrong dosage."

Cassian's posture shifted, holding his hand up to silence Markson, before turning to me. "Rosalie, if you don't want to hear this, then please go upstairs. I'll come find you when we are finished."

Cassian's words hung in the air, his tone gentle but firm. His gray eyes met mine, their usual sharpness softened with an unspoken plea. He was giving me an out, a chance to distance myself from whatever grim details were about to unfold.

But as much as I wanted to escape the weight of his world, I couldn't. My insatiable curiosity stirred, gnawing at me with relentless questions. This was the thread that connected his life to mine now—the unspoken dangers, the secrets whispered in dark corners. Turning away felt like pretending it didn't exist, and I wasn't sure I could live with that.

"I'll stay," I said, my voice steady despite the unease pooling in my stomach.

Cassian's jaw tightened, the muscles feathering briefly before he gave a single nod. He didn't argue, though the flicker of reluctance in his eyes didn't escape me.

Markson's gaze shifted to me, his expression unreadable. "You sure about that?" he asked, his voice carrying the faintest edge of doubt.

"I'm sure," I replied, lifting my chin slightly.

Cassian sighed, rubbing the back of his neck before gesturing for Markson to continue. "Fine. Let's hear it."

Markson's posture straightened, his tone returning to its measured cadence. "We've been tracking a new supplier moving product through Salvatori's club. It's coming in small, unmarked shipments—easy to overlook, even easier to move without raising suspicion. The stuff is dangerous, Cassian. Pure enough to hook someone on their first hit, lethal if they miscalculate."

"Who's running it?" Cassian asked, his voice hardening.

Markson shook his head. "We don't have names yet, but we've got a few leads. The problem is, they're cautious—paranoid. They don't trust anyone new, and they've been switching locations frequently. They know we're closing in."

Cassian's brow furrowed, his arms uncrossing as he leaned against the table, his knuckles brushing the edge. "And you think I can flush them out," he said flatly, not phrasing it as a question.

"I know you can," Markson replied, his tone unwavering. "Your reputation gives you leverage. They'll listen to you."

"Leverage works both ways," Cassian muttered, his gaze darkening. "And when this goes sideways—and it will—they'll come after me, my people, and anyone connected to me." His eyes flicked briefly to me before settling back on Markson.

"We'll make sure it doesn't come to that," Markson said, though the faint tension in his jaw betrayed the weight of his own doubts. "We've already got officers stationed nearby, ready to move in the second we have a solid lead. We just need you to set the stage."

The room fell into a tense silence, the air thick with unspoken risks. Cassian's fingers tapped lightly against the wood, his thoughts clearly running a mile a minute.

I couldn't stop myself from stepping closer, the words spilling out before I could think better of them. "How would you do it? Set the stage, I mean."

Both men turned to look at me, Cassian's expression hardening instantly. "This doesn't involve you, Rosalie," he said sharply, though there was an edge of worry beneath his tone.

"Maybe not," I admitted, standing my ground, "but I'm already here. And I'm curious how the plan would unfold, not necessarily to be involved in it."

Cassian exhaled sharply, running a hand through his hair. "Curiosity hasn't always serve you well in the past," he muttered, though his voice had softened slightly.

Markson, meanwhile, regarded me with a faint trace of amusement. "She's got guts," he said, glancing at Cassian. "You could do worse."

Cassian shot him a glare before turning back to me. "This isn't a game, Rosalie. People are going to get hurt—or worse. You're not part of this."

"I'm not trying to be," I said quickly, my voice firm. "But if it's happening, I'd rather know than be blindsided later."

His eyes searched mine for a long moment, the tension between us palpable. Finally, he nodded, though his expression made it clear this wasn't a victory. "Fine. But you stay out of it. No involvement, no risks. Understand?"

I nodded, though my stomach churned with unease.

Markson cleared his throat, breaking the moment. "The plan's simple," he said, his tone brisk. "We use Cassian's connections to set up a meeting. Something low-stakes, just enough to get them to show up. Once they're there, we close in and take them down."

"And if they run?" Cassian asked, his voice sharp.

"They won't get far," Markson replied, though the faint tightness in his expression suggested he wasn't as confident as he sounded.

Cassian didn't respond immediately, his gaze shifting back to the window overlooking the lake. The sunlight caught in his gray eyes, making them seem colder, more calculating. Finally, he turned back to Markson, his jaw set.

"Fine," he said, his tone clipped. "But if this goes wrong, don't expect me to clean up your mess."

Markson gave a faint nod, his expression unreadable. "Fair enough."

The room fell into a strained silence, the weight of the conversation settling heavily between us. Cassian's hand found mine briefly, his grip firm but fleeting, as though grounding himself for what was to come.

And as the two men continued to hash out the details, I stood there, a strange mix of fear and determination coursing through me. Whatever this was, it felt like a point of no return. And despite the risks, I couldn't bring myself to step away.

CHAPTER EIGHTEEN

The hum of the car engine filled the silence, a steady undercurrent to the soft strains of classical music playing in the background. I glanced out the window as the trees blurred past, my mind still tangled with everything that had happened. Markson had gone his separate way, leaving me with more questions than answers. Beside me, Cassian sat focused on the road, his profile sharp in the fading light.

I studied him quietly—the way his hands rested on the wheel, his fingers relaxed despite the tension still evident in his jaw. He hadn't said much since we'd left, but the stillness between us wasn't uncomfortable. It felt like we were both waiting for the right moment to break it.

Eventually, the city lights began to creep back into view, and I shifted in my seat, the leather cradling my body as if it were trying to comfort me.

"Where are we going?" I asked softly, my voice breaking the quiet.

Cassian glanced at me, the faintest hint of a smirk tugging at his lips. "Home."

His answer sent a flicker of unease through me. *His home.* Not mine. The distinction lingered in the air, unspoken but undeniable.

When we arrived at the penthouse, I followed him

inside, the familiar luxury of his space wrapping around me like an elegant cocoon. The faint scent of something savory and rich wafted through the air, and I stopped short, glancing at him.

"You cooked?"

Cassian's lips curved into a sly smile. "Hardly. I had dinner prepared. I thought you might be hungry after the long day."

He gestured for me to follow, and I did, my curiosity growing as he led me down a hall I'd never ventured into before. The door he opened revealed a room that was every bit as stunning as the rest of the penthouse—a formal dining room with sleek lines and understated luxury, the soft glow of candlelight bouncing off delicate glassware.

"You have a dining room?" I asked, my voice tinged with surprise.

Cassian chuckled softly, stepping aside to let me in. "What, did you think I ate all my meals on the couch?"

"Honestly? Yes," I admitted, earning a faint shake of his head as he pulled out a chair for me. "That's what most people do these days..."

"Sit," he said, his tone warm but firm.

I complied, watching as he moved with practiced ease, pouring wine into a pair of crystal glasses before taking the seat across from me. The tension from earlier seemed to have melted away, replaced by a calm that felt almost foreign.

The table was set with precision, every detail immaculate, from the polished silverware to the crisp linen napkins folded neatly beside the plates. The first course was a delicate butternut squash bisque, its velvety texture and hint of nutmeg warming me from the inside out. I sipped it slowly, letting the subtle sweetness of the squash meld with the faint savoriness of sage as the quiet between us stretched comfortably.

Cassian, however, was less inclined to linger. He spooned the bisque with methodical precision, his movements measured and efficient. There was no sign of tension in his hands—they were as steady as ever—but his silence was heavier than mine, weighted by thoughts I couldn't yet read.

The second course was a beautifully plated grilled salmon, its skin perfectly crisp, paired with a medley of roasted vegetables that carried a hint of caramelized sweetness. The delicate aroma of lemon and dill wafted up as I cut into the fish, the first bite melting on my tongue. I felt the tension in my shoulders easing, the richness of the food grounding me in the moment and offering a reprieve from the day's earlier chaos.

Cassian ate sparingly, his focus split between the meal and some distant thought that lingered just behind his storm-gray eyes. His knife cut cleanly through the salmon, but there was no savoring in the way he ate—just a deliberate consumption, as though fueling his body was an obligation rather than a pleasure.

"Good?" he asked suddenly, breaking the silence, his gaze flicking up to meet mine.

I nodded, setting my fork down. "It's delicious," I replied, meaning it.

He gave a faint smile, but it didn't quite reach his eyes. He leaned back slightly, one hand resting on the table as his other cradled the stem of his wineglass.

As the main course was cleared away and dessert arrived—a decadent chocolate mousse garnished with a dollop of whipped cream and a single raspberry—I allowed myself to sink further into the moment. The bittersweet richness of the chocolate was indulgent, a perfect finish to the meal.

But while my body relaxed, lulled by the comfort of good food and wine, Cassian remained sharp-edged, his posture deceptively casual but his gaze too alert. He took a single bite of the mousse, then set his spoon down, his fingers lightly tapping the base of his glass.

The contrast between us was stark—I, unwinding with each passing moment, and he, seemingly coiled tighter, as though bracing for a storm only he could see. The food may have satisfied the physical hunger, but whatever gnawed at him wasn't so easily sated.

"Move in with me," he said, his voice low but direct, the words cutting through the quiet like a blade.

I froze, my wineglass halfway to my lips. "What?"

"You heard me," he said, his gray eyes steady as they met mine. "I want you to move in with me. Permanently. No more of the back and forth—your place or mine. I want it to be our place."

"Cassian..." I set the glass down carefully, my heart thudding against my ribs. "We've talked about this."

"And I'm bringing it up again," he countered, his tone calm but unyielding. "You're already here more often than not. It makes sense."

"It's not about what makes sense," I said, leaning forward slightly. "We are just now reexploring this, learning to make things work. I don't want to rush into something that could damage what we have already."

His jaw tightened, but he didn't interrupt. I took a deep breath, trying to put my thoughts into words.

"Your world, Cassian... it's intense. Complicated. I'm still trying to find my footing in it. Moving in with you—it's a commitment that I'm not sure I'm ready for. I'd be stepping even deeper into your life, your world. And I need time to figure out if I'm ready for that."

For a moment, he said nothing, his gaze locked on mine with an intensity that made my stomach twist. Then he exhaled slowly, setting his glass down with deliberate care.

"I understand," he said finally, though his tone was laced with reluctance. "But I'm not going to stop asking."

The corners of my lips twitched despite myself. "I didn't expect you to."

A faint smile touched his lips, and for a moment, the tension between us eased. The conversation wasn't over, not by a long shot, but for now, it felt like enough.

As the night wore on, we drifted back into lighter topics, the weight of the day gradually lifting. But as I sat there, watching the way the candlelight flickered against the sharp planes of Cassian's face, I couldn't help but wonder if my hesitation wasn't just about his world—but about the part of me that was afraid of getting too close. Too attached.

The wineglass in my hand felt cool and grounding as I swirled its contents absently, watching the crimson liquid catch the light. I glanced up at Cassian, his sharp features still tense, his thoughts clearly elsewhere despite the calm setting. The air between us carried an unspoken tension, and I couldn't help but voice the concern gnawing at me.

"So... this drug sting," I started, hesitating slightly when his gray eyes flicked to mine. "Is it really a good idea? It sounds dangerous."

His lips pressed into a faint line before he leaned forward, resting his elbows on the table. "It's a cut-and-dry process," he said, his tone brisk but steady. "Markson's done this a dozen times before, and his team knows how to handle it."

I frowned, my fingers tightening slightly around the stem of the glass. "Yeah, but doesn't that worry you?"

The question hung in the air, unanswered. Cassian's gaze drifted past me, his expression unreadable as though he hadn't heard me at all. But I knew better—he was choosing not to respond.

I studied him for a moment, the way his jaw tightened ever so slightly, the subtle crease between his brows deepening as his fingers tapped rhythmically against the table. Whatever thoughts were running through his mind, he wasn't sharing them.

Realizing I wouldn't get more out of him, I sighed softly and set my glass down. "You should get to it, then," I said, my voice quieter now. "I can tell you're ready to start planning, ready to analyze every variable and hatch your masterplan..."

Cassian's eyes snapped back to mine, and for a fleeting moment, something unspoken passed between us. Gratitude, perhaps, or acknowledgment that I understood the part of him that always needed to stay three steps ahead.

He walked over and wrapped his fingers into my hair before kissing my forehead, "I'll be in my office if you need me."

I pushed back my chair and rose, feeling the stiffness in

my legs from the long day. "I'll be fine, I'm going to take a bath," I said lightly, offering a faint smile as I stepped away from the table.

His gaze followed me briefly before he turned his attention to the papers waiting on a side table. The weight of his focus shifted entirely to the task at hand, and I knew that for Cassian, there would be no pause until every detail was meticulously planned.

The bathroom was a haven of quiet and warmth as I filled the deep tub with steaming water, adding a generous pour of lavender-scented oil that swirled into the water in silky ribbons. The faint sound of classical music from earlier still played faintly in my mind, mingling with the soft splash of the water against porcelain.

I stepped in slowly, the heat enveloping me and soothing the ache in my muscles. As I sank down, the tension of the day began to dissolve, leaving me alone with my thoughts.

Cassian's world was one of calculated risks, and though he spoke of Markson's plan with the confidence of someone who'd seen it all before, I couldn't shake the unease curling in my chest. *Doesn't that worry you?* I'd asked, and his silence had been louder than any answer.

I tilted my head back against the edge of the tub, letting the lavender-scented steam rise around me as I closed my eyes. I couldn't change who Cassian was, nor the world he operated in, but that didn't make it easier to live with the constant undercurrent of danger.

As much as I wanted to push those thoughts away, I knew they'd linger, waiting in the corners of my mind. For now, though, I let the water cradle me, its warmth the only comfort I allowed myself. And in the quiet of the bathroom, I tried to forget the storm I knew was coming.

The water was cooling, its warmth fading into the steam still clinging to the mirrors. I ran a hand along the rim of the tub, tracing lazy patterns as I tried to will away the knot of tension still lingering in my chest. Cassian hadn't come back.

With a soft sigh, I rose from the tub, the water cascading down my skin as I stepped onto the plush bath mat.

Wrapping a towel around me, I padded to the counter and wiped a hand over the fogged mirror. My reflection stared back at me, flushed from the heat of the bath, but the shadows beneath my eyes told their own story.

I dried off quickly, tying the soft robe Cassian had left on the door around me. The fabric was luxurious, the kind that felt like it was meant to be lived in forever. But even its comfort couldn't distract me for long. Cassian was still holed up in his office, no doubt consumed by whatever he and Markson had concocted.

As I tightened the sash of the robe, a thought struck me, impulsive and slightly wicked.

He wanted to dive into his world and leave me to navigate mine? Fine. But that didn't mean I couldn't remind him of what was waiting on this side of the door.

CHAPTER NINETEEN

The hallway leading to Cassian's office was quiet, save for the faint murmur of voices drifting through the partially open door. I paused just outside, my heart racing—not from nerves, but from anticipation. Adjusting the robe so it sat loose against my skin, I stepped inside.

Cassian was seated at his desk, his focus locked on the papers spread before him. Two other men stood near the corner of the room, speaking in hushed tones, their expressions serious. None of them noticed me at first.

I moved with deliberate slowness, positioning myself directly in Cassian's line of sight but far enough from the others that only he could see me clearly. His gaze flicked up, his sharp features softening just slightly when he saw me.

I held his eyes as my hands moved to the sash of the robe, tugging it free with a teasing slowness. The fabric slipped open, revealing bare skin beneath.

Cassian's gray eyes darkened instantly, the corner of his mouth twitching as though he were trying to hold back a smirk. He straightened in his chair, his posture suddenly more alert, and raised a hand to silence the men mid-sentence.

"We're done here," he said, his tone calm but carrying an

authority that left no room for argument.

The men exchanged quick glances, clearly confused but smart enough not to ask questions. They gathered their things and slipped out of the office without another word, the door clicking shut behind them.

Cassian's gaze never left mine.

The moment we were alone, he pushed his chair back slightly and crooked a finger at me. "Come here," he said, his voice low and filled with promise.

I let the robe slip from my shoulders entirely as I moved toward him, the fabric pooling at my feet. Cassian's eyes roamed over me with a hunger that made my skin tingle, but he didn't say anything. Instead, he reached out, his hands firm but gentle as they guided me into his lap.

The leather of his chair was cool against my legs, a stark contrast to the heat of his hands as they settled on my hips. I looped my arms around his neck, my fingers playing with the ends of his hair as I met his gaze.

"You're supposed to be working," I teased, though my voice was playful and light—I knew exactly what I was doing.

"And you're supposed to be relaxing," he countered, his lips curving into a faint smirk.

"I was. Until I realized you'd forgotten all about me."

Cassian's hands tightened on my hips, his smirk fading as his expression grew more serious. "I could never forget about you, Rosalie," he said, his voice rougher now. "Not now, not ever. I told you, you're mine—and I meant it."

The intensity in his tone made my breath catch, but before I could respond, he leaned in, his lips capturing mine in a kiss that was both commanding and tender. His hands moved slowly, deliberately, as though he was memorizing every inch of me.

Whatever plans he'd been making moments ago, they seemed to evaporate, leaving only us. And for the first time all evening, the tension that had been lingering since we'd left the woods finally began to dissolve.

Cassian's lips pressed against mine with a fire that seemed to melt away every thought but him. His hands slid from my hips to the small of my back, pulling me flush against him as the kiss deepened, his tongue teasing mine in a rhythm that left me breathless.

The tension that had simmered all evening finally erupted into something raw and consuming, his touch igniting every nerve in my body. I shifted in his lap, the heat between us building with every kiss, every brush of his hands.

My fingers trailed down his chest, slipping beneath the open collar of his shirt to feel the warmth of his skin. He groaned softly against my lips, his grip tightening, but I was already moving, sliding off his lap and sinking onto my knees between the chair and the desk.

Cassian's breath hitched, his gray eyes darkening as he looked down at me, his expression a mix of surprise and raw desire. "Rosalie... you never cease to amaze me," he murmured, his voice rough with restraint.

I didn't answer, my hands already working at his belt. The soft clink of the buckle filled the charged silence, followed by the whisper of fabric as I freed him from the confines of his pants.

Cassian's length stood rigid and thick, the heat of him palpable as I wrapped my hand around him. His head tilted back slightly, a low growl escaping his throat as my tongue flicked across the tip, tasting him.

His hands curled into fists against the arms of the chair, his control fraying as I took him deeper, my lips sliding down his shaft with deliberate slowness.

"Fuck, Rosalie," he groaned, his voice a husky rasp as his hips shifted involuntarily.

I looked up, meeting his gaze as I moved, my tongue swirling with each stroke. His expression was pure intensity, his usually sharp features softened by the pleasure overtaking him. The sight sent a thrill through me, and I quickened my pace, hollowing my cheeks as I took him deeper.

Cassian's hand found its way to my hair, his fingers threading through the strands as he guided me, his movements still gentle despite the tension coiling in his body. His breath came in ragged bursts, his control unraveling with every flick of my tongue, every stroke of my lips.

"Rosalie," he said again, his voice rougher now, almost a plea. "You're going to—"

I didn't stop, my focus entirely on him, on the way his body responded to every touch. His hand tightened in my hair, his jaw clenching as his hips bucked slightly, his restraint slipping further with every passing second.

When he finally shattered, his release came with a deep groan, his body trembling beneath my hands. I stayed with him, my movements softening as I helped him ride out the waves of pleasure.

The room was quiet again, save for the sound of his breathing as it slowed, his chest rising and falling heavily. Cassian's hand loosened in my hair, his fingers brushing lightly against my scalp before he guided me back to my feet.

He pulled me into his lap again, his arms wrapping around me as he pressed a kiss to my forehead. "You're going to ruin me," he murmured, his voice still thick with emotion.

Cassian's arms tightened around me as he stood, lifting me effortlessly off the floor. His lips found mine again, the kiss stronger, more commanding than before. His hands gripped my waist as he pressed me against his chest, his movements full of a hunger that sent shivers through my entire body.

My fingers curled into his shirt, pulling him closer as his tongue teased mine, the kiss deepening with every second. His dominance was unrelenting, each touch and kiss making it clear that he wasn't holding back anymore.

Without breaking the kiss, he carried me around the desk, his stride steady and deliberate until my back met the cool surface of his desk. Papers and pens were brushed aside with a swift movement of his hand, scattering onto the floor.

He pulled back just enough to look at me, his gray eyes dark and stormy, filled with a need that mirrored my own.

"You have no idea what you do to me, Miss Quinn," he murmured, his voice low and gravelly as his hands slid down the sides of my body, slipping the robe from my shoulders.

The cool air against my bare skin was nothing compared to the heat radiating from him. His gaze swept over me, possessive and reverent all at once, before he stepped between my legs and claimed my lips again.

Cassian's hands moved with purpose, gripping my thighs and pulling me closer to the edge of the desk. The hard surface beneath me was a stark contrast to the warmth of his body as he leaned into me, his lips leaving a trail of fire along my neck and collarbone.

"Look at me," he commanded softly, his hand tilting my chin upward.

I met his gaze, my breath catching at the intensity in his eyes. He positioned himself against me, the heat and pressure making me gasp as he slid into me with one fluid motion.

The stretch was exquisite, a perfect blend of pleasure and pain as my body adjusted to him. His grip on my hips tightened, anchoring me in place as he began to move, each thrust deep and deliberate.

My hands flew to his shoulders, clutching him tightly as he set a rhythm that left me gasping. The desk creaked faintly beneath us, the sound lost in the symphony of our breaths and soft moans.

"Cassian," I breathed, my voice breaking as he drove me closer to the edge.

"Eyes on me," he growled, his tone a mixture of dominance and desire. His hand slid to the small of my back, pulling me even closer to him. "I want to see you fall apart."

His words sent a shiver racing through me, the pressure building with every thrust until I felt like I might shatter. His movements became faster, harder, his control slipping as his own need took over.

When I finally unraveled, the release was overwhelming, my body trembling as waves of pleasure crashed over me. Cassian followed moments later, his grip on me tightening as he groaned deeply, his release drawing mine out even further.

We stayed like that for a moment, our bodies entwined, the aftershocks of pleasure rippling through us both. His forehead rested against mine, his breathing heavy as he whispered my name softly, almost reverently.

"Rosalie," he murmured, his lips brushing against my temple.

I leaned into him, my hands sliding down his back as I tried to catch my breath. The world outside the office felt distant, unimportant, as if nothing else existed but us in this moment.

Cassian pulled back slightly, his gaze softening as he looked at me. "You're incredible," he said, his voice a low rumble.

I smiled, my fingers brushing against his jaw. "So are you."

For once, he didn't argue, just kissed me again, slower this time, the fire replaced by something gentler. And as the tension melted away, I felt a sense of connection that went deeper than words, a silent promise lingering between us in the quiet glow of the room.

CHAPTER TWENTY

The morning light streamed through the windows of Ivy & Bloom, casting soft, golden hues over the counter and the carefully arranged displays of flowers. The shop felt like a haven of peace, a stark contrast to the tension that had hung in the air since Cassian started preparing for the drug sting.

It had been three days of watching him slip further into his world, his focus razor-sharp and impenetrable. And though he hadn't said it outright, I knew his refusal to let me anywhere near Salvatori's club, Nocturne today was as much about protecting me as it was about staying in control.

So here I was, at the shop, reviewing the stack of documents Cassian had left for me. The amended contract lay on the counter, its crisp edges and meticulously worded clauses staring up at me like a challenge.

I ran my fingers over the pages, my eyes scanning the terms for what felt like the hundredth time. Cassian had been true to his word—the language was clearer now, the loopholes I'd once bristled at carefully sealed. The terms gave me full operational control of Ivy & Bloom, while Cassian retained a silent, financial stake—with the majority of the power seated with me rather than him.

It was more than I'd expected. He'd signed it over to me, trusting me with something I wasn't sure I fully deserved but couldn't bring myself to refuse.

My pen hovered over the bottom line for a moment, hesitation flickering briefly before I exhaled and signed my name. The motion felt final, like closing a door on one chapter and stepping into another.

I set the pen down, my gaze lingering on the document. A strange mix of emotions swirled in my chest—relief, pride, and a faint undercurrent of unease. This was mine now, truly mine. But at what cost?

The hum of activity in the shop carried on as I worked, the familiar routine comforting me. Lena had popped in earlier to drop off a shipment of supplies, her usual efficiency tempered by an almost uncharacteristic softness when she asked about Cassian. I'd brushed her off with a vague answer, not wanting to share details I wasn't sure I fully understood myself.

By mid-afternoon, the shop was quiet again, the faint scent of roses and eucalyptus filling the air. I leaned back in my chair, stretching out the stiffness in my shoulders as I glanced toward the window.

Cassian's world felt so far away from this one, yet I couldn't shake the weight of it. Somewhere across the city, he was preparing for something dangerous, something I couldn't be part of. The thought twisted in my stomach, but I pushed it down, focusing instead on the familiar comfort of the shop.

As the hours passed, I found myself glancing at my phone more often than I wanted to admit. There were no updates from Cassian, no reassurance that everything was going according to plan.

The quiet was almost deafening, and though I tried to stay busy, a gnawing sense of anticipation crept in. Signing the contract had felt like a step toward stability, but the uncertainty of Cassian's world loomed over me, a reminder that nothing about this life would ever truly be simple.

And as the clock ticked on, I couldn't help but wonder— what would happen if this sting didn't go as planned?

The shop was my usual sanctuary, but today, it felt like a fragile bubble—a quiet place I couldn't trust to hold against the storm brewing in Cassian's world. Still, I kept my hands busy, completing orders with the same dedication I'd learned from years of working under my father's watchful eye.

A bouquet of ivory roses sat on the counter in front of me, their velvety petals catching the soft, golden light filtering through the shop's wide windows. I carefully trimmed their stems, arranging them alongside eucalyptus and delicate sprigs of lavender, my hands moving on autopilot.

The details of the day blurred together—phone calls, client requests, rearranging a display of hydrangeas near the front. I escaped to my office during a lull, the familiar scent of coffee and ink greeting me as I surveyed the small but functional space.

The desk was cluttered with receipts and order forms, the ledger tucked beneath a stack of inventory reports. With a sigh, I pulled it out, running my fingers over the worn cover before opening it.

As the hours passed, I updated the accounts, cross-referencing numbers with shipments, my pen scratching against the pages in a steady rhythm. Yet, no matter how focused I tried to be, a faint unease prickled at the edges of my thoughts. The tension wasn't mine alone—I'd caught glimpses of it in Marcus and Sierra, who lingered near the shop's entrance like sentinels.

By the time the sun began to set, the golden light in the shop had shifted to a deep amber, the shadows stretching long across the wooden floor. I straightened a stack of invoices on my desk, glancing at the clock. Cassian hadn't called, and though I knew he was preoccupied, the silence gnawed at me.

I stepped out of the office, my eyes falling on Marcus and Sierra. They were standing near the front door, their postures stiff, their movements clipped.

"What's going on?" I asked, my voice steady despite the unease coiling in my chest.

Marcus glanced at Sierra before turning to me, his expression unreadable. "We need to leave, Miss Quinn," he said, his tone low but firm.

"Leave?" I frowned, glancing around the shop. "Why? What's happening?"

Sierra stepped forward, her eyes scanning the street outside before looking back at me. "Cassian's orders. It's a simple precaution."

"A precaution for what?" I pressed, frustration creeping into my voice. "What aren't you telling me?"

Neither of them answered directly. Marcus reached for the keys hanging near the counter while Sierra moved closer to me, her hand lightly brushing my arm. "Please, Miss Quinn," she said quietly. "We'll explain in a bit, but not here, not now."

My pulse quickened, but I nodded, the urgency in their voices enough to silence further questions. Marcus locked up the shop behind us, and Sierra guided me toward the waiting car parked along the curb.

The ride was tense and silent, the city lights blurring past the tinted windows as we drove. Sierra sat beside me, her phone in hand, while Marcus navigated through the streets with a calm that felt forced.

"Where are we going?" I asked finally, unable to stand the silence.

"We'll explain everything soon enough; you just need to trust us," Marcus replied curtly, his gaze fixed on the road.

The answer did little to settle my nerves.

When we arrived, the car pulled up to The Peninsula Chicago, a landmark of elegance and discretion in the heart of the city. The sleek, modern facade rose into the night sky, its towering glass windows reflecting the golden glow of streetlights and the faint shimmer of Lake Michigan in the distance. A uniformed doorman nodded respectfully as Marcus stepped out first, his sharp gaze sweeping the surrounding streets before he opened my door.

Sierra guided me inside, her pace brisk and purposeful. The moment we entered, the world seemed to shift. The lobby was a masterpiece of understated luxury, designed to make you feel cloaked in exclusivity the second you crossed its threshold.

Marble floors gleamed under a soft glow of recessed lighting, their creamy hues complemented by rich accents of mahogany and bronze. Towering floral arrangements of orchids and lilies filled the space with a faint, sophisticated fragrance, their petals perfectly arranged as though untouched by human hands.

My footsteps were muffled by the thick Persian rugs that framed the reception area, their intricate patterns a nod to timeless craftsmanship. The low hum of classical piano music drifted from somewhere nearby, soothing and unobtrusive, adding to the serene ambiance.

Despite the grandeur, there was a quiet intimacy to the space. Conversations were hushed, and the staff moved with professional strides, their smiles polite but never intrusive. Everything about the hotel exuded privacy and control, the kind of place where secrets were both kept and expected. A place only Cassian would approve of.

Sierra strode to the reception desk, where a well-dressed concierge greeted her with a professional nod. Their conversation was brief and low, Sierra signing in under an alias without so much as a flicker of hesitation. The concierge handed over the keycards with a small, knowing smile, gesturing toward the private elevators.

"This way," Sierra murmured, her hand brushing lightly against my arm as she led me toward the elevators.

The mirrored doors reflected my faintly frazzled appearance, a stark contrast to Sierra's calm, composed demeanor. The elevator rose smoothly, the quiet hum of its ascent punctuated only by the faint chime as we passed each floor.

When we reached the suite, the doors opened to reveal a space that could only be described as opulent. The living area was expansive, its plush furnishings arranged around a glass coffee table that reflected the soft, ambient lighting. Floor-to-ceiling windows framed a breathtaking view of Chicago's skyline, the city lights twinkling like a sea of stars.

The bedroom was equally stunning, dominated by a king-sized bed draped in crisp white linens and accented with soft, muted tones of gold and slate gray. A private dining area and a marble-tiled bathroom with a deep soaking tub completed the space, each detail designed to cater to the kind of clientele who valued both luxury and privacy.

Sierra stood near the door, her expression steady as she turned to me. "You'll stay here until we get word from Cassian," she said, her tone firm but not unkind.

I nodded, my gaze lingering on the glittering cityscape outside the window. The Peninsula wasn't just a hotel—it was a fortress of tranquility, a place where the outside world couldn't reach. And yet, as I stood there, the tension in my chest refused to dissipate, the glittering lights below a stark contrast to the uncertainty that loomed above them.

The room was silent except for the soft ticking of a sleek wall clock and the muted hum of the city below. I perched on the edge of the expansive couch, my hands twisting in my lap as I stared out at the dazzling skyline. The Peninsula's luxury might have been comforting in any other situation, but now, it only felt like a gilded cage.

Sierra and Marcus stood by the door, their postures stiff, their expressions carefully blank. They'd barely spoken since escorting me to the suite, their silence only adding to the weight pressing down on me.

Finally, I couldn't take it anymore. "What's going on?" I asked, my voice sharper than I intended. "Why am I here, and where is Cassian?"

Marcus exchanged a glance with Sierra, something unspoken passing between them. Sierra stepped forward, her normally composed expression tinged with hesitation.

"Cassian..." She paused, as though searching for the right words. "He's been arrested."

The words hit me like a physical blow, stealing the breath from my lungs. "Arrested?" I echoed, my voice barely above a whisper.

"For what?"

Sierra took a deep breath, her hands clasped tightly in

front of her. "He was charged with possession of narcotics with intent to distribute, conspiracy to traffic controlled substances, and money laundering. The DEA was involved. They've been building a case against him for months."

I stared at her, the room spinning slightly as the weight of her words sank in. "What?" My voice broke, the disbelief clear in the single word. "How can you be so calm right now?"

Marcus stepped closer, his tone relaxed but grim. "The sting at Salvatori's club—it was compromised. They moved in on him before Markson's team could act. The evidence they presented..." He hesitated, glancing at Sierra.

"It's enough to keep him held without bail," Sierra finished, her tone quieter now.

My stomach churned, a wave of nausea rolling through me. "This doesn't make sense," I said, shaking my head. "Cassian wouldn't—"

"Rosalie," Marcus interrupted gently, his voice steady. "Whether he would or wouldn't doesn't matter right now. What matters is that they've got enough to make it stick. He's not walking out of this without a fight."

My hands curled into fists in my lap, my nails digging into my palms. The details of Cassian's world had always felt distant, abstract—things I could observe without fully stepping into. But this? This was real, undeniable, and impossible to ignore.

"What happens now?" I asked, forcing the words out despite the lump in my throat.

Marcus sighed, his shoulders relaxing slightly. "Now, we wait. His legal team is already working on it, but it's going to take time."

"And in the meantime?"

Sierra stepped forward, her expression softening. "Cassian's orders were clear. You're to stay here, under our protection, until we know it's safe."

"Safe from what?" I demanded, my voice rising. "Stop tiptoeing around me like I'm fragile. Cassian was just arrested, now tell me everything you know."

"There are a lot of moving parts," Marcus said carefully.

"With Cassian out of the picture, it leaves a vacuum. People are going to notice, and not all of them will be friendly."

The implication hung heavily in the air.

I stood abruptly, pacing to the window as I tried to make sense of the storm that had just engulfed my life. The glittering cityscape suddenly felt cold, menacing, as though every light below was another piece of this world I couldn't escape.

"How long am I supposed to stay here?" I asked finally, my voice quieter now.

"Until Cassian says otherwise," Sierra replied, her tone leaving no room for argument.

I turned to face them, my chest tight with frustration and fear. Whether I wanted to or not, I'd been dragged further into Cassian's world—thrown into the chaos that surrounded him. And as much as I wanted to deny it, to run from it, I couldn't.

Cassian was in trouble, real trouble, and no amount of denial would change that. All I could do now was wait—and figure out where I stood in a life that had just become infinitely more complicated.

CHAPTER TWENTY-ONE

The faint glow of the city lights spilled into the suite, casting long shadows across the room as the hours dragged on. I paced near the window, the cold marble floor biting against my bare feet. A single glass of untouched wine sat on the coffee table, its rich burgundy color glinting faintly in the dim light.

Across the room, Cassian's lawyer—Harrison Blackwell, an older man with graying hair and a no-nonsense demeanor—sat at the desk, his reading glasses perched low on his nose as he rifled through a thick stack of documents. His tailored suit, slightly rumpled from the long day, spoke of a man who rarely let himself relax.

"This doesn't look good, Miss Quinn," he said finally, his gravelly voice breaking the tense silence.

I stopped pacing and turned to face him, my arms crossed tightly over my chest. "What do you mean 'doesn't look good'?"

Harrison pulled off his glasses, pinching the bridge of his nose as though he were trying to ease an invisible pressure. "The evidence against Cassian is..." He hesitated, choosing his words carefully. "It's thorough. Insurmountable, even."

I sank onto the edge of the couch, my legs feeling unsteady. "What kind of evidence?"

Harrison set the papers down, his gaze sharp and unyielding. "They've got his fingerprints on a significant quantity of the product seized at Salvatori's club. Surveillance footage placing him near multiple suspected drop points. Records that link large sums of money from his accounts to known drug suppliers."

"That doesn't make sense," I argued, my voice trembling. "Cassian wouldn't be that careless. He wouldn't—"

"Precisely," Harrison interrupted, leaning forward slightly. "Cassian is too meticulous to leave a trail like this. Which is why I believe this was a setup—a damn good one."

His words hit me like a punch to the gut. "A setup?"

Harrison nodded grimly. "Someone wanted him behind bars, and they went to great lengths to make it happen. Everything aligns too perfectly—too conveniently."

I pressed my fingers to my temples, my mind racing. "Who would do this? And why?"

"Enemies—he has a fair amount of them," Harrison said simply, shrugging as though the question were irrelevant. "Rivals. People who want Cassian out of the way. Take your pick."

The suite was heavy with silence, the weight of Harrison's grim assessment settling in my chest like lead. I tried to focus on the papers spread across the desk, the endless lines of legal jargon blurring together, but the sharp ring of Marcus's phone shattered the quiet.

My head snapped up as Marcus, standing near the suite door, answered with a brisk, "Yeah."

A pause followed, his expression tightening as he listened. "No, she's fine," Marcus said, his tone clipped but professional. "And no, you don't need to know where she is."

Sierra, standing near the window, exchanged a glance with me, her brow furrowed.

Marcus's gaze flicked to me briefly before he turned his back, his voice dropping lower. "I'll pass it along. Anything else?"

Another pause, and then Marcus's lips thinned. "Goodbye, Detective." He ended the call without waiting for a response, slipping the phone back into his pocket with a controlled motion that hinted at frustration.

"What was that about?" I asked, my voice quieter now.

"Markson," Marcus replied, his tone curt. "He wanted to know how you were holding up and where you were."

"And you didn't tell him," I said, though it wasn't a question.

"Of course not," Marcus said, folding his arms across his chest. "Cassian's orders were clear—you're to stay off everyone's radar, including his, but he was adamant I let you know that he had nothing to do with this."

Markson's call, brief as it had been, now felt less like a lifeline and more like another layer of uncertainty.

Harrison cleared his throat, drawing my attention back to the desk. "Focus, Miss Quinn. If we're going to help Cassian, we can't waste time worrying about who called whom."

I nodded slowly, though the unease didn't fade. As the night dragged on, the unanswered questions swirled in my mind. Markson's motives, the evidence against Cassian, and the shadowy figures pulling the strings—it all felt like a web tightening around us.

And no matter how hard I tried to untangle it, I couldn't shake the feeling that I was already caught in it.

The room felt colder as the hours dragged on, the weight of uncertainty pressing down on me like an invisible hand. I hadn't been able to talk to Cassian since his arrest, and the absence of his voice felt sharper with every passing minute. Harrison had returned from his visit to Cassian earlier that night, carrying nothing but a folded piece of paper and an expression that told me I wouldn't like what I was about to read.

Now, the note lay open on the desk, its contents written in Cassian's sharp, deliberate handwriting.

Rosalie,
This is the only message I can send. I need you to act in my place. No one else can take this on—not the way you can. Marcus and Sierra will follow your lead. You'll need to call a meeting of my inner circle, and you know where it needs

to happen. I trust you, Rosalie.
   -Cassian

The words felt like a punch to the gut. Cassian trusted me—more than anyone—but stepping into his world like this, truly stepping into it, was something I'd never anticipated. My heart raced as I stared at the note, the gravity of his request settling over me.

"Miss Quinn?" Marcus's voice cut through my thoughts. He stood by the door, his sharp gaze assessing me carefully.

I folded the note and slipped it into my pocket, turning to face him. "We need to gather Cassian's closest men," I said, my voice steadier than I expected. "And we need to meet at the distillery. Tonight."

Marcus's brow furrowed, his arms crossing over his chest. "The distillery?"

"Yes, I trust you'll make the calls?" I said firmly, stepping closer to him. "He's trusting me to handle this, and I'm trusting you to help me do it."

For a moment, Marcus didn't respond, his expression unreadable. Then, with a slow nod, he said, "I'll make the calls."

Sierra stepped forward, her eyes narrowing slightly. "Do you know what you're walking into?"

"No," I admitted, my stomach twisting. "But Cassian does. And if he says the distillery is where we need to be, then that's where we'll go."

The drive to the distillery was quiet, the tension in the car palpable. Marcus sat in the passenger seat, his phone pressed to his ear as he confirmed details with Cassian's inner circle. Sierra drove, her eyes flicking to the rearview mirror every few minutes, her hand resting near the firearm at her side.

The distillery loomed ahead, its massive structure a mix of old-world charm and modern function. The scent of oak barrels and faint traces of whiskey hung in the air as we pulled into the gravel lot, the crunch of tires loud in the stillness.

Inside, the space was cavernous, the high ceilings and

dim lighting casting long shadows over the rows of barrels. The faint hum of machinery filled the air, blending with the sound of footsteps as Cassian's men began to arrive.

One by one, they entered—men I recognized from fleeting glances and whispered conversations. Their presence was intimidating, their loyalty to Cassian clear in the way they carried themselves.

When the last man arrived, Marcus gestured for everyone to gather near a long wooden table in the center of the room. They stood in a loose circle, their eyes shifting between me and Marcus, their expressions guarded.

"This is her meeting," Marcus said, stepping back slightly to let me take the lead.

All eyes turned to me, and for a moment, the weight of their attention threatened to crush me. But then I thought of Cassian—his trust in me, his belief that I could handle this—and I straightened my shoulders, meeting their gazes one by one.

"Cassian's instructions were clear," I began, my voice steady despite the nerves coiling in my stomach. "Until he's back, I'm in charge. And we have work to do."

The room was silent, the men waiting for me to continue. The enormity of the task ahead loomed, but I knew there was no turning back now. Cassian had handed me the reins to his empire, and whether I was ready or not, it was time to take command.

CHAPTER TWENTY-TWO

The hum of voices in the distillery fell silent as I stepped forward, the echo of my boots against the bare floor the only sound. Cassian's men—tough, seasoned, and loyal to a fault—stood in a loose circle around the room. Their faces were a mix of curiosity and caution, though the tension in their postures betrayed the unease none of them dared to show outright.

I stopped at the center of the circle, the faint scent of whiskey and aged oak hanging in the air. My heart pounded, but I kept my shoulders back and my chin high, channeling every ounce of confidence Cassian had instilled in me. If I faltered now, I'd lose them—and him.

"Let me be clear," I began, my voice steady but firm. "Cassian trusted you. Every single one of you. And now, with him locked up, I'm trusting you too. But that trust isn't blind. Not today."

A ripple of unease passed through the group. I could see it in the subtle shifts of their bodies—the way one man adjusted his stance, another crossed his arms too quickly, as if to shield himself. Good. Let them feel the weight of what was coming.

I reached into my pocket and pulled out the folded note Cassian had written. Unfolding it slowly, I let their curiosity grow as I skimmed my eyes over the familiar handwriting.

"This is from Cassian," I said, holding it up for them to see. "He made it clear that his empire is at risk. Someone inside this circle—someone he trusted—is working against him."

Murmurs broke out, low and agitated. I let them simmer for a moment before raising a hand, cutting through the noise with a sharp look.

"I'm giving you the chance to come clean now," I continued, pacing slowly within the circle. "If you confess, we'll deal with it here, in this room. If you wait until the evidence comes to light—and trust me, it will—you'll deal with Cassian himself."

The silence that followed my words was suffocating, stretching longer than anyone in the room seemed comfortable with. I kept my stance steady, my gaze firm, scanning their faces like a spotlight sweeping over a stage.

The first reaction came from the man closest to me—a broad-shouldered enforcer with tattoos snaking up his neck. He shifted his weight subtly from one foot to the other, his fingers brushing against the hem of his jacket. His jaw clenched tightly, the muscle ticking as though he was physically biting back words.

Another man near the back let out a faint huff of air, crossing his arms over his chest with a sharpness that felt defensive rather than annoyed. His eyes darted to the floor, then to Marcus, then back to the floor again, as though avoiding my gaze entirely might make him invisible.

The scarred man, the one who had challenged me earlier, was less subtle. He took a deliberate step forward, his boots scraping against the concrete, and fixed me with a hard stare. "This is bullshit," he muttered, though his voice lacked the conviction it should have had.

I didn't flinch, meeting his glare head-on. "Is it?" I said evenly, my tone carefully measured. "Because your reaction tells me otherwise."

His lips curled into a sneer, but he said nothing further, stepping back with a faint shrug as if to brush off the accusation.

Near the edge of the group, a younger man—barely out of his twenties—rubbed at the back of his neck, his eyes flickering nervously between the others. His hands wouldn't stay still, moving from his neck to his pockets and back again, his fidgeting so conspicuous it drew the attention of the man next to him, who elbowed him sharply in the ribs.

"Stop squirming," the older man hissed under his breath, his voice just loud enough to carry.

The younger man stammered something incoherent, his face flushing, but I caught the flicker of panic in his eyes before he looked down at his feet.

Across the room, a tall man with graying hair remained unnervingly calm, his hands clasped loosely in front of him. His expression was neutral, almost bored, but his gaze never left mine, and the corners of his mouth twitched faintly as though he were suppressing a smile. He said nothing, did nothing, but the stillness of his demeanor stood in stark contrast to the unease radiating from the others.

I tucked that observation away, my focus shifting to the group as a whole.

"Cassian's lawyer has already found clues," I said, my voice cutting through the tension like a whip. I let the lie roll off my tongue with practiced ease, watching the ripple it sent through the room. "They've traced the leak to information that only a select few of you had access to. The details were too specific, too well-timed, for it to be anyone outside this room."

The reactions were immediate. One man rubbed at his temples, his shoulders slumping slightly as though the weight of the accusation had settled squarely on his back. Another swore under his breath, his eyes narrowing as he glanced suspiciously at the others.

Marcus remained still, his sharp gaze tracking the movement of each man like a hawk circling prey. Sierra, standing by the doorway, leaned casually against the frame, but the hand resting near her sidearm betrayed her readiness to act.

The scarred man spoke again, his tone louder now. "So what, you're accusing one of us?"

I turned my attention to him, keeping my expression calm but unyielding. "I'm saying the evidence doesn't lie," I replied. "And if it was one of you, you should have the guts to admit it now before things get worse."

A tense laugh broke from someone in the back, sharp and derisive. "You think we're gonna take the fall for something we didn't do?"

My eyes flicked to the source of the laugh, a wiry man with a faint limp. He leaned against a barrel, his arms crossed tightly, his lips pulling into a sneer. But even as he spoke, his gaze darted toward the scarred man, a flicker of unease betraying his bravado.

"I think the guilty party already knows they're caught," I said, tilting my head slightly, letting the weight of my words settle. "And I think they're wondering how much I know."

The room tensed again, the undercurrent of suspicion growing stronger. The men began glancing at each other, their unease palpable as the silence stretched. I let it linger, knowing the pressure was enough to make even the most hardened among them crack.

This wasn't about finding the mole in that exact moment. It was about planting the seed of doubt, forcing the guilty party to question whether they'd been outed. And as I watched the room unravel, I knew it was only a matter of time before someone slipped.

The tension in the room was a living thing now, pressing down on everyone like a suffocating fog. The faint hum of the distillery's equipment in the background seemed louder against the silence that followed my words. I let it stretch just long enough to make the discomfort unbearable before taking another step forward, closer to the group.

"If you think you're safe," I said, my tone sharper now, "you're mistaken. Cassian's system is built on trust, loyalty, and obedience. Every move is tracked. Every detail accounted for. You think you can slip through the cracks?

You can't. Not with me watching."

I gestured to Marcus, who stepped forward with the faintest smirk playing at the corner of his mouth. He held up a small device—a simple black thumb drive—and turned it over in his hand for effect.

"We've already started pulling logs," Marcus said, his voice steady but deliberate. "Every call, every shipment, every key card swipe in the security system. If you've been sloppy, it'll show up. And when it does..." His smile widened, just enough to send a chill through the room.

I didn't know if what Marcus said was true. Hell, I didn't even know if the thumb drive held anything at all. But the ripple it sent through the group was enough. The wiry man near the barrel shifted uncomfortably, his arms tightening across his chest. The younger one—still fidgeting—rubbed his palms against his jeans, his eyes darting toward the door for the briefest moment.

"I'll give you one last chance," I said, my voice carrying a sharp finality. "Come clean now, and maybe—just maybe—you'll walk out of here with something to bargain with. But if you wait until we have proof..." I trailed off, letting the weight of my silence fill the gap.

Most of the men avoided my gaze, their unease spilling into their body language. The scarred man tried to mask his discomfort by standing straighter, his shoulders squaring as though bracing for impact. His jaw tightened, his eyes narrowing in a way that screamed defiance.

The room felt like a coiled spring, each passing second ratcheting the tension higher. And then, just as I thought the silence might snap, the younger man—the one with the restless hands—moved.

It happened so fast that for a moment, I wasn't sure what I'd seen. He bolted toward the door, his footsteps echoing sharply against the concrete. Sierra moved instantly, her hand snapping to her weapon as Marcus blocked his path with the force of a battering ram.

The younger man stumbled back, his breath coming in ragged gasps as he raised his hands, palms out in surrender. "I wasn't—It's not—" He stammered, his words tumbling over each other in a frantic mess.

Sierra stepped forward, her expression cold as she leveled her weapon at him. "I'd think real carefully about your next words."

The others stared, their shock genuine, though it was quickly swallowed by suspicion. Whispers broke out among the group, a low murmur of voices that made the room feel even more suffocating.

I stepped toward the man slowly, my heart pounding in my chest, though I forced my voice to remain steady. "What were you planning to do?" I asked, keeping my gaze locked on his.

"N-nothing," he stammered, his hands trembling as they remained in the air. "I just—this is all wrong. I didn't—"

"You didn't what?" Marcus barked, his tone sharp enough to cut through the man's rambling.

The man flinched, his eyes darting to the others before settling on me. "I didn't mean for it to happen like this," he whispered, his voice barely audible.

My blood ran cold. "What did you mean?"

Before he could answer, Marcus grabbed him by the collar, hauling him forward. The younger man gasped, his hands scrambling to grip Marcus's wrists.

"You'd better start talking," Marcus growled, his voice low and deadly. "Because the only thing between you and the worst day of your life is her."

I coiled at the evil sentiment, but I couldn't let them see me break my composure now.

He jerked his head toward me, and the younger man's panicked eyes met mine. For a moment, the room seemed to hold its breath.

And then, in a trembling voice, he said, "I didn't think they'd actually arrest him."

The words hit like a hammer, shattering the silence and sending a ripple of shock through the group. My heart pounded in my chest, the weight of what he'd just admitted sinking in like a stone.

I took a slow step forward, my voice colder than I'd ever heard it. "Who?"

His lips trembled, his gaze darting between me and Marcus. "I don't know their names," he said quickly. "They reached out—said they'd make it worth my while if I gave them something. I didn't think—"

I cut him off, my tone sharp enough to make him flinch. "You didn't think. You just sold out Cassian and this entire operation for a quick payday."

He shook his head violently, his breath coming in short gasps. "No! It wasn't like that. They—"

"Enough," Marcus snapped, shoving him toward one of the barrels. The younger man stumbled, collapsing against the cold steel as Sierra moved to restrain him.

The room erupted into angry murmurs, the other men's expressions ranging from disgust to fury. I turned to Marcus, my chest tight with a mix of adrenaline and rage.

"Secure him," I said, my voice hard. "And find out everything he knows. I want names, contacts, and locations. Everything." He started to turn away when I added, "And Marcus, keep him remote and under guard until this is all over with."

Marcus nodded, his expression grim. "On it."

As Sierra dragged the younger man toward the back of the distillery, I turned to the remaining group, my gaze sweeping over them. "Let this be a lesson," I said, my voice cold and steady. "Cassian trusted you. I trusted you. Don't make me regret it."

The room was silent, their eyes fixed on me, the weight of my authority settling over them.

And as I stood there, the echoes of the betrayal still ringing in my ears, I knew one thing for certain: the storm was far from over.

I moved to the next group, dividing them into teams to trace the drugs back to their supplier. "Start with the shipments Cassian flagged last month. Look for anything unusual—altered manifests, unexplained delays, new players. And don't just follow the product; follow the money. That's where we'll find our answers."

They nodded, their expressions grim but determined as they moved to their tasks.

Finally, I turned to Marcus again. "I'll handle Salvatori and his staff personally," I said, my voice quieter but no less firm. "If anyone knows how this setup came together, it's him."

Marcus hesitated for a moment, his brow furrowing. "Are you sure? He's not exactly the cooperative type."

"Exactly why it has to be me," I said.

His gaze lingered on mine, searching for something, before he finally nodded. "Just be careful."

"I will," I said, though the knot in my stomach betrayed my calm exterior.

As the men dispersed, I found myself standing alone in the now-empty center of the distillery. The faint hum of machinery and the distant echo of footsteps filled the silence. I exhaled slowly, my hands brushing against the cool steel of a nearby barrel.

For the first time since this nightmare had begun, I felt the enormity of the situation settle fully into my chest. Cassian was gone, and everything he'd built—everything he'd fought to protect—was now in my hands.

I wasn't sure if I was ready for this. But as I straightened my shoulders and walked toward the exit, one thought steadied me: *Cassian trusted me. Now it was time to prove him right.*

The early morning was cold as I stepped outside, the crisp air biting against my skin. I slid into the waiting car, my mind already racing with questions for Salvatori. The men at the distillery were working to unravel the web around us, but for now, I had one goal: to make Salvatori talk.

And I wasn't leaving until I had answers.

CHAPTER TWENTY-THREE

The early morning light filtered weakly through the heavy curtains, bathing the suite in a muted gray glow. I sat on the edge of the bed, the cool fabric of my blouse clinging to my skin, sticky from the adrenaline that had fueled me through the night. Exhaustion weighed heavily on me, but sleep felt impossible.

The tray of room service on the table remained untouched, save for the faint smudge of a fork dragged halfheartedly through the mashed potatoes. Marcus hovered near the window, his posture stiff, his sharp gaze flicking between his phone and the city skyline as though expecting danger to announce itself at any moment.

"You've been running on fumes for hours," he said without looking at me. "You need to eat something."

"I'm fine," I muttered, my voice hoarse from lack of rest.

"No, you're not," he snapped, turning to face me fully. "You're human, Rosalie. Cassian may trust you to take the reins, but he wouldn't want you collapsing in the middle of it."

I glared at him but said nothing, the fire in my response fizzling out before it reached my lips. He was right, of course, but food felt irrelevant when my mind was a swirling storm of Cassian's arrest, the mole's betrayal, and the delicate balance of an empire teetering on the edge.

"I'll order some breakfast while you shower."

I glared at him but said nothing, the fire in my response fizzling out before it reached my lips. He was right, of course, but food felt irrelevant when my mind was a swirling storm of Cassian's arrest, the mole's betrayal, and the delicate balance of an empire teetering on the edge.

"I'll order some breakfast while you shower."

When I returned to the suite, the smell of freshly brewed coffee and warm toast greeted me. Marcus stood by the small table, his arms crossed as he waited for me to approach. A tray of breakfast sat neatly arranged—eggs, toast, fruit, and a steaming mug of coffee.

"You're eating," he said simply, his tone leaving no room for argument.

I sighed, sinking into the chair he'd pulled out for me. "You're worse than Cassian," I muttered, though the bite in my words was absent.

"I faintly remember him threatening me on my first day of work if anything were to happen to you—no offense, but I'm much more terrified of him than you." Marcus replied, his voice soft but firm. "But I'll admit, that was impressive work in there."

I nodded, not feeling like it was rewarding work at all. It only made me realize we would always be surrounded by a pit of vipers.

I picked up a piece of toast, nibbling at the edges without much enthusiasm. My stomach churned at the thought of the day ahead, but Marcus's unwavering gaze forced me to take a few more bites.

"Better," he said, satisfied.

I ignored him, reaching for the coffee instead. The bitter warmth was a small comfort, cutting through the haze in my mind as I forced myself to focus, but my stomach was not settling. That's what I get for not eating regularly through the night.

"What's the latest from Harrison?" I asked, setting the mug down.

Marcus shook his head. "Nothing good. He's still trying

to poke holes in the evidence, but it's slow going. Whoever set this up, they didn't leave much room for error."

My grip on the mug tightened. "Then we can't wait for him to figure it out. Salvatori knows something. He has to."

"Rosalie—"

"I'm going," I said firmly, cutting him off before he could argue. "He's the last piece of this puzzle, and I'm not going to sit around while he ties up his loose ends."

Marcus sighed heavily, rubbing a hand over his face. "Fine. But you're not going in there alone. Salvatori doesn't play nice, especially not with someone he sees as an outsider."

"Perhaps that was your interaction with him, but I found him to be civil—not obstinate," I said, my voice braver than I felt. "I just need him to talk."

Twenty minutes later, we in the car, pulling out onto the busy Chicago streets. The drive to Nocturne was quieter than I expected. The streets were bathed in the soft light of the morning, the city springing to life around us. I stared out the window, the buildings blurring together as I tried to steel myself for what was to come.

"Salvatori's not going to make this easy," Marcus said, breaking the silence. "If he thinks you're coming in there to dig, he'll shut you down before you can even ask the first question."

"Then I won't give him the chance," I replied, my voice steady despite the storm raging in my chest.

Marcus glanced at me, his brow furrowing slightly. "Just... be careful, Rosalie. This isn't your world."

"It is now," I said softly, my gaze fixed on the horizon.

When we arrived, the car rolled to a stop in front of Nocturne's sleek, unassuming facade. The club looked innocuous in the daylight, its dark windows and simple exterior giving little away about the chaos that brewed inside after dark.

Marcus cut the engine, his fingers drumming once against the steering wheel before he turned to me. "Ready?"

"No," I admitted, unbuckling my seatbelt. "But I'm going in anyway."

As I stepped out of the car and into the cool morning air, I took a deep breath, steeling myself for the confrontation ahead. Salvatori had answers—and I was determined to get them, no matter what it took.

The door to Nocturne loomed ahead, its sleek black frame stark against the muted morning light. As I approached, the bouncer—a towering man with a shaved head and arms that looked capable of crushing steel—stepped forward, blocking my path.

"We're closed," he said gruffly, his tone leaving no room for argument.

"I need to speak with Salvatori," I said, keeping my voice steady and firm.

He didn't move, his dark eyes narrowing slightly. "I don't think you understand. Nobody gets in. Not now."

Before I could argue, a familiar voice cut through the tension.

"Let her through."

The bouncer's stance shifted slightly, his shoulders relaxing as Salvatori stepped out from the shadows behind him. Dressed in a sharp suit and holding a steaming cup of coffee, Salvatori looked as put-together as ever, his expression calm and unreadable.

"Miss Quinn," he said smoothly, a faint smile playing on his lips. "I wasn't expecting you this early."

"I'm sure you weren't," I replied, my tone sharper than I intended.

He chuckled softly, motioning for the bouncer to step aside. "Come in."

The tension in my chest didn't ease as I followed Salvatori into the club. The interior was dark and hushed, the usual pulse of music and chatter replaced by an eerie stillness. The scent of spilled alcohol and faint traces of smoke lingered in the air, mingling with the aroma of freshly brewed coffee.

He led me to one of the private booths tucked in a shadowed corner of the club. The plush green velvet seating was immaculate, and the low, ambient lighting cast long shadows across his sharp features as he gestured for me to sit.

"Coffee?" he offered, setting his own cup down with a deliberate clink against the polished surface of the table. His voice was smooth, the kind of tone that invited trust while keeping its true intentions hidden just out of reach.

Salvatori looked like he belonged in a movie about powerful men and their untouchable empires. His dark suit, tailored to perfection, hugged his lean frame, the crisp white shirt beneath it unbuttoned just enough to suggest casual elegance without straying into carelessness. A sleek silver watch peeked out from beneath his cuff, understated but undeniably expensive.

I hesitated briefly before nodding. "Sure."

With a faint smile, Salvatori reached for the coffee pot. His hands were steady, his fingers long and precise as they gripped the handle. The faint aroma of rich, freshly brewed coffee filled the air as he poured, the steam curling like smoke in the dim light. He didn't rush, his movements measured and confident, as though every action was a calculated part of a performance only he understood.

Sliding the cup across the table with practiced ease, he leaned back into his seat, crossing one leg over the other. His polished leather shoes caught the light briefly as he settled into the booth, the faintest smirk playing at his lips.

His dark hair was perfectly combed, a streak of silver cutting through the temples like a deliberate touch of refinement. His eyes—sharp and piercing—were the color of aged whiskey, warm on the surface but with a depth that hinted at something colder. As he regarded me, there was a quiet intensity in his gaze, like he was already three steps ahead, watching to see how I'd catch up.

He picked up his own cup, taking a slow sip before setting it down again with the same unhurried grace. "You look tired," he said, his voice as smooth as the coffee, but carrying an edge of detached observation that made the comment sting just a little more. "Rough night, I take it?"

It wasn't a question. Salvatori didn't ask questions he didn't already know the answers to.

I took a sip of the coffee, its warmth cutting through the

chill that had settled in my chest. "You could say that," I replied.

His lips curved into a faint smile. "I'm guessing this isn't a social visit."

"No," I said bluntly, setting the cup down. "I need answers, Salvatori."

He leaned back slightly, his posture relaxed, but his eyes were sharp, assessing. "Answers about what?"

"You know what," I said, my voice hardening. "The drugs. The setup. Cassian's arrest. It all starts here."

His smile didn't waver, but there was a flicker of something—amusement, perhaps, or irritation—in his eyes. "You give me a lot of credit, Miss Quinn," he said smoothly. "But I don't have as much control over these things as you seem to think."

"You and I both know that's not true," I said calmly, my frustration on the edge of breaking through. "This is your club. Nothing moves through here without your knowledge."

He raised an eyebrow, his expression calm despite the sharpness of my words. "I'm flattered that you think so highly of me, but the truth is, I run a business. What happens beyond these walls isn't always in my control."

"You're lying," I said, leaning forward. "And you're stalling."

Salvatori's smile widened slightly, his fingers tapping idly against the rim of his coffee cup. "You're tired, Miss Quinn," he said again, his tone almost patronizing. "Perhaps you should take a moment to rest before jumping to conclusions."

I clenched my fists beneath the table, the anger bubbling just below the surface. He was playing with me, dodging my questions and hiding behind his carefully constructed mask.

"Cassian trusted you," I said, my voice low but steady. "And right now, I'm giving you the chance to show me that trust wasn't misplaced. But if you don't start talking, I'll assume you're part of the reason he's behind bars."

Salvatori's smile faded slightly, his eyes narrowing as he

regarded me. For a moment, the silence between us felt suffocating, the weight of his gaze pressing down on me like a challenge.

But he didn't speak, and the longer the silence stretched, the more my frustration grew. He was stonewalling me, and I was running out of patience.

Salvatori's gaze lingered on me, the smirk tugging at his lips softening as he leaned forward slightly. His movements were still deliberate, but there was a shift in his demeanor—a flicker of something deeper beneath the polished facade.

"You think I had a hand in this," he said, his tone quieter now, almost reflective. "That I sold Cassian out to save myself, or worse, that I orchestrated the whole thing."

"It's hard not to," I said as calmly as I could muster, though my voice had lost some of its edge. "The drugs came through your club. The setup leads straight here. Tell me how that happens without you knowing."

He nodded slowly, his fingers tracing the rim of his coffee cup. "You're right to ask. If I were in your position, I'd be questioning me too." His eyes flicked up to meet mine, steady and unflinching. "But you're wrong about me, Rosalie. I've done a lot of things in my life, things I'm not proud of—but betraying Cassian? That's a line I'd never cross."

His words carried a weight that made me pause, but I wasn't ready to let him off the hook just yet. "Then prove it," I said, my voice firm. "Give me something that shows you're not part of this."

A faint smile curved his lips, though it didn't carry the same amusement as before. "You don't trust me yet," he said simply. "That's fair. But let me tell you something about Cassian and me—something you don't know."

I stayed silent, my curiosity piqued despite myself.

"I met Cassian twenty years ago," Salvatori began, his gaze distant as though he were looking through the years. "He was barely more than a kid then—sharp as hell, but reckless, with a chip on his shoulder the size of this city. I was running a small operation back then, nothing like what you see now, but it was enough to keep me in trouble."

He chuckled softly, shaking his head. "Cassian showed up one night at one of my clubs, trying to muscle his way into my business. Thought he was tough enough to take it all on his own." He leaned back, his hand brushing against the silver watch on his wrist. "He underestimated me, of course. I let him think he had the upper hand, just long enough to teach him a lesson."

My brows furrowed, but I didn't interrupt.

"That lesson," Salvatori continued, "wasn't about power or territory. It was about respect. Cassian thought I was his enemy, but what I saw in him was potential. I didn't crush him, didn't run him out—I brought him in. Taught him the things no one else would. The things he needed to survive in this world."

He met my eyes again, his expression more serious now. "I didn't just help him survive. I helped him build the foundation for everything he has now. Cassian owes me nothing—he's more than paid me back over the years. But what we have? It's loyalty. And that's not something I take lightly."

I processed his words, the weight of his story settling into the cracks of my doubt. "So, you're saying you knew the drugs were coming through here?" I asked, my voice quieter but still sharp.

Salvatori nodded, his gaze steady. "I did. But not how, and not by whom." He leaned back in his seat, his polished demeanor cracking just enough to show frustration beneath the surface. "That's why I called Cassian. I needed someone I could trust—someone who wouldn't immediately see this as an opportunity to exploit me or my business."

"Why Cassian?" I pressed, folding my arms across my chest.

"Because I knew he'd understand," Salvatori replied, his tone softening slightly. "He's been there—on the edge, trying to balance power and survival while keeping the rot out. Cassian knows the stakes, and he doesn't take shortcuts. That's why I asked him to get Markson involved. The detective has connections I don't, and I thought he'd keep the operation clean."

The mention of Markson sent a flicker of unease through me. "And now Cassian's in jail, the DEA is breathing down your neck, and I'm supposed to believe this wasn't part of your plan?"

Salvatori's lips pressed into a thin line, his frustration flaring briefly before he let out a breath. "If I'd wanted to set Cassian up, do you think I'd be sitting here with you, trying to untangle this mess? If I were behind this, I'd be halfway out of the city by now."

The sincerity in his voice gave me pause, but the doubt still lingered. "You've been in this business a long time, Salvatori. Why not get out before it got this bad?"

He chuckled darkly, shaking his head. "The same reason Cassian never got out. This world doesn't let you walk away. You don't survive as long as I have without making enemies, and leaving doesn't make them disappear. The only way to stay alive is to stay relevant. Lose your footing, and you're gone."

His words cut deeper than I wanted to admit. As much as I hated to acknowledge it, Salvatori's reasoning made sense.

"So, what now?" I asked, my voice softer, but the determination behind it clear.

"Now," Salvatori said, setting his coffee cup down with a deliberate clink, "we work together. You want to find out who set Cassian up? So do I. The first step is figuring out exactly how those drugs got into my club—and who's pulling the strings."

He stood, smoothing the front of his suit with a practiced motion as he looked down at me. "I have access to things you don't, and I know people you'd never reach on your own. You've got fire, Rosalie, but you're new to this world. Let me help."

I studied him, my chest tightening as I weighed his offer. Trust didn't come easily, and even now, suspicion lingered in the back of my mind. But Salvatori had resources—and knowledge—I didn't. If he was telling the truth, he might be the ally I desperately needed.

"All right," I said finally, standing to meet his gaze. "To a new partnership."

"New partnerships," Salvatori interrupted smoothly, a faint smirk tugging at his lips. "Cassian would not approve of me working together with such a beautiful woman—his woman no doubt."

The reminder of Cassian sent a pang through my chest, but I pushed it aside. "That's the least of his concerns," I said firmly.

Instead of turning to lead me out, Salvatori reached into his jacket pocket, pulling out a small, clear packet and setting it on the table between us. Inside were neon pink pills, their surface stamped with the faint image of a rose.

"This fell from one of the DEA agents' hands when they were walking Cassian out," Salvatori said, his voice lower now. "I don't know what they are, but I thought they might help you figure it out."

I stared at the pills, their garish color a stark contrast to the polished surface of the table. "You're saying the DEA had this?"

"I'm saying it shouldn't have been anywhere near them," he replied, his tone darkening. "And if they're tied to what's happening at Nocturne, someone in their ranks is playing both sides."

The implications hit me like a punch to the gut. Markson, the DEA, the drugs—everything was connected, but the pieces didn't fit yet. I slipped the packet into my pocket, the plastic crinkling faintly beneath my fingers.

"This could be the leverage we need," I murmured, more to myself than to Salvatori.

"It's a start," Salvatori said, his voice carrying an edge of warning. "But if you're going to use it, be careful. This isn't just about Cassian anymore. It's about whoever set him up—and they're playing a game far bigger than you realize."

As we left the booth and stepped into the dim quiet of the club, the weight of what lay ahead settled heavily on my shoulders. Trusting Salvatori felt like a gamble, but the stakes were too high to play it safe.

With the pills pressing against my pocket like a reminder, I knew one thing for certain: I'd have to learn to play the game—and fast—if I wanted any chance of saving Cassian and taking down whoever was behind this.

CHAPTER TWENTY-FOUR

The hotel suite felt too quiet as I stepped inside, the weight of Salvatori's revelations pressing heavily on my shoulders. The neon pink pills burned a metaphorical hole in my pocket, their garish color seared into my mind like a warning sign I couldn't ignore.

Marcus and Sierra were already inside, both standing near the window with postures that screamed tension. Sierra glanced up first, her sharp gaze immediately flicking to the bag in my hand.

"What's that?" she asked, her tone cutting through the silence.

I set the bag down on the coffee table, the pills shifting slightly in the clear plastic as Marcus stepped closer. "Salvatori found these," I said, my voice steady despite the knot in my stomach. "They fell from one of the DEA agents while they were walking Cassian out."

Marcus leaned forward, his eyes narrowing as he examined the pills without touching them. "Neon pink with a rose imprint," he murmured, his tone laced with suspicion. "That's new."

"What do you mean?" I asked, my gaze shifting between them.

Sierra crossed her arms, her expression grim. "I've seen

designer drugs with flashy imprints before—it's a branding tactic. But a rose? That's not just branding. That's a signature. Whoever made these wants their work recognized."

Marcus pulled out his phone, scrolling through his contacts with a practiced ease. "I know someone who might have a lead on this," he said, typing quickly. "Give me a second to reach out."

As he stepped into the corner to make the call, Sierra took the seat across from me, her gaze never leaving the bag of pills. "If the DEA had these, they either confiscated them during a bust or..." Her voice trailed off, the implication hanging in the air like a heavy weight.

"Or they're involved," I finished for her, my stomach twisting at the thought.

She nodded, her jaw tightening. "Either way, it's not good. If they confiscated them, why would one of their agents be carrying them out in the open? And if they're involved in distributing them..."

I shook my head, trying to push down the rising tide of frustration. "Then this is bigger than getting Cassian out of the way. And the people who set him up aren't just playing dirty—they're playing smart. I'm afraid this might just be the beginning."

Marcus returned a moment later, his phone still in hand. "I spoke to my contact," he said, his tone grim. "These pills are a new designer drug that's been popping up in underground circles. Potent, expensive, and dangerously addictive. But the rose imprint? That's new. No one's seen it before."

"Which means what?" I asked, leaning forward.

"It means this is either a new batch from an established player, or someone new is trying to make their mark," Marcus replied. "Either way, it's deliberate. They want to be noticed."

Sierra leaned back, her eyes narrowing as she processed the information. "So, someone's making waves with these, using Nocturne as a pipeline, and the DEA's either complicit or too blind to see the bigger picture. *Great.*"

My fingers brushed against the edge of the coffee table where the small bag of pills lay, the vibrant pink and delicate rose imprint mocking me with their quiet power.

I pulled my phone from my pocket, scrolling through my contacts until Harrison Blackwell's name appeared. Cassian's lawyer was as sharp as they came, but even he couldn't work miracles—not without the right tools. I needed his insight, his ability to see the game from every angle, and most importantly, his discretion.

The line rang twice before his gravelly voice answered. "Rosalie. I was wondering when I'd hear from you."

"I need to talk to you about something," I said, my voice low but steady. "Something big."

There was a pause, followed by the faint sound of shuffling papers on his end. "Go on."

I glanced at Marcus and Sierra, who turned to watch me silently, their eyes sharp and expectant. "I have something that might connect the DEA to Cassian's setup. Salvatori found these..." I hesitated, reaching for the bag and holding it up as though Harrison could see it. "Neon pink pills. They fell out of a DEA agent's hands when they were walking Cassian out."

The other end of the line went quiet, the silence stretching long enough to make my chest tighten.

"Did you say DEA?" Harrison asked finally, his tone shifting into something sharper, more dangerous.

"Yes," I said firmly. "And it gets worse. Marcus's contact says these pills are a new designer drug—potent, addictive, and fresh to the market. The rose imprint? It's a signature, like someone staking a claim. And Salvatori thinks Nocturne was being used as a pipeline."

"Damn it," Harrison muttered, and I could practically hear the wheels turning in his mind. "If the DEA had those pills, either they're part of an ongoing investigation, or someone inside their ranks is dirty."

"Exactly," I said, leaning forward as my frustration bubbled to the surface. "But how do we prove it? And what do we do with these?"

"You don't prove anything," Harrison said bluntly. "Not

yet. If you go public with this, you're putting a target on Cassian's back—and yours. Accusing the DEA without solid proof? It's a death sentence in this game, Rosalie."

I swallowed hard, gripping the phone tighter. "So what are you saying? We just sit on this and hope for the best?"

"No," Harrison said, his tone firm. "I'm saying you use it as leverage. Keep the pills close, but don't let anyone outside your circle know you have them. If the DEA is involved, they'll be watching you, waiting for a move. If you can find more concrete connections—something that ties these pills directly to someone high up in the chain—then we strike. Until then, you play the long game."

The thought of holding onto such a dangerous secret made my stomach churn, but Harrison's reasoning was sound. If we exposed our hand too early, we'd be crushed before we had a chance to fight back.

"Markson?" I asked hesitantly.

"He's a wild card," Harrison said. "If he's clean, he's a liability—he could report this and bury you in legal red tape. If he's dirty, he's even more dangerous. Either way, don't trust him until we know where he stands."

I nodded, even though he couldn't see me. "Understood."

"Rosalie," Harrison said, his voice softer now. "Cassian's world is a minefield, and right now, you're standing at the center of it. One wrong move, and this whole thing goes up in flames. Be careful."

"I will," I said quietly.

The call ended, leaving me staring at the pills once more. Their bright color seemed to pulse under the dim light, a stark reminder of the precarious path ahead.

Marcus crossed the room, his expression grim as he sat beside me. "What did he say?"

"He said we keep the pills close but don't make a move yet," I replied. "We use them as leverage, not evidence. Not until we know more."

Sierra leaned against the wall, her arms crossed. "And Markson?"

"We can't trust him," I said firmly. "Not until we figure out whose side he's on."

For a moment, the room was silent, the weight of Harrison's warning pressing down on all of us.

"We need to trace these back to their source," I said, my voice steady despite the storm brewing inside me. "Find out who's behind them, how they got into Nocturne, and who's benefiting from all this. If we can figure that out, maybe we can figure out who set Cassian up."

Marcus nodded, his expression serious. "I'll keep digging into the drug's distribution network. Someone has to know who's behind this signature."

"And I'll start looking into the DEA's involvement," Sierra added. "If they're complicit, there'll be a trail— maybe not an obvious one, but enough for us to follow."

I exhaled slowly, the tension in my chest easing slightly as the pieces of a plan began to fall into place. The pills were a lead—a dangerous one—but they were also a chance to unravel the setup that had ensnared Cassian.

"Let's move quickly," I said, my gaze shifting between them. "The longer we wait, the more ground they gain— and the longer Cassian stays in that hellhole."

Marcus and Sierra nodded in unison, their focus razor-sharp.

As they left to begin their respective tasks, I turned back to the pills on the table. Their garish color and delicate rose imprint mocked me, a reminder of just how precarious this situation was.

But precarious or not, I wasn't going to stop. Cassian's freedom depended on it—and so did my ability to survive in his world.

The pills sat on the table like a silent challenge as I scrolled through my contacts, my finger hesitating over Julian's name. If anyone knew the underbelly of the party scene well enough to offer insight, it was him. Still, I hated pulling him into this—it wasn't his problem, and Julian had always danced on the edges of Cassian's world without stepping fully into its shadows—or so I thought.

But I had no choice.

I pressed the call button, my heart pounding as the line rang.

"Rosalie," Julian answered, his voice as smooth as ever. "To what do I owe this unexpected pleasure?"

"I need your help," I said, skipping past the pleasantries. "Something's come up, and I need information about a designer drug circulating in the underground scene. It's pink, with a rose stamped on the pills. Have you heard of it?"

There was a long pause on the other end, and I could hear faint music in the background—a reminder that Julian was rarely far from a party. "I've heard whispers," he said finally, his tone more serious now. "Nothing concrete, but people are talking. It's new, expensive, and apparently making waves. Why?"

"I can't get into details," I said, lowering my voice. "But it's tied to Cassian. I need to trace it back to its source."

Julian sighed, the sound heavy with resignation. "Rosalie..."

"I wouldn't ask if it wasn't important," I said, my voice softening. "Please, Julian. You might be the only person who can help me with this. If not for me, then for Cassian."

There was another pause, then a faint rustling as he moved. "Fine. I'll make some calls. I'll reach out when I have something."

"Thank you," I said, relief washing over me.

It didn't take Julian long to get back to me. Less than an hour later, my phone buzzed with a encrypted message. I followed the link with a timer on the top of the screen; the message was going to self-destruct in thirty seconds.

Julian: Got a lead. Low-level distributor, works out of a warehouse on the outskirts of the city. He's small-time but might know more about the supply chain. Be careful. Details attached.

I quickly jotted down the address and name just as the message disappeared forever.

CHAPTER TWENTY-FIVE

The warehouse loomed in the distance, its metal walls rusted and streaked with graffiti, standing in stark contrast to the clean lines of the industrial buildings that surrounded it. The faint hum of machinery from nearby factories filled the night air, blending with the crunch of gravel beneath Marcus's tires as he pulled the car to a stop a few hundred feet away.

"Stay here," Marcus said firmly, his hand brushing the weapon holstered at his side as he scanned the area.

"No," I replied, my voice sharper than I intended. "This is my lead. I'm going in."

"Rosalie—"

"She's right," Sierra interrupted, her tone clipped but calm. "It's her call. But we do it smartly. Marcus and I will cover you. You stay close and if we give you a command, you follow it. We're not taking chances."

Marcus glared at Sierra for a moment before letting out a sharp breath. "Fine. But if anything goes sideways, we're pulling you out. No arguments."

"Deal," I said, unbuckling my seatbelt and stepping out of the car.

The cool night air sent a shiver through me as I adjusted my jacket, my gaze locked on the warehouse. The faint glow of a light inside spilled out through a cracked window, casting faint shadows that flickered like specters.

"Let's move," Marcus said, nodding toward Sierra as they flanked me, their movements silent and precise.

Inside the warehouse, the air was thick with the smell of oil and damp concrete. Stacks of crates lined the walls, their wooden frames battered and marked with smudged shipping labels. The faint buzz of a fluorescent light overhead added to the eerie atmosphere, casting harsh shadows that danced across the room.

The man we assumed was the distributor sat at a makeshift desk in the far corner, his wiry frame hunched over a tablet. He didn't notice us at first, too focused on whatever he was scrolling through.

"Hey!" Marcus barked, his voice echoing through the space.

The man jumped, nearly knocking over a stack of papers as he shot to his feet. His wide eyes darted between us, his hands raised defensively. "Whoa, whoa! Who the hell are you?"

"I'm the one asking questions," I said, stepping forward. My voice was calm, but the steel beneath it was unmistakable.

The man's gaze flicked to Marcus and Sierra, both of whom stood behind me like silent sentinels. He swallowed hard, his Adam's apple bobbing as he tried to steady his breathing.

"What do you want?" he asked, his voice trembling.

I pulled the bag of the pink pills from my pocket, holding it up so he could see. "These. Who's making them? Where are they coming from?"

The man's eyes widened slightly, his hands lowering just enough to betray his nervousness. "I—I don't know," he stammered.

"Try again," I said, stepping closer. My tone was colder now, sharper. "You're moving product, and I know you're tied to this supply chain. So start talking."

His gaze darted toward the door, his body tensing as though he was considering running. Marcus took a step forward, his presence looming enough to make the man freeze.

"Okay! Okay," the distributor said, raising his hands again. "What are you cops? I don't know much. I swear. I'm just a middleman."

"Then tell me what you do know," I said, my voice softening slightly.

He hesitated, his eyes flicking to Marcus and Sierra before settling back on me. "The pills—they're coming from a lab outside the city. Small operation, but it's run by someone big. Calls himself 'The Broker.' He handles everything—the manufacturing, the distribution, the branding."

"The Broker?" I repeated, my stomach tightening.

The man nodded quickly. "Yeah. That's all I know. The Broker doesn't deal with small-timers like me. We just move the product."

"And what's in it for you?" Marcus asked, his tone sharp.

"Money," the distributor replied, his voice shaking. "A lot of it. Look, I don't ask questions. I just do the job and get paid."

I stared at him for a long moment, weighing his words against the anger simmering in my chest. He was giving me information, but his involvement in this operation couldn't be ignored.

"Here's the deal," I said finally, my voice steady. "You keep your mouth shut about this conversation. No calls, no warnings, no sudden disappearances. If I find out you've run or tried to warn anyone, I'll make sure The Broker knows you're talking. And we both know what that would mean."

The man paled, his hands trembling as he nodded quickly. "I won't say anything. I swear."

"Good," I said, stepping back.

As we left the warehouse, the night air felt sharper, colder. The weight of the distributor's words pressed heavily on my mind, and for the first time, I felt the true magnitude of the world Cassian operated in.

The Broker was out there, pulling strings in ways I

couldn't fully grasp yet. But one thing was clear: I was stepping deeper into this world, and there was no turning back.

The night air clung to my skin as Marcus pulled the car out of the gravel lot. I sat in the back seat, the hum of the engine filling the silence between us. My gaze flickered to the neon lights of the city as they blurred past the windows, but my mind was elsewhere—circling The Broker, the lab, and the tangled mess Cassian had left me to unravel.

The warehouse encounter had given us a name, but no address, no location, no real way forward. The Broker remained a phantom, pulling strings from the shadows, always one step ahead. My chest tightened with frustration. It wasn't enough.

"We're close, but not close enough," I said aloud, breaking the silence.

Marcus glanced at me in the rearview mirror. "We've got a name. That's a start."

"But it's not actionable," I countered, leaning forward slightly. "The Broker isn't going to show up on a list of known associates. He's careful, cautious, even. We need to force him into the open."

"And how do you propose we do that?" Sierra asked, her voice calm but tinged with curiosity as she turned in her seat to look at me.

I leaned back, my eyes fixed on the city lights but unfocused as my thoughts churned. "The lab is the key," I said, more to myself than to them. "Whoever's running the lab is working directly with The Broker. If we can find the lab, we can find him."

"But we don't have an address," Marcus pointed out, his tone patient but firm.

"Not yet," I replied. My fingers tapped lightly against my thigh as an idea began to take shape. "But maybe we don't need it. Maybe we can make The Broker come to us."

Marcus and Sierra exchanged a glance, their expressions skeptical.

"How?" Marcus asked.

I didn't answer immediately, my mind spiraling through

the possibilities. Drawing The Broker out wasn't just about strategy—it was about risk. A misstep could tip him off or put us in his crosshairs before we were ready. But waiting wasn't an option either.

Cassian wouldn't wait, I thought, the weight of his absence pressing down on me. *He'd act, knowing the risk and owning the consequences. If I'm going to lead this, I have to do the same.*

I thought back to everything I'd learned in the past days—the pills, the distribution chain, the careful branding that marked this as a calculated operation. The Broker didn't just want power; he wanted control, dominance, and visibility. That kind of ambition left a trail, even if it was faint.

"We use the pills," I said finally, my voice steady as I leaned forward, the weight of the idea settling over me. "They're his product, his signature. If we plant rumors that someone's making a move on his supply chain—someone trying to cut him out—it might force him to act."

The words hung in the air, their weight amplified by the silence that followed. Marcus's brow furrowed, his hand tightening on the steering wheel, while Sierra's expression sharpened, her arms crossing over her chest.

Sierra raised an eyebrow, the faintest flicker of skepticism crossing her face. "You want to bait The Broker?" she asked, her tone calm but edged with caution. "That's bold, Rosalie. Dangerous."

"Every move we make is dangerous," I countered, my voice firmer now, the determination in my chest solidifying. "But it's calculated. If The Broker thinks his operation is compromised, he'll try to protect it. We use that to get closer to him."

Marcus glanced at me through the rearview mirror, his gaze heavy with doubt. "And if he doesn't take the bait?"

"Then we'll be back where we started," I admitted, "but at least we'll know. The Broker is careful—meticulous—but that means he's predictable in one way: he'll act to preserve his empire. If we press the right buttons, we can force him to show his hand."

Sierra shifted in her seat, her sharp gaze locking on mine. "And how do you propose we press those buttons? People like The Broker don't scare easily. They're not the kind to make rash moves."

"We don't need him to panic," I replied. "We just need him to pay attention."

"And how do we spread those rumors?" Marcus asked, his tone more measured now as he considered the plan.

"Through Salvatori," I said without hesitation. "He knows the channels, the people who would carry that kind of message. He can feed it to the right ears—low enough in the chain to avoid suspicion, but high enough that it'll get back to The Broker. We keep it subtle, just enough to get under his skin."

Sierra leaned back, her arms still crossed as she processed the idea. "You're assuming Salvatori is on board with this."

"He will be," I said firmly. "This affects him as much as it does us. If The Broker is using Nocturne as a pipeline, then Salvatori's business is already in jeopardy. He has every reason to help."

"And if he doesn't?" Marcus asked, his tone low but pointed.

I met his gaze through the mirror, the weight of his question sinking into me. "Then we find someone else who will. But Salvatori has the most reach—and the most to lose. He's our best shot."

The car fell into silence again, the hum of the engine filling the space as Marcus and Sierra exchanged a look.

"It's risky," Sierra said finally, her tone softer now but still cautious. "If The Broker catches wind that we're baiting him, he won't just protect his operation—he'll come after us."

"I know," I said, my voice quieter but no less resolute. "But Cassian trusted me to handle this. If we don't push back, we'll lose any chance we have of finding The Broker and getting Cassian out of this mess."

Sierra's eyes softened slightly, though her expression remained guarded. "Then we'd better make sure this works."

Marcus sighed, his grip on the wheel tightening as he turned his focus back to the road. "If Salvatori's in, we'll need to move fast. The longer we wait, the more time The Broker has to cover his tracks."

"Agreed," I said.

As the city lights blurred past the window, the weight of the plan settled over me. It was bold, risky, and dangerous, but it was also necessary. The Broker had pulled Cassian into his web, and now it was my turn to pull the strings.

For the first time, the fear that had been clawing at the edges of my resolve began to quiet, replaced by a steady, determined rhythm. I wasn't just navigating this world anymore—I was shaping it, one move at a time.

CHAPTER TWENTY-SIX

The faint pulse of music reverberated through the walls of Nocturne as I stepped inside for the second time today, the dim lighting casting long shadows across the sleek black-and-green interior. The club wasn't alive with its usual energy—this time of night, it was quiet, the crowd replaced by Salvatori's men. They lounged in corners or leaned against the bar, their sharp gazes snapping to me the moment I walked in.

My heels clicked against the polished floor as I made my way toward the private booths at the back. Salvatori was already there, seated casually with a drink in hand, his dark suit impeccable as always. A faint smile tugged at his lips as he saw me, but it didn't reach his eyes.

"Miss Quinn," Salvatori said smoothly, his voice rich and controlled, like the low hum of a cello. He set his glass down with deliberate precision, the faint clink of crystal against wood punctuating his words. His sharp eyes tracked my approach, his lips curling into a faint smile that danced on the edge of amusement. "Twice in one day—to what do I owe the pleasure?"

I paused a few feet from his table, clasping my hands in front of me to keep them steady. "We need to talk," I said, my voice softer than I'd intended but carrying enough weight to show I wasn't here to waste time. My gaze flicked to the two men standing on either side of him. They were watchful, their relaxed stances a thin veil over their readiness to act.

"Alone," I added, my tone quiet but firm.

Salvatori raised an eyebrow, his smile widening ever so slightly. He leaned back in his chair, draping one arm over the backrest as though settling in to enjoy a performance. "You don't trust my company?" he asked, his tone laced with mild amusement but free of malice.

I met his gaze, my own unwavering. "I don't know them," I said carefully. "And we need discretion. This isn't something I want to discuss with an audience."

He regarded me for a long moment, his expression thoughtful, almost contemplative. Then he nodded once, a small, deliberate gesture that carried the weight of unspoken understanding.

"Gentlemen," he said lightly, the warmth in his voice belying the firmness of his command. "Give us some space."

The two men hesitated, exchanging a glance before stepping back. Their movements were unhurried, deliberate, but the subtle tension in their postures betrayed their reluctance. With a final glance my way, they turned and left, the faint echo of their footsteps disappearing as the door clicked shut behind them.

The silence that followed was thick but not uncomfortable. Salvatori adjusted his cuffs, the motion smooth and precise, before gesturing to the chair across from him. "Please, sit," he said, his voice softer now, almost inviting. "You have my full attention."

I took the offered seat, smoothing the front of my jacket as I settled in. "Thank you," I said, meeting his gaze. "I appreciate you taking the time."

He tilted his head slightly, his eyes glinting with curiosity. "For you, Rosalie, I can always make time. Now, tell me—what's on your mind?"

The warmth in his tone eased the knot in my chest, and I found myself relaxing, if only slightly. Salvatori wasn't just a business associate of Cassian's—he was someone who understood the weight of the decisions I was about to make. And for the first time, I felt like I wasn't facing this fight entirely alone.

I took a steadying breath, clasping my hands in my lap to keep them from fidgeting. Salvatori's gaze remained fixed on me, his expression patient but attentive, the faint curl of his lips suggesting he was waiting for something clever—or reckless—to come out of my mouth.

"We need to draw out The Broker—the man responsible for all of this," I began, my voice calm but resolute. "He's careful, but I think if we press the right buttons, we can make him act. And the best way to do that is by going after his supply chain—by making him think someone's making a move on it."

Salvatori tilted his head slightly, his expression sharpening. "Sounds like something Cassian would do," he said softly, his fingers tapping idly against the arm of his chair. "Dangerous, but ballsy. And how exactly do you plan to accomplish that?"

I leaned forward, my voice dropping slightly as though the walls themselves might be listening. "We spread rumors. Whisper through the right channels that someone's stealing product, undercutting prices, trying to edge him out. Make it seem like a coordinated attack on his operation."

He chuckled, the sound low and warm, as though he'd heard an amusing joke. "You think he'll fall for it?"

"I think he won't have a choice but to pay attention," I countered. "The Broker doesn't seem like the type to ignore a threat to his empire. If we make it look real enough, he'll move to protect it—and when he does, we'll be waiting."

Salvatori nodded slowly, his smile fading into something more serious. "It's a clever plan, I'll give you that. But rumors are tricky. Spread them too wide, and they lose credibility. Too narrow, and they might not reach him in time. We'll need to strike the right balance—and use the right voices."

"That's why I came to you," I said. "You know this world better than anyone. You know the channels, the people who can make this believable. I can't do this without you."

His eyes flickered with something unreadable, and for a moment, I thought he might refuse. Then he leaned forward, resting his elbows on the table as his expression shifted into something more calculating.

"There are a few ways we could play this," he said thoughtfully. "The clubs are always a good place to start. Dealers, suppliers, buyers—they all talk. If we plant the right story in the right ears, it'll spread fast enough to reach The Broker."

"But we need it to look like more than just talk," I said. "We need it to feel real."

Salvatori nodded, a faint smirk tugging at the corner of his mouth. "Then we give it weight. Have someone stage a fake heist—just enough to make it look like product is going missing. Leave a trail for The Broker to follow, but not one he can trace back to us."

I considered his suggestion, the pieces of the plan falling into place in my mind. "And the rumors—how do we make sure they're believable?"

"I know a few people," Salvatori said, his tone casual but laced with confidence. "People who know how to talk just loud enough to be heard by the right ears. Let me handle that part."

I nodded, relief washing over me as the plan began to take shape. "Thank you," I said, my voice softer now.

He waved a hand dismissively, leaning back in his chair. "Don't thank me yet. This is risky, Rosalie. If The Broker catches on, he'll retaliate—and it won't be subtle."

"I know," I said firmly. "But I'm willing to take that risk. We don't have time to play it safe anymore."

Salvatori studied me for a long moment, his sharp gaze cutting through the tension in the room. Then, slowly, he nodded. "All right. I'll start making calls tonight. But once this starts, there's no turning back."

"There hasn't been a way back for a long time," I said, standing as I smoothed my jacket.

Salvatori stood as well, his expression softening just slightly. "You've got guts, Rosalie. Cassian chose well."

"Let's hope that counts for something," I said, my voice steady despite the storm brewing inside me.

As I walked out of Nocturne, the weight of what we'd just set in motion pressed heavily on my shoulders. The Broker would come—but when he did, I had to be ready to meet him head-on. There was no other choice.

The car was quiet, save for the low hum of the engine and the occasional sound of Marcus shifting in his seat, sparing glances back at me whenever he thought I wasn't looking, but I could feel him. The glow of the city lights blurred past the windows, casting fleeting reflections inside the cabin. I leaned back against the seat, my thoughts circling the plan Salvatori and I had just set in motion. The Broker was going to feel the heat, and I needed to be ready for whatever came next.

My phone buzzed in my pocket, jolting me from my thoughts. I hesitated for a second, glancing at the screen before answering.

"Markson," I said, my tone neutral but firm.

"Rosalie," he greeted warmly, his voice carrying a casual familiarity that made my stomach twist. "I thought I'd check in. I know things have been... difficult lately."

"Difficult doesn't quite cover it," I replied, keeping my voice steady.

His chuckle was soft, almost disarming. "Fair enough. I just wanted to make sure you're holding up. I know you're probably stressed out with Cassian's arrest, but you have every right to be."

I frowned, glancing out the window as I tried to piece together his angle. "I'm managing," I said carefully.

"That's good," he said, his tone light but carrying an undertone I couldn't quite place. "You're strong. Cassian's lucky to have someone like you in his corner."

I didn't respond immediately, letting the silence linger long enough for him to continue.

"I know you're working hard to clean up the mess," he added, his voice softening. "But just remember—not everything needs fixing. Sometimes it's better to let certain things fall apart."

The comment hit me like a sudden chill, my grip on the phone tightening. There was nothing overtly wrong with what he'd said, but the way he'd phrased it—the weight behind his words—set my instincts on edge.

"Good advice," I said finally, my tone colder now. "Anything else?"

"No," he replied smoothly. "Just wanted to let you know I'm here if you need anything. Anytime."

"Thanks," I said shortly, ending the call before he could say more.

I stared at the phone in my hand, my heart pounding as the conversation replayed in my mind. Something about his tone, his choice of words, didn't sit right. *Let certain things fall apart.* What was he trying to imply?

Marcus's voice cut through the silence, pulling me back to the present. "You're running on fumes, Rosalie," he said, glancing at me in the rearview mirror. His tone wasn't judgmental—just observant, almost concerned.

I met his gaze in the reflection, forcing a faint smile. "I'm fine."

He raised an eyebrow, clearly unconvinced. "You've been saying that for days. You need sleep, even if it's just for a couple of hours."

"I can't," I admitted, my voice quieter now. "Not yet. There's too much to do."

Marcus sighed, his grip on the wheel tightening. "At this pace, you're going to burn out before we even get to The Broker."

"I'll rest when this is over," I said firmly, though my own words felt hollow.

The rest of the drive was quiet, but my mind refused to settle. Markson's voice echoed in my head, his subtle comment playing on repeat. It was too carefully worded to be casual, too pointed to be meaningless.

By the time we pulled up to the hotel, the exhaustion weighing on me had been replaced by a sharp, restless energy. Whatever Markson's angle was, I couldn't shake the feeling that he wasn't just checking in. He was testing me—and I needed to figure out why.

CHAPTER TWENTY-SEVEN

Two days had passed, and the walls of the hotel suite felt smaller with each hour. I paced the length of the living room, my bare feet brushing over the soft carpet as I chewed the inside of my cheek. The weight of waiting pressed down on me—waiting for whispers to turn into waves, for The Broker to feel the tremors of what we'd set into motion.

Harrison sat at the small dining table, his glasses perched low on his nose as he thumbed through a stack of papers. He was meticulous, his pen scratching faintly against the margins as he made notes, but his presence added to the heaviness in the air.

Marcus leaned against the counter near the kitchenette, his arms crossed and his expression unreadable, while Sierra sat by the window, scrolling through something on her phone. Their calmness only amplified my restlessness.

I stopped mid-step, turning toward Harrison. The question had been gnawing at me for days, but I hadn't let myself voice it—not until now. "How is he?" I asked, my voice quieter than I intended.

Harrison didn't look up immediately, his pen pausing briefly on the page before he finished a note. Then he removed his glasses, setting them down beside the stack of papers. "Cassian's holding up," he said, his tone measured but guarded.

"That's not an answer," I pressed, stepping closer. "Is he okay? Is he..." I trailed off, unsure how to finish the question.

Harrison sighed, leaning back in his chair. "He's not okay, Rosalie. He's in prison. A man like Cassian doesn't belong in a place like that, and he knows it."

The weight of his words settled over me like a stone, and I sank into the chair across from him. "Why hasn't he tried to contact me?" I asked, my voice breaking slightly. "It's been days, Harrison. I haven't heard a word from him."

Harrison's gaze softened, and for the first time, the sharp edges of his demeanor dulled. "He's protecting you."

"Protecting me?" I repeated, disbelief creeping into my tone.

"Yes," Harrison said firmly. "The situation he's in—it's volatile. The people around him are watching his every move, waiting for a crack in his armor. If he reaches out to you, it could be seen as a weakness. It could make you a target, Rosalie."

I swallowed hard, the knot in my chest tightening. "That doesn't make it easier," I murmured, my hands twisting in my lap.

"I know it doesn't," Harrison said quietly. "But Cassian's playing the long game. He's keeping his distance because he trusts you to hold things together out here. And whether you realize it or not, that trust says everything."

His words struck a chord, but they didn't ease the ache in my chest. I nodded slowly, my gaze dropping to the table. "Just... tell him I'm doing everything I can," I said softly.

Harrison nodded, picking up his glasses again. "He already knows."

I leaned back in my chair, exhaling slowly as the tension in the room settled over me once more. Harrison's reassurance should have been enough, but the silence from Cassian felt like a void I couldn't fill. And until we brought The Broker to light, that silence was all I'd have.

A sharp knock at the door jolted me from my thoughts.

Marcus was there in an instant, his hand brushing the weapon holstered at his side before he opened the door.

A courier stepped in, carrying a sleek black folder with Lena's name embossed on the front. He handed it to Marcus, nodded politely, and left without a word.

"What's this?" I asked, stopping mid-step.

"From Lena," Marcus replied, flipping the folder open and skimming the top document. "Looks like paperwork for the Ivy & Bloom expansion."

I sighed, rubbing my temples. The timing couldn't have been worse. "Let me see."

Marcus handed me the folder, and I dropped into the chair across from Harrison, flipping through the papers with quick, distracted movements. Expansion plans, budget outlines, leasing agreements—it was all there, and I knew it was important, but my mind refused to focus.

"You don't have to deal with this now," Sierra said gently, glancing up from her phone.

"No," I replied, shaking my head. "It needs to get done."

I signed where Lena had marked, barely skimming the details. My trust in Lena wasn't blind, but I didn't have the bandwidth to question every line of text. As I handed the folder back to Marcus, a thought struck me.

"Tell Lena," I began, my tone steady despite the whirlwind in my mind, "to prepare Ivy & Bloom for a massive grand opening. Something big, well-publicized. Invite everyone—past clients, Julian, Salvatori, Markson, and Cassian's men. Anyone who will come."

Marcus raised an eyebrow, his grip tightening slightly on the folder. "You're throwing a party?"

"I'm creating an event," I corrected. "Something too loud to ignore. The kind of thing that someone might notice if they're paying attention."

Harrison glanced up from his papers, his sharp gaze narrowing slightly. "And what's the purpose of this event, exactly?"

"To celebrate Ivy & Bloom's growth" I said simply. "But there can be other reasons beneath the surface. If the rumors we planted are working, maybe the Broker want to see who's pulling the strings. And if he's as careful as we think, he won't send someone else to watch—he'll come himself."

"And if he doesn't?" Marcus asked, his tone cautious.

"Then we've lost nothing," I replied, standing again as the restless energy surged back. "But if he does, we'll be ready."

Sierra leaned forward, her elbows resting on her knees. "You're betting on a big 'if,' Rosalie. This could backfire."

"Everything about this could backfire," I said, meeting her gaze. "But we're out of options. If we don't make him move, we'll be stuck waiting for him to strike—and I'm not willing to give him that advantage."

Marcus nodded slowly, his expression softening slightly. "I'll pass the message to Lena."

As he left the room, I caught Harrison watching me, his pen poised above the papers in front of him.

"You're playing a dangerous game," he said finally, his tone quiet but firm.

"I know," I replied, my voice softer now. "But it's the only game I have left."

He didn't respond, turning back to his work as I resumed my pacing, the weight of the plan settling heavily on my shoulders. The Broker was out there, somewhere, watching. And if this event didn't force his hand, I wasn't sure what else would.

I sat on the edge of the bed, gripping my phone tightly as my thoughts churned. The tension in the room had become a constant drain on my body—Marcus pacing near the window, Sierra scrolling on her phone, Harrison back at the table with his papers. The weight of my decisions pressed against my shoulders like an anchor, and I needed air, a break, something to clear my head.

I unlocked my phone and tapped the screen a few times before pressing it to my ear. "Yes, this is Rosalie Quinn in the penthouse suite. I'd like to schedule a massage for this evening," I said loudly, ensuring my voice carried across the room. "Something relaxing. As soon as possible."

I ended the call and set my phone down on the bed with

a deliberate motion, turning to face the room. Marcus and Sierra were both watching me, their postures stiff with unspoken suspicion.

"You're scheduling a massage?" Marcus asked, raising an eyebrow.

"Yes," I said simply. "I've been running on fumes, as you so kindly pointed out, and I need to unwind."

"You want me to check out the spa first?" Sierra offered, her tone neutral but her meaning clear.

"No," I replied, standing and smoothing the front of my jacket. "It's in the hotel. I'm not leaving the building, and I'll have my phone on me. You don't need to babysit me."

Marcus crossed his arms, his jaw tightening. "I don't like this."

"You don't have to," I said, flashing a faint smile as I grabbed my purse. "I'll be fine. Just stay here, and I'll check in when I'm done."

Before either of them could argue further, I slipped out the door, letting it close behind me with a quiet click.

The spa was two floors down, its sleek and tranquil decor visible from the elevator as I passed by. But I didn't stop. Instead, I turned down a side corridor marked with an unobtrusive sign: *Employees Only*.

My footsteps echoed faintly against the tiled floor as I moved through the narrow hallway. It smelled faintly of cleaning supplies and laundry detergent, the kind of scent that would go unnoticed by most guests.

The side exit came into view, a plain metal door with a push bar. I glanced over my shoulder, half-expecting Marcus or Sierra to appear, but the hallway remained empty. Taking a deep breath, I pushed the door open and stepped into the cool night air.

The city was alive with sound—car horns, distant laughter, the faint thrum of music spilling from a nearby bar. I pulled my jacket tighter around me and merged into the flow of pedestrians on the sidewalk, keeping my head down and my pace brisk.

I didn't have a specific destination in mind—just a need to escape the suffocating confines of the hotel and the ever-present weight of expectation. My phone buzzed in my pocket, but I ignored it, focusing instead on the rhythm of my steps and the energy of the city around me.

For once, I wanted to feel like myself—not the woman Cassian had left in charge of his empire, not the strategist plotting against The Broker, but just Rosalie, moving through the world with purpose and anonymity.

The thought was fleeting, though, as reality settled back in. I wasn't just Rosalie anymore. Not really. The choices I made now didn't just affect me—they rippled outward, touching Cassian, Marcus, Sierra, and everyone else caught in the web of this world.

As I turned a corner, I caught sight of a café tucked into the side of a building, its warm light spilling onto the sidewalk. It was small, unassuming, and perfect.

I stepped inside, the bell above the door chiming softly. The aroma of freshly brewed coffee wrapped around me like a blanket, momentarily easing the tension in my chest. I ordered a latte, paying in cash to avoid leaving a trail, and took a seat by the window.

For the first time in days, I allowed myself to pause, to breathe, to simply exist without the weight of everything pressing down on me. But even as I sipped my coffee, a part of me remained on edge, waiting for the next move, the next threat, the next decision.

The city moved around me, its rhythm constant and unyielding, and for a brief moment, I let myself get lost in it. But I knew it wouldn't last. It never did.

The café was warm, a bubble of peace that stood in stark contrast to the chaos I'd been swimming in for weeks. The latte in my hand was already cooling, but I didn't care. My attention was drawn to the activity outside, the steady rhythm of the city as it pulsed with life.

Across the street, a reporter stood under the glow of a streetlamp, her professional poise stark against the casual movements of pedestrians weaving around her. A cameraman adjusted his equipment while she reviewed notes, the faint hum of her voice just audible through the glass.

Something about the scene caught my attention—the way she commanded the moment, the way her presence turned the mundane backdrop into a stage. It wasn't just a news segment; it was a story being shaped in real time, designed to grab the attention of whoever was watching.

An idea sparked in the back of my mind, flickering like a match that had just caught flame. I straightened in my chair, my fingers tightening around the cup as the thought grew, bold and insistent. If I wanted The Broker's attention—if I wanted to control the narrative—I needed to make my own stage.

I glanced at the clock on the wall. I didn't have much time before Marcus and Sierra started questioning my absence. If I was going to act, it had to be now.

Draining the last of my coffee, I rose from my seat, leaving a few bills on the table before slipping out the door. The reporter was still across the street, now mid-segment, her voice animated as she gestured toward the camera. I didn't linger to watch. My focus was already elsewhere, my mind racing as I navigated the crowded sidewalks.

The idea felt reckless, ambitious—but if it worked, it could be the move that changed everything. I pulled my jacket tighter against the night air, my pace quickening as I set my sights on my destination.

The Chicago Tribune.

The name alone carried weight, a legacy of influence that stretched back generations. If I wanted a platform, there was no better place to start. I didn't have a plan yet, but I didn't need one—not entirely. All I needed was the spark, and the Tribune could provide the fuel.

The city buzzed around me, the sound of horns and footsteps and distant conversations blending into a symphony of urgency. I didn't stop, didn't hesitate, until I rounded a corner and saw the building rise before me, its iconic sign gleaming against the night sky.

I stood on the sidewalk, staring up at it, the enormity of the moment pressing against my chest. This wasn't just about drawing out The Broker anymore. It was about controlling the narrative, shaping the story before anyone else could.

As I looked up at the sign, the faint glow of its letters reflected in the glassy surface of my determination. The next step was clear. It was time to make my move.

CHAPTER TWENTY-EIGHT

The sound of running water filled the hotel suite as I scrubbed at a plate left behind from breakfast. The mundane task offered a brief reprieve from the relentless hum of tension that had followed me for days. The scent of soap mingled with the faint aroma of coffee lingering in the air, and for a moment, I focused solely on the plate in my hands—the cool ceramic against my skin, the steady rhythm of my scrubbing.

But even in the quiet, my thoughts churned.

The Broker. Cassian. The plan.

I'd set the wheels in motion, but the weight of it all sat heavy on my chest, the what-ifs clawing at the edges of my resolve. What if the rumors didn't reach The Broker? What if he saw through them? What if, instead of drawing him out, I'd only painted a target on Cassian's empire—and on myself?

The plate slipped slightly in my grasp, the sound of ceramic against porcelain startling me. I set it down carefully, drying my hands on a towel as I exhaled slowly.

"Focus," I muttered to myself. "You've got this."

I had barely settled onto the couch when Marcus walked in, his expression guarded. The door clicked shut behind him, the faint sound of Sierra's voice trailing off from wherever she was stationed.

"Anything?" I asked, leaning forward slightly.

Marcus nodded, pulling out his phone and scrolling through a message. "Salvatori's contacts are talking. Word on the street is that someone's making moves on The Broker's supply chain. Dealers are spooked, and there's chatter about shipments being rerouted."

"That's a good sign," I said, though my chest tightened at the thought of what that chatter might provoke.

"It's more than that," Marcus added, glancing up at me. "One of Salvatori's guys said a few of The Broker's people have been pulling back from their usual spots. Whatever you've stirred up, it's making them nervous."

I nodded, my fingers gripping the edge of the couch. "And Salvatori? What's he saying?"

"Same thing," Marcus replied. "He thinks the rumors are spreading faster than we expected. Too fast, maybe."

"What does he mean by 'too fast'?" I asked, my voice sharper than I intended.

Marcus shrugged, his expression neutral. "It means you might be getting his attention sooner than you wanted."

The weight of his words settled heavily over me. I had prepared for The Broker to respond, but the speed of it sent a ripple of unease through my chest.

The door opened again, this time to Sierra, her phone in hand and her pace brisk. "Just got word from Salvatori," she said, her tone clipped. "There's been movement near one of the drop points he flagged earlier. It's not much, but it's enough to suggest they're scrambling."

"Scrambling," I repeated, standing as the pieces began to fit together.

"Exactly," Sierra replied, meeting my gaze. "Your plan's working, Rosalie. The Broker's people are reacting, and they're not subtle about it."

"That's good, but this isn't over," I said, though the tightness in my chest refused to ease. "That means we're close."

Sierra's eyes narrowed slightly. "Close, yes. But it also means we need to be careful. If they're pulling back, they're watching, and they're going to want to know who's behind this."

"I know," I said, my voice quieter now.

I stepped away from the couch, pacing to the window as the city lights sparkled against the night sky. The plan was moving faster than I'd anticipated, and while that meant progress, it also meant risk.

"Marcus," I said, turning back to him. "Reach out to Salvatori. Tell him to keep watching those drop points, but to stay low. The last thing we need is for them to catch wind of us before we're ready."

Marcus nodded, already pulling out his phone as he stepped into the other room.

Sierra stayed where she was, her sharp gaze fixed on me. "What's the next move?" she asked.

I exhaled slowly, the weight of the moment pressing down on me. "We wait," I said, though the words tasted bitter on my tongue. "We let them come to us."

The Broker's network was shifting, reacting, showing the cracks in its carefully constructed facade. And as much as I wanted to act, to push harder, I knew the next move wasn't mine to make.

Not yet.

*   *   *

The next morning brought little relief. Sleep had been elusive, the weight of the previous day pressing down on me even as the sun rose over the city. My phone buzzed on the nightstand, the screen lighting up with Salvatori's name.

"Rosalie," he said, his voice as smooth as ever, but there was an edge to it this time. "Swing by the club when you can. We need to talk."

"Is everything all right?" I asked, already sensing the answer.

"Just get here," he replied, and the line went dead.

Nocturne was quiet when I arrived, its usual buzz replaced by a tension I could feel the moment I stepped inside. Salvatori was waiting near the bar, leaning against the counter with a drink in hand. His sharp suit and composed demeanor gave little away, but his eyes—piercing and alert—told a different story.

"Miss Quinn," he greeted, gesturing for me to join him. "Thanks for coming."

"What's going on?" I asked, cutting straight to the point.

He didn't answer immediately, instead motioning toward the back. "Let's talk in private."

I followed Salvatori into his private office, the heavy door clicking shut behind us with a finality that made my pulse quicken. The room was exactly as I remembered it: sleek, minimalist, and expensive. The faint scent of leather and polished wood filled the air, mingling with a hint of Salvatori's cologne—something sharp and undeniably commanding.

The centerpiece of the room was the massive desk, its dark mahogany surface immaculate save for a single silver pen and a black leather-bound notebook. Behind it, a wall of floor-to-ceiling bookshelves displayed not just books but artifacts—small sculptures and relics that spoke to a life filled with power plays and calculated risks.

Salvatori didn't waste time. He moved to the sideboard, pouring himself a drink with practiced ease before gesturing toward the leather chair opposite his. "Sit, please" he said, his voice firm but not unkind. "Would you like a drink?"

I shook my head no, but complied, sinking into the familiar chair. The faint scent of leather and wood polish wrapped around me, a reminder of the last time I'd sat here, negotiating on Cassian's behalf. Now, I wasn't just here for Cassian—I was here for all of us.

Salvatori swirled the amber liquid in his glass, his sharp eyes fixed on me as he spoke. "The rumors you started—they're working," he began, his tone even. "But not without consequences."

I leaned forward slightly, my pulse quickening. "What

kind of consequences?"

"For one, there's been unusual activity around the club," he said, setting his glass down with a deliberate clink. "My men have noticed strangers hanging around at odd hours— watching, waiting. It's subtle, but it's enough to make them nervous."

I frowned, the weight of his words settling heavily on my chest. "Are they making any moves?"

"Not yet," Salvatori replied, his tone darkening. "But they're not just here for the nightlife. They're trying to figure out where the rumors are coming from, and Nocturne is at the top of their list."

I glanced toward the window, my reflection barely visible against the city skyline. "What about the drop points?"

Salvatori nodded grimly. "Increased security. They've added extra men, rerouted shipments, tightened schedules. It's a calculated response—one that shows they're feeling the pressure but aren't panicking. Not yet."

I swallowed hard, processing the implications. The Broker was responding exactly as I'd hoped, but the calculated nature of his moves meant he wasn't acting recklessly. He was watching, waiting, just like we were.

"And there's more," Salvatori continued, his voice dropping slightly. "One of my men reported being followed yesterday. Whoever it was didn't make contact, but it's clear they're watching us closely."

My stomach twisted, the thrill of progress mingling with the sharp edge of danger.

Before I could respond, the door opened, and Marcus stepped inside. His expression was tense, his jaw set as he closed the door behind him.

"We've got another issue," he said, his gaze shifting between Salvatori and me.

"What is it?" I asked, my voice sharper than I intended.

"One of Cassian's lieutenants reached out just now," Marcus replied. "He's concerned about the strategy. Says some of them are under surveillance by the DEA. He's questioning whether any of this was a good idea. They're questioning you."

I clenched my fists in my lap, forcing myself to remain calm. "Did he give a reason?"

Marcus nodded. "He thinks the organization's exposure is putting everything at risk. Says Cassian wouldn't have allowed it."

A flash of anger flared in my chest, but I pushed it down. "And did he suggest an alternative?"

"No," Marcus admitted. "But he made it clear that if this goes south, the fallout will be on you."

I leaned back in the chair, the tension in the room thick enough to choke on. The plan was working, but the speed of its success was testing the loyalty of those still clinging to Cassian's shadow.

Salvatori broke the silence, his tone calm but pointed. "You've got The Broker's attention, Rosalie. But now you need to decide how far you're willing to push him."

I met his gaze, my resolve hardening. "We keep going," I said firmly. "Backing off now only gives him time to regroup. We've come this far. We finish it."

Salvatori studied me for a long moment, the faintest flicker of approval in his sharp eyes. "Then I'll handle things on my end," he said. "But you'd better be ready for what comes next. The Broker isn't just playing defense anymore—he's looking for someone to blame."

"Let him look," I replied, standing as I smoothed my jacket. "We'll be ready."

As I left the office, Marcus trailing silently behind me, the weight of the plan pressed heavily on my shoulders. The Broker's moves were calculated, deliberate—but so were mine.

The question wasn't whether he would retaliate. It was when. And I had to be ready to meet him when he did.

I left Salvatori's office with a tightness in my chest, the weight of his words settling over me like a lead blanket. My steps quickened as I moved down the hall, the polished wood floors gleaming under the faint light. The air felt heavier, oppressive, pressing down with every breath I took.

"Rosalie—" Marcus's voice came from behind me, but I barely heard him.

A sudden wave of nausea swept through me, sharp and unrelenting. My stomach twisted violently, and I broke into a near run, my heels clicking loudly against the floor as I pushed through the door to the women's restroom.

The cool air hit me as I gripped the edge of the sink, my knuckles white against the porcelain. My reflection stared back at me in the mirror, pale and wide-eyed, a sheen of sweat on my brow.

It hit again, stronger this time, and I barely made it to the nearest stall before the nausea won. I doubled over, the sound of retching filling the small, tiled space.

The restroom door opened, and I heard Marcus's voice, tense and commanding. "Sierra, get in there. Now."

Sierra's heels clicked quickly across the floor, and a moment later, she was at my side, her hand lightly brushing my back as I gripped the sides of the stall for balance.

"Rosalie," she said softly, her voice a mix of concern and curiosity. "What's going on? Are you okay?"

I shook my head, wiping my mouth with the back of my hand as I leaned back against the stall door. "It's fine," I muttered, my voice hoarse. "Just the nerves. And not eating regularly."

Sierra raised an eyebrow, her sharp gaze scanning my face. "Nerves don't usually make you puke your guts out."

"They do when you're running a criminal empire and have no idea what the fuck you're doing," I said with a weak attempt at a smile.

She didn't laugh, her expression remaining serious. "You've been pushing yourself too hard, Rosalie. This isn't sustainable."

"I'll be fine," I said firmly, straightening as I tried to regain some composure. The nausea had passed, but the knot of tension in my stomach remained. "I just need to get back to the hotel and rest."

Sierra studied me for a moment longer before nodding reluctantly. "All right. But I'm keeping an eye on you. And you're eating something as soon as we're back."

"You all have an unhealthy obsession with my eating habits," I said, the words barely a whisper as I splashed cold water on my face.

As I left the restroom, Marcus was waiting just outside the door, his arms crossed and his expression unreadable. He glanced at Sierra, who gave him a small shake of her head, then back at me.

"You need to take care of yourself," he said, his tone gruff but not unkind.

"I know," I replied, though the words felt hollow.

The three of us walked in silence back through the quiet halls of Nocturne, the distant hum of the city outside a sharp contrast to the storm brewing inside me. I was holding the threads of Cassian's empire together, but for how long?

As the car pulled up to the curb, I couldn't help but wonder if the nausea was just the stress—or a warning that I was pushing myself too close to the edge.

CHAPTER TWENTY-NINE

The distillery loomed ahead, its steel and concrete walls stark against the early evening light. My stomach twisted as Marcus parked the car, the engine's low hum fading into the silence that followed. This wasn't the first time I'd come here, but it felt different now—heavier, like the air carried the weight of every decision I'd made in the past week.

The faint tang of alcohol and metal greeted me as I stepped inside, the door closing behind me with a hollow clang. The cavernous space stretched out before me, its rows of stacked crates and dormant machinery casting long shadows under the high, dim lights. The hum of distant equipment vibrated faintly through the floor, barely masking the low murmur of voices near the center of the room.

They were waiting for me.

Cassian's men stood in a loose cluster, their postures stiff with tension. Some leaned against crates, their arms crossed, their eyes sharp and calculating. Others paced, their boots scuffing against the concrete with restless energy. Their faces were a mix of suspicion, frustration, and barely concealed defiance. They didn't look at me like a leader—they looked at me like an outsider.

I straightened my shoulders, squaring my jaw as my

heels clicked sharply against the floor. The sound echoed in the cavernous space, cutting through the quiet and drawing every gaze toward me. I felt the weight of their stares, the silent judgment in the way their eyes tracked my every step.

Marcus and Sierra flanked me, their presence a steadying force as I approached. Marcus's expression was unreadable, his body language calm but coiled, like a spring ready to snap. Sierra's sharp gaze swept the room, her hand resting lightly near her holster.

I stopped a few feet from the group, planting my feet firmly on the concrete. My voice had to carry, but my presence had to speak louder.

"Gentlemen," I began, my tone steady, "I understand some of you have concerns about my decisions."

A ripple of murmurs moved through the group, low and indistinct, but it was enough to set my teeth on edge. One of the men—a shorter, stocky guy with tattoos that climbed his forearms—stepped forward, his jaw tight and his eyes hard.

"Cassian wouldn't be stirring the pot like this," he said, his tone edged with doubt. "He'd be playing it smart, not dragging us into some risky game."

I met his gaze, forcing myself to hold it steady. "Is that what you think this is? A risky game?"

He nodded, his chin jutting out slightly. "You're poking a bear, and when it wakes up, it's us who'll have to deal with the fallout."

A murmur of agreement rose from a few others, their nods small but visible.

I let the silence stretch, letting their words settle as I gathered mine. Then I stepped forward, closing the space between us until my heels stopped just shy of the circle they'd unconsciously formed.

"You're right about one thing," I said, my voice firm but measured. "This isn't how Cassian would handle it. But Cassian isn't here."

The statement cut through the air like a blade, silencing the murmurs and forcing their eyes back to me.

I continued, my gaze sweeping over them. "He trusted me to hold things together while he's gone. To make the decisions that will keep this organization intact—not just for today, but for tomorrow and every day after that. Do you think he would've left that responsibility with someone he didn't trust?"

The stocky man shifted his weight, his jaw tightening as he broke eye contact. Another man—taller, with a scar cutting through his left brow—pushed off the crate he was leaning on, stepping forward with a faint smirk.

"And what happens if this blows up in your face?" he asked. "If The Broker doesn't take the bait, or comes back harder than we can handle?"

I turned to him, my chin lifting slightly. "Then we fight. And we keep fighting until we win or there's nothing left to fight for. Because that's what Cassian would expect—and it's what I expect from all of you."

The words burned as they left my mouth, but they were true. This wasn't about safety or guarantees. It was about survival, and survival didn't come with certainties.

The scarred man's smirk faded, replaced by a grudging nod. The others exchanged glances, their postures shifting slightly, the tension in their stances easing just a fraction.

Marcus stepped forward, his voice cutting through the heavy quiet. "Cassian trusted her. If you have a problem with her decisions, you have a problem with him."

The shorter man glanced at Marcus, then back at me. "It's not that we don't trust her," he muttered, his tone softer now. "It's just... a lot to take in."

"I know it is," I said, my voice softening but remaining firm. "But if we hesitate, if we falter, we lose. And I don't know about you, but I'm not willing to let that happen."

The scarred man nodded again, his expression shifting toward reluctant respect. "You've got guts," he said, his tone grudging. "But if this goes sideways, don't expect us to be the ones cleaning it up."

I met his gaze, holding it steady. "It won't come to that," I said, my voice calm but firm. "This will all be over soon enough. All I need from you is to trust me for a few more days."

A ripple of murmurs spread through the group, quieter now but laced with curiosity. The scarred man's brow furrowed, and the shorter, stocky one shifted his weight uncomfortably.

"What do you mean, 'over soon'?" he asked, his voice edged with suspicion.

I took a step forward, my gaze sweeping over the group. "I have a plan," I said, letting the weight of my words settle over them. "A plan to get Cassian out of jail and to stop The Broker before he can do any more damage. But to make it work, I need all of you to stay the course. No doubts, no hesitations—just trust. Can you do that?"

The silence that followed was heavy, their expressions a mix of skepticism and guarded hope.

"You've got a plan?" the scarred man asked, crossing his arms over his chest.

"Yes," I said firmly, meeting his gaze. "And it's already in motion. Cassian trusted me to handle this, and I'm asking you to do the same. Give me a few more days, and I promise you, this will be behind us."

The scarred man didn't speak, but his nod was enough. One by one, the men began to disperse, their movements slower, less tense. The tension in the room didn't disappear completely, but it shifted—lighter, more manageable.

I exhaled slowly, the knot in my chest easing just slightly.

Marcus stepped closer, his voice low enough that only I could hear. "You're putting a lot on the line, Rosalie."

"I know," I replied, watching as the last of the men disappeared around a corner. "But if I'm right, it'll be worth it."

He studied me for a long moment, his expression unreadable. "I hope you are."

"So do I," I admitted, my voice barely above a whisper.

The faint hum of machinery filled the quiet as Marcus and I turned to leave. The men had given me their trust—tentative as it was—but the clock was ticking. And if my plan didn't work, it wasn't just my trust on the line. It was everything.

The tension in the room thickened as I scanned the faces of Cassian's men. The defiance I'd sensed earlier had softened into guarded curiosity, their postures no longer rigid with resistance but tense with anticipation. They were waiting—for me, for answers, for something to hold onto.

I took a deep breath and stepped closer, ensuring my voice would carry across the cavernous space. "The Broker is finally taking the bait," I said, my tone steady despite the pounding in my chest.

The murmurs quieted instantly, all eyes snapping to me.

"A new shipment of the drug Cassian was suspected of being involved with is being moved," I continued, locking eyes with the scarred man who'd challenged me earlier. "And it's being protected heavily. That means the rumors are working. He's tightening his grip on the operation, trying to safeguard his supply chain."

"What's the play?" one of the men asked, his voice cautious but laced with urgency.

I let the question hang for a moment, ensuring I had their full attention before I answered. "We intercept the shipment," I said firmly. "Before the night ends."

The room buzzed with low murmurs again, the men exchanging glances. The shorter man, still standing near the front, frowned. "You're talking about hitting his operation directly. That's reckless."

"It's necessary," I replied. "If we let this shipment move unchecked, he regains control, and we lose the advantage we've worked so hard to gain. This is our chance to weaken his grip and gather the intel we need to bring him down."

The scarred man stepped forward, his expression skeptical but curious. "How do you know where the shipment is? And how do you know it's connected to him?"

"Because I have eyes on the ground," I said, meeting his gaze head-on. "Salvatori's network flagged the movement, and every detail points back to The Broker. The pills, the security—it's him. And we can't afford to let this slip through our fingers."

The room fell into silence, the weight of my words pressing down on all of us. The men exchanged glances again, some nodding, others shifting uncomfortably.

"What's the plan?" Marcus asked, his voice steady as he stepped forward.

"We split into teams," I said, my mind already working through the logistics. "One team shadows the shipment, tracking its movements while staying out of sight. Another sets up a blockade at the rendezvous point to cut them off. Sierra and I will coordinate from the ground, ensuring communication stays clear and the teams stay in position."

"And what about the cargo?" the scarred man asked.

I hesitated for only a moment before answering. "We seize it. Secure it. Once we have it, we'll figure out how to use it to dismantle his operation."

The shorter man glanced at Marcus, then back at me. "That's a big risk," he muttered.

"It's a calculated one," I said. "And if we pull this off, it will bring us one step closer to getting Cassian out of jail and taking back control of this organization."

The silence that followed was thick with unspoken tension, but no one spoke up to challenge me further.

"Get ready," I said, my tone sharp and final. "We move before the night ends. I want every man in position and prepared to act. This is our moment—let's make it count."

The men began to disperse, their movements purposeful now, the hesitation I'd seen earlier replaced by resolve. Marcus lingered near the edge of the group, his gaze fixed on me as I turned to leave.

"You're putting a lot on the line," he said quietly, falling into step beside me.

"I know," I replied, my voice steady despite the knot tightening in my stomach. "But if we wait any longer, we'll lose everything. This is the only way forward."

Marcus nodded, his expression unreadable. "Then let's make it happen."

As we stepped out of the distillery and into the cool night air, I exhaled slowly, the weight of the plan settling fully on my shoulders. The stage was set, the players in motion.

All that was left was to see it through—and hope that the risks I'd taken would be enough to tip the scales in our favor.

The night air was cool against my skin as I stepped outside the distillery, the distant sounds of the city blending with the quiet rustle of leaves in the dark. Marcus and Sierra trailed behind me, their footsteps steady, their silence a reflection of the weight we all carried.

I paused near the car, my gaze lifting to the inky sky above. The stars were faint, their light dimmed by the glow of the city, but they were there—constant, unchanging, even as my world spun out of control.

I leaned against the car, closing my eyes for a moment. The voices of Cassian's men echoed in my mind—their doubts, their questions, their tentative trust. They had seen a version of me tonight that I hadn't even recognized. Calculating, decisive, willing to risk lives for a single move on a chessboard I barely understood.

How had it come to this?

When I first stepped into Cassian's world, I'd clung to a belief that I could navigate it without losing myself—that I could hold onto the person I was before, no matter how dark things became. But now, that person felt like a stranger.

I had made choices I couldn't take back. I had lied, manipulated, and played a dangerous game with people far more ruthless than me. And for what? To save a man who had pulled me into this storm in the first place.

I opened my eyes, the sharp sting of guilt mingling with a fiercer, deeper emotion. Loyalty. Love.

Cassian wasn't just a man. He was the gravity that held this chaotic world together, the force that had drawn me in and refused to let me go. I had fought for him because I couldn't imagine a world without him in it. But in doing so, I'd become someone I barely recognized—someone willing to cross lines I once swore I'd never approach.

And yet, I didn't regret it.

I stared out into the night, my hands curling into fists at my sides. The choices I'd made had changed me, and there was no undoing that. But if it meant saving Cassian, if it meant holding onto the fragile empire he'd built with blood and sweat, I'd make them again.

Even if it cost me the last pieces of who I used to be.

Marcus's voice pulled me back to the present. "Rosalie," he said, his tone quiet but steady. "We need to move."

I nodded, straightening as I pushed the thoughts away. There was no room for reflection now, no time for second-guessing. The plan was in motion, and there was only one way forward.

As we got into the car and the engine roared to life, I cast one last glance at the distillery behind us. The shadows stretched long across the pavement, swallowing everything in their path.

For Cassian, I'd learned to walk in those shadows. And I wasn't afraid of what they'd turn me into anymore.

CHAPTER THIRTY

The night was unnervingly quiet, the rush of the city fading as we left the bustling streets behind. The industrial district loomed ahead, its warehouses and empty lots cloaked in shadows. I sat in the back seat of SUV with Marcus at the wheel, my pulse steady but my chest tight with anticipation.

Ahead of us, the convoy rolled forward: a large box truck sandwiched between two black SUVs. The lead vehicle moved deliberately, its tinted windows giving no clue as to what—or who—was inside. The rear SUV followed closely, its headlights cutting through the darkness like a warning.

Sierra's voice crackled through the earpiece, her tone sharp and professional. "The convoy just passed marker six. No deviations from the route so far."

I glanced at Marcus, who kept his focus on the road ahead, his jaw set. "How close are we to the choke point?" I asked, keeping my voice low.

"Two minutes," Marcus replied, his tone clipped.

The Interception Team was already in position at the underpass up ahead, waiting for the signal. They'd prepared for this moment carefully: two large vehicles parked strategically to block the road, forcing the convoy to a stop.

The glow of the truck's taillights flickered in the distance, the convoy moving at a steady, cautious pace. It was a routine run on the surface, but the heavy security presence told a different story.

As we approached the choke point, Marcus slowed the car, staying just far enough back to avoid suspicion. "Sierra, any signs of reinforcements?" he asked into the comms.

"None yet," Sierra replied. "But we're keeping our eyes open."

The lead SUV entered the underpass first, the truck following close behind. My fingers tightened around the edge of my seat as we rolled to a stop just out of sight.

"Go," I said, my voice steady despite the tension coiling in my chest.

Marcus nodded, giving the signal through the comms. A faint hum filled the air as the Interception Team's vehicles roared to life, pulling out of their hidden positions to block the road at both ends of the underpass. The lead SUV braked hard, its tires screeching against the pavement as the truck skidded to a halt behind it. The rear SUV tried to reverse, but it was already boxed in.

"Move!" Marcus barked, throwing the car into park.

The Interception Team moved quickly, their vehicles boxing in the convoy as planned. The screech of brakes and the faint murmur of shouting filled the air as the guards spilled out of the SUVs, their weapons raised but their movements hesitant.

"Drop your weapons!" Marcus barked, his voice cutting through the chaos as he stepped out of the car.

I followed, my heart hammering in my chest as I kept my focus on the scene ahead. Sierra moved alongside Marcus, her weapon drawn but pointed low, her gaze scanning the guards with cold precision.

The guards hesitated, exchanging glances as the tension thickened. For a moment, it seemed like they might comply.

Then, the first shot rang out.

The sound was deafening, echoing through the underpass like a thunderclap. But it didn't come from us—

or the convoy.

I froze, my breath catching as the guards around the convoy crumpled to the ground in quick succession. It happened so fast—too fast—that it took me a moment to process what I was seeing.

"Get down!" Marcus shouted, shoving me behind the cover of a nearby crate as another round of gunfire lit up the night.

From the shadows, they emerged—another team, their movements swift and surgical. Dressed in dark tactical gear, their faces obscured by masks, they moved like predators, silent and efficient.

"Who the hell are they?" Sierra hissed, crouched beside me as she scanned the scene.

"They're not ours," Marcus growled, his hand gripping his weapon tightly.

I peeked around the crate, my stomach sinking as I watched the team close in on the convoy. They didn't hesitate, taking out every guard and driver with ruthless precision. Blood pooled beneath the vehicles, the scent sharp and metallic in the air.

"We need to move," Marcus said, his voice low and urgent.

"No," I said quickly, my hand gripping his arm. "Look at them. They're too organized. If we go in now, we'll get slaughtered."

He clenched his jaw but didn't argue.

The team worked quickly, their leader—a tall figure with a commanding presence—barking orders that were just audible over the chaos. They surrounded the truck, moving the bodies aside with an eerie efficiency before unloading the cargo.

The boxes were lifted into sleek, unmarked vehicles that had appeared seemingly out of nowhere, their engines purring like predators waiting to strike.

"We're losing the shipment," Sierra whispered, her voice tight with frustration.

"I know," I said, my teeth clenched. "But I'd rather lose that then anyone from the team."

We watched, helpless, as the last of the boxes were loaded into the vehicles. The team didn't linger. They moved with the same precision they'd arrived with, disappearing into the night as quickly as they'd come.

The convoy was left behind, a graveyard of blood and broken bodies.

Marcus exhaled sharply, his hand running through his hair as he leaned back against the crate. "What the hell just happened?"

"The Broker," I murmured, my voice shaking slightly. "Or someone just as dangerous."

Sierra's gaze snapped to me, her eyes narrowing. "How could they know? How could they be ready for this?"

I didn't have an answer, the knot in my chest tightening as I replayed the scene in my mind. Every move they'd made, every shot fired—it was calculated, deliberate, and terrifyingly effective.

"They were waiting," Marcus said grimly, his voice heavy. "They knew we'd be here."

"Or someone told them," Sierra added, her tone sharp.

The words hit me like a punch to the gut. A mole. It was the only explanation that made sense.

I stood slowly, my legs unsteady beneath me as I surveyed the carnage. The plan had been flawless—or so I'd thought. But we'd been outmaneuvered, outplayed.

And now, the game had changed.

"We need to regroup," I said finally, my voice barely above a whisper. "And we need to figure out who's feeding them information."

As we retreated into the shadows, my mind raced. The Broker's people—or whoever they were—had sent a message tonight.

And I wasn't sure we'd be ready for the next one.

The distant wail of sirens cut through the night, sharp and unmistakable. My heart sank as red and blue lights began to flicker faintly on the horizon, growing brighter with each passing second.

"Cops," Marcus muttered, his voice low but urgent. He turned to me, his expression grim. "We need to go. Now. We can't stay here any longer, Rosalie."

I hesitated for half a breath, my eyes scanning the carnage ahead of us. The blood, the bodies, the destroyed convoy—it was a scene that screamed betrayal, chaos, and loss. Whoever had swooped in had left us nothing but a disaster.

"Pull everyone back," I said finally, my voice steadier than I felt. "We can't be here when they arrive."

Marcus nodded, already signaling the others. Sierra moved quickly, her sharp voice directing the remaining men to retreat.

I followed Marcus to the SUV, climbing into the back seat as the engine roared to life. The tension in the air was palpable as the vehicle sped away from the underpass, the sirens growing louder behind us.

The drive was silent, save for the hum of the engine and the distant echo of police sirens fading into the background. I sat in the back seat, my hands gripping the edge of the seat, my mind racing.

The scene replayed in my head on a loop: the tactical team's precision, the blood pooling beneath the convoy, the boxes disappearing into sleek, unmarked vehicles. It wasn't just a failure—it felt like a message, a carefully orchestrated statement.

My stomach twisted as a darker thought crept into my mind. Was this part of the plan? Not mine—but theirs.

The Broker wasn't just reacting to the rumors we'd spread. He was dismantling our efforts piece by piece, turning them against us. The interception wasn't just a failure—it was another nail in Cassian's coffin.

"Rosalie," Marcus said, glancing at me through the rearview mirror. "You okay?"

I nodded automatically, though the tightness in my chest told a different story. "Just thinking," I murmured.

Sierra twisted in her seat to look at me, her gaze sharp. "They were ready for us," she said. "This wasn't random."

"No," I agreed, my voice quiet. "It wasn't."

I leaned my head back against the seat, my eyes closing for a moment as the weight of the night pressed down on me. Every decision I'd made had led to this moment, and now it felt like the ground beneath my feet was crumbling.

"They're smarter than I gave them credit for," I said softly. "More calculated."

"They're sending a message," Marcus said, his voice steady but grim. "And it's not just for us. This is for Cassian too."

The thought made my chest tighten further. Cassian was already in a cage, his name tied to an empire that felt like it was unraveling. And now, this—more blood, more chaos—would only strengthen the case against him.

Sierra nodded slowly, though her expression remained guarded. "We don't have a choice."

As the SUV wove through the quiet streets, the weight of the night settled heavier on my shoulders. The Broker wasn't just an opponent—he was a predator, circling, waiting for the right moment to strike.

And I wasn't sure if I was the hunter or the prey.

CHAPTER THIRTY-ONE

The midday sun hung high in the sky as I stepped out of the SUV, the familiar storefront of Ivy & Bloom coming into view. The glass gleamed, reflecting the vibrant spring flowers displayed in neat rows along the sidewalk. For a moment, the sight calmed me—the simple beauty of the shop, a stark contrast to the chaos I'd left behind.

I pushed open the door, the faint chime of the bell above announcing my arrival. The familiar scent of fresh blooms and greenery enveloped me, and for the first time in days, I felt like I could breathe.

Lena stood behind the counter, flipping through a stack of papers. Her sharp eyes snapped up at the sound of the bell, her expression softening when she saw me.

"Rosalie," she said warmly, setting the papers aside. "You're just in time."

"In time for what?" I asked, stepping further inside.

"The expansion," she replied, her tone laced with excitement. "It's ready. Come see."

I followed her through the shop, past the displays of roses, hydrangeas, and lilies that filled the air with their delicate fragrances. As we approached the back, Lena stopped near the wall that once divided Ivy & Bloom from the neighboring space.

Or what used to be the wall.

"Ready?" she asked, a faint smile tugging at her lips.

I nodded, my curiosity outweighing my exhaustion.

Lena pushed open the door, leading me into the newly expanded section of the shop. My breath caught as I stepped inside.

The space was stunning.

The wall that had once divided the two shops was gone, replaced by an open, seamless layout that flowed effortlessly between the original Ivy & Bloom and the new addition. The polished hardwood floors stretched the length of the space, their rich, dark grain gleaming under the natural light that streamed in from above. Skylights dotted the ceiling, their placement deliberate, casting dappled sunlight that shifted gently with the breeze outside.

The ceiling rafters were exposed, painted a crisp white to give the space a rustic, airy charm. Recessed lighting was tucked along the beams, adding warmth to the already inviting atmosphere. It created a perfect balance of industrial and elegant, modern and timeless.

Along the walls, the shelving was a continuation of the shop's signature aesthetic—handcrafted wood with delicate carvings, each unit housing neatly arranged rows of floral arrangements, potted plants, and unique decorative pieces. Antique furniture from the old shop had been repurposed and integrated into the design: an ornate writing desk served as a checkout station, its brass inlay polished to perfection, while a refurbished apothecary cabinet displayed small vases, handmade candles, and packets of seeds.

"It's breathtaking," I murmured, running my fingers along the edge of a refinished side table, its weathered texture smoothed to perfection.

"I wanted to keep the charm of Ivy & Bloom—for you," Lena explained, her voice laced with pride. "The antique pieces you had were too beautiful to replace. They deserved a second life."

In the center of the room stood a grand display—a cascading arrangement of seasonal blooms in shades of blush, lavender, and cream. The flowers spilled out of a vintage claw-foot bathtub, a touch of whimsy that drew the eye and demanded admiration.

Near the far wall, Lena had added a cozy seating area: two tufted armchairs and a small table, surrounded by plants that hung in macramé holders from the rafters. It was a space designed for lingering, for conversations that could stretch long past the time it took to choose a bouquet.

The finishing touch was the mural. Stretching across the back wall, it depicted a field of wildflowers, their soft petals reaching toward a watercolor sky. The words *Ivy & Bloom: Where Beauty Grows* were written in elegant script, their placement perfect—centered, commanding attention without overwhelming the rest of the design.

"I had to hire contractors to work around the clock," Lena said, her tone brimming with satisfaction. "But it was worth it. The grand opening is going to blow everyone away."

I nodded, my gaze traveling over every detail, every choice Lena had made. It was more than an expansion—it was an evolution. Ivy & Bloom had always been beautiful, but now it was something else entirely.

It was a statement. A declaration.

"It's perfect," I said, my voice barely above a whisper.

Lena's smile widened, the pride in her eyes unmistakable. "I thought you'd like it."

As I stood there, the sunlight catching on the polished wood and vibrant blooms, I felt a flicker of hope. This wasn't just a shop—it was a symbol of everything I was fighting for.

And I wasn't about to let anyone take it away.

Lena turned to me, her excitement still evident as she gestured toward the vibrant floral arrangements scattered throughout the space. "We've already started prepping for the grand opening," she said. "But there's still plenty to do. With the new additions, it'll take at least a couple of days to get everything perfect."

"Two days is all we have," I said, stepping closer to one of the displays. The soft petals of blush roses brushed against my fingertips, their scent calming but fleeting against the storm brewing in my mind. "We need to have everything ready by then—every arrangement, every detail."

Lena nodded, pulling out her notebook. "That's doable," she said, jotting something down. "But it'll be tight. We'll need all hands on deck."

"That's fine," I said, my tone steady. "But I need one more thing."

Lena looked up, her pen hovering over the page. "What's that?"

I turned to face her fully, my voice lowering. "Leave the doors unlocked the night before the grand opening."

The words hung in the air like a slap, and Lena's expression shifted instantly, her brow furrowing in confusion. "Leave the doors unlocked?" she repeated, her tone incredulous. "Rosalie, are you serious?"

"I am," I said firmly, holding Lena's gaze as steadily as I could. My voice carried conviction, but I felt the weight of her doubt pressing against me like a solid wall.

She shook her head slowly, her frustration radiating in the sharp set of her jaw. Her arms crossed over her chest, the notebook in one hand tapping against her elbow in a restless rhythm. "That's a terrible idea," she said, her tone low but clipped. "Do you know how much we have in here? The flowers, the furniture, the decorations—someone could steal everything or vandalize the place."

Her body angled slightly away from me, a subconscious retreat, but her gaze remained locked on mine, filled with incredulity and a hint of betrayal.

"I know," I replied, keeping my voice calm and even despite the tension twisting in my gut. "But it's crucial for everything to happen the way it needs to."

Lena's lips pressed into a tight line, her shoulders stiffening as her fingers gripped the notebook tighter. "Why?" she demanded, the sharp edge in her voice cutting through the air. "What's so important that you're willing to risk everything we've built here?"

I hesitated, feeling the weight of her words settle on my

chest. Her fingers stilled, clutching the notebook as she leaned slightly forward, her eyes narrowing as though trying to read the thoughts I wasn't saying aloud.

"It's complicated," I said finally, my voice quieter but no less resolute. "But trust me, Lena. This isn't a decision I'm making lightly."

Her brow furrowed, and she shifted her weight, planting one foot slightly forward as if bracing herself against the force of my insistence. The tension in her arms didn't ease, and her grip on the notebook was so tight I could see the faint tremor in her knuckles.

"You're asking a lot," she said quietly, the words almost a whisper. Her gaze didn't soften, but there was something in the way she tilted her head, just slightly, that betrayed her internal conflict.

"I know," I admitted, letting my tone match the honesty in her words. "And I wouldn't ask if it wasn't necessary. But this is bigger than the shop. Bigger than me."

Her shoulders sagged just a fraction, and her gaze flickered to the floral arrangements before coming back to me. The tension in her posture didn't leave entirely, but there was a faint shift, a tiny crack in the armor of her resistance.

"You're sure about this?" she asked, her voice quieter now, though the doubt lingered in her eyes.

"I am," I said, nodding firmly. "Leave the doors unlocked. Just for one night."

Lena let out a long, frustrated sigh, her free hand raking through her hair as she looked away, her gaze scanning the shop as though searching for an escape. She shifted her stance, uncrossing her arms and letting the notebook hang at her side.

"You're putting me in a tough spot, Rosalie," she said, her voice low but weighted with resignation. Her eyes flicked back to mine, and the faintest hint of defeat showed in the way her shoulders dipped slightly, a reluctant acceptance in her stance.

"I know," I replied softly, stepping closer. "But you've trusted me this far. Trust me now."

She didn't move for a long moment, her fingers twitching slightly against the notebook. Then, with another sigh, she gave the faintest nod, her shoulders dropping fully as she let the tension ease out of her frame.

"Fine," she said, her voice laced with reluctant resolve. "But I hope you know what you're doing."

"Me too." I said more under my breath than anything.

Lena gave me one last look, her lips pressed tightly together, before turning back to her notebook, her pen moving briskly across the page. Her movements were deliberate but sharp, her body language screaming both frustration and reluctant loyalty.

As I watched her, a mix of gratitude and guilt churned inside me. I knew what I was asking was risky—maybe even reckless—but it had to be done. And whether Lena believed that or not, she was standing by me.

For now, that was enough.

The bell above the door chimed softly as I stepped out of Ivy & Bloom, the cool midday air brushing against my skin. The sun was bright, casting long shadows on the sidewalk, but my thoughts were anything but light. Lena's reluctant agreement lingered in my mind, and I couldn't shake the unease that had settled in my chest.

I slipped my hand into my jacket pocket, pulling out my phone. My thumb hovered over the screen for a moment before scrolling to Julian's name. This wasn't the kind of call I ever imagined I'd make, but if anyone could pull it off, it might just be Julian.

Pressing the call button, I brought the phone to my ear. It rang twice before Julian's smooth, familiar voice came through.

"Rosalie," he greeted, a note of curiosity in his tone. "How are you doing?"

"Julian," I said, keeping my voice steady as I stepped to the side of the sidewalk, away from the flow of pedestrians. "I need your help. And I'll be upfront—it's a bit of an unusual request."

His low chuckle was warm, laced with intrigue. "You certainly know how to pique my interest. Go on."

I glanced back at the shop, the bright blooms in the window a stark contrast to the storm swirling in my mind. "You're always at the center of the party scene," I began. "You know people—people who know things."

"That's one way to put it," he replied, the faint sound of glasses clinking in the background. "What exactly are you getting at?"

"Think you could help me with something?" I asked carefully, choosing my words with precision. "And I need it fast. There's something big happening, and I need to make sure the right people are watching when it unfolds."

Julian was silent for a moment, his breath audible over the line. "You're planning something," he said finally, his voice quieter but no less sharp.

"Yes," I admitted. "And I need your help to set the stage. Can you do that for me?"

"I'd be honored to help however I can."

CHAPTER THIRTY-TWO

The mirror reflected a version of myself I wasn't sure I recognized. The black dress fit like a second skin, the faint embossed pattern of roses catching the light just enough to create a subtle texture. It was understated, elegant—everything I wanted to project tonight. The fabric was soft against my skin, offering a comfort I desperately needed amid the chaos swirling inside me.

I adjusted the neckline, smoothing the fabric over my hips as I tilted my head, studying my reflection. My makeup was minimal, just enough to brighten my face, and my hair fell in loose waves over my shoulders. The simplicity felt like armor, a way to remind myself that this wasn't about standing out—it was about standing firm.

A faint knock at the door broke through my thoughts.

"It's almost time," Sierra said, her voice steady as she stepped into the room. She paused, her sharp eyes scanning me before offering a faint smile. "You look perfect."

"Thanks," I said softly, turning back to the mirror.

Sierra crossed her arms, leaning against the doorframe. "You ready for this?"

I exhaled slowly, my gaze lingering on my reflection. "As ready as I'll ever be."

She nodded, her expression unreadable. "Marcus is at

Ivy & Bloom already. He says the place is packed already. You pulled it off, Rosalie."

"Not yet," I replied, my voice firm. "Tonight is just the beginning."

Sierra's eyes narrowed slightly, but she didn't press. "Then let's make it count."

The atmosphere at Ivy & Bloom was electric. The soft hum of conversations and the delicate clinking of glasses filled the air, mingling with the sweet scent of flowers that seemed to bloom in every corner. The newly expanded space was alive with light and color, the grand opening drawing more people than I'd anticipated.

Julian had outdone himself, his connections ensuring that the event wasn't just well-attended but strategically curated. Familiar faces mingled with unfamiliar ones, a mix of past clients, potential partners, and a few who were clearly more curious than invested.

The mural at the back of the shop drew many admiring glances, its vibrant colors catching the light from the elegant chandeliers above. Beneath it, the sleek coffee station buzzed with activity, the barista skillfully pouring drinks for guests as they browsed the displays.

Lena caught my eye from across the room, her expression a mix of pride and nervous energy. She was dressed in a deep green dress that complimented the floral theme perfectly, her hair pinned back to keep her movements efficient as she navigated the crowd.

I made my way through the guests, offering polite smiles and brief conversations as I worked the room. Each interaction felt like a performance, a carefully measured balance of warmth and poise.

Marcus and Sierra lingered near the entrance, their sharp eyes scanning the room as they blended in with the crowd.

"You're holding up well," Marcus said as I passed by, his voice low enough for only me to hear.

"Thanks," I replied, my lips curving into a faint smile.

"Let us know if anything feels off," Sierra added, her gaze sweeping over the guests.

I nodded, though the knot in my stomach hadn't eased since I stepped into the room. This was a moment to celebrate, but it was also a test—a chance to see who was watching, who might be lurking in the shadows, and who would show their hand.

As I reached the center of the room, Julian appeared at my side, his easy smile a welcome distraction. But this time, something was different. A sleek black dog, a German Shepherd by the looks of it, walked beside him, wearing a clearly marked service vest. The dog moved gracefully, its focus unwavering despite the noise and bustle of the crowded shop.

"You've outdone yourself," Julian said, his voice warm but carrying an edge of something I couldn't place. "The place looks incredible."

I glanced down at the dog, then back at Julian, raising an eyebrow. "Is this our new friend?" I asked, keeping my tone light.

Julian smirked, his hand briefly brushing over the dog's head. "Not exactly. He's more of a partner."

I studied him for a moment, noting the subtle tension in his shoulders, the way his smile didn't quite reach his eyes. "Partner for what?"

Julian let out a soft chuckle, shaking his head. "You were right," he said cryptically, his tone dropping just enough to send a ripple of unease through me.

"You were right," Julian said again, his tone carrying a weight that pressed down on me, though his easy demeanor didn't falter.

I opened my mouth to ask more, but something about the subtle tension in his frame stopped me. Julian's hand rested on the service dog's harness, his fingers brushing the material as if grounding himself. Whatever he wasn't saying, it was deliberate—and pressing would only make him retreat further.

Instead, I let out a soft sigh, forcing a faint smile as I shifted the conversation. "Well, I'm glad you're here. The party wouldn't be the same without you."

Julian's smirk returned, his shoulders relaxing ever so

slightly. "You flatter me. But tonight, Rosalie, this is all you. Look around—every single person here is either impressed or jealous, and both are good for business."

I chuckled lightly, grateful for the pivot. Together, we turned toward the room, surveying the crowd. The soft hum of conversations mingled with the scent of fresh flowers, and glasses clinked faintly as servers moved through the crowd with trays of champagne.

"Impressed, jealous—or suspicious," I murmured, my eyes scanning the room. "Let's hope they don't spill their drinks on the furniture."

Julian chuckled, his gaze sharp as it swept over the guests. "You've got an interesting mix tonight," he said, his voice low. "Some familiar faces, some less so."

I nodded, my pulse quickening as my eyes landed on Markson near the edge of the crowd. He was dressed sharply, his dark suit blending in with the other well-dressed guests. But his stance—relaxed yet too deliberate—gave him away. He wasn't just here to admire the flowers.

Markson caught my gaze, offering a faint nod and a smile that didn't quite reach his eyes. My chest tightened, but I returned the gesture, forcing my expression to remain neutral.

"Friend of yours?" Julian asked, following my gaze.

"Not exactly," I replied, my voice measured. "That's Detective Markson. He's been... involved in Cassian's case."

Julian's brow lifted slightly, but he didn't respond immediately. Instead, his gaze shifted, subtly scanning the group surrounding Markson. A few of the men and women nearby seemed out of place—polished, yes, but their movements too coordinated, their postures too rigid.

"Let me guess," Julian said, his voice barely above a whisper. "DEA?"

I swallowed hard, my eyes narrowing as I studied them. "Probably," I muttered. "I don't recognize most of them, but they're not here for the grand opening."

Julian's smirk faded, his expression turning serious.

"They're watching," he said. "Question is, what are they waiting for?"

"That's the question," I replied, my mind racing.

Julian's hand brushed the dog's harness again, a faint tension returning to his frame. "You're playing a dangerous game, Rosalie. I hope you've stacked the deck."

"I'm trying," I said quietly, keeping my gaze fixed on the group. "But it feels like everyone's holding cards I can't see."

Julian turned his head slightly, his voice low and even. "Then make them show their hand."

Before I could respond, a server passed by with a tray of champagne. Julian plucked a glass with practiced ease, offering it to me with a faint smile. "For now, though, let them think you're untouchable. If they're watching, give them something worth watching."

I took the glass, my fingers brushing against the cool surface. "You always know what to say."

"It's a gift," Julian replied with a wink, the tension in his posture easing just enough to reassure me.

As we mingled back into the crowd, my gaze darted back to Markson and the strangers near him. They weren't blending in as well as they thought, and the weight of their presence settled heavily in my chest. The grand opening had been designed to draw attention—but now, I wasn't sure I wanted to know who else had decided to show up.

I let Julian's words linger as I shifted my focus back to the crowd. The mingling guests moved in graceful currents, their laughter and polite conversation creating a pleasant hum. My gaze darted from face to face, searching for one in particular.

And then I saw her.

She stood near the back, partially obscured by a group of chattering women admiring a floral centerpiece. Her sharp, angular features were softened slightly by her navy blue jacket and khaki pants, her dark hair pulled into a sleek chignon. She was poised, calm—watchful, but didn't exactly blend into the rest of the guests attire, perhaps that was why she stayed to the back.

But it was her, the woman I'd invited for this very moment.

My pulse quickened as I met her gaze across the room. She didn't smile, but there was the faintest tilt of her head, an acknowledgment that she'd seen me. It was time.

I took a steadying breath and turned toward the center of the room where a small platform had been built. It was understated, just a few steps leading up to a simple podium draped in soft white fabric, but it commanded attention.

Julian caught my movement and raised an eyebrow as I passed. He didn't say anything, but his faint smirk told me he'd figured out I was about to make a move.

The conversations around the room began to quiet as I ascended the platform. The light from the chandeliers caught the faint embossed roses on my dress, adding a subtle sheen to the fabric as I turned to face the crowd.

"Ladies and gentlemen," I began, my voice carrying easily across the room. The hum of conversation ceased entirely, all eyes turning to me. "Thank you for being here tonight to celebrate the grand opening of Ivy & Bloom's expansion."

I let my gaze sweep over the crowd, catching Markson's subtle shift of posture as he leaned slightly closer to listen.

"This shop has always been more than just a business," I continued, my tone warm but measured. "It's a reflection of community, growth, and beauty—the kind of beauty that reminds us of the strength it takes to thrive in uncertain times."

A few polite nods greeted my words, the faint rustle of clothing as guests adjusted their stances.

"The expansion you see tonight wouldn't have been possible without the dedication of so many. Lena, my incredible team, and everyone who has supported Ivy & Bloom over the years—you've made this dream a reality."

I gestured toward Lena, whose cheeks flushed as a small ripple of applause spread through the room.

"But tonight isn't just about flowers and design," I added, letting a slight edge creep into my tone. "It's about something much bigger—connection, family, friends. The kind of connection that brings people together, even when everything else seems to be pulling them apart."

Scanning the crowds again, my eyes fell on my father, Abram who'd made his first visit back to this shop since Cassian forbid him from being involved due to his gambling addiction. I gave him a knowing, loving smile, but my heart pained that he had to watch the rest of the evening unfold.

I let the words hang in the air, my gaze darting back to the woman at the rear of the room. She was still, her eyes locked on me, her expression unreadable.

"We've all faced challenges," I said, softening my tone. "But challenges are what give us the opportunity to rise, to adapt, to grow."

A murmur of agreement rippled through the crowd, but my focus remained steady.

"So tonight," I concluded, my voice firm, "let this space remind us of the strength in growth, the beauty in resilience, and the power of community."

The applause that followed was warm, polite. I stepped down from the platform, my heart racing as I forced a calm smile. The speech had done its job—set the tone, established my control over the room—but the real work was just beginning.

The woman near the back tilted her head slightly again, an almost imperceptible gesture. It was time to move forward, and as I rejoined the crowd, I couldn't help but feel the weight of every step, every word, every choice.

The stage was set. Now, it was time to see who would take the first move.

The party was in full swing, the room alive with chatter, laughter, and the occasional burst of applause. I moved through the crowd with a practiced ease, shaking hands, exchanging pleasantries, and keeping an eye on every face I didn't recognize. The woman from earlier had vanished into the sea of guests, but her presence lingered at the back of my mind.

I was mid-conversation with a former client—an elderly woman who'd commissioned one of my first floral designs— when the first sign of trouble reached me. It wasn't a loud commotion or sudden panic, but a subtle shift in the air. The hum of conversation began to falter, replaced by uneasy murmurs as people turned toward the windows and the doors.

I followed their gazes, my chest tightening at the sight of flashing blue and red lights outside. Police cars and unmarked vehicles lined the street, their presence too numerous and deliberate to be coincidence.

Marcus appeared at my side, his expression grim. "We've got a problem," he said, his voice low.

Before I could respond, the front doors of the shop burst open. A swarm of men and women in DEA jackets filed in, their movements efficient and calculated. Behind them, uniformed police officers fanned out, their hands hovering near their holsters as they began securing the exits.

The hum of the crowd turned into a dull roar as panic rippled through the room. Guests stepped back, their murmurs growing louder as they exchanged nervous glances.

"Ladies and gentlemen," one of the DEA agents announced, his voice cutting through the noise. "Please remain calm. This is a federal operation. We're here to conduct a search of the premises."

I stepped forward, my heart pounding as I forced a calm expression onto my face. "What is the meaning of this?" I demanded, my voice steady but firm.

The agent turned to me, his gaze sharp. "Ms. Rosalie Quinn?"

"That's me," I said, lifting my chin.

"We're executing a search warrant," he said, handing me a folded piece of paper. "The DEA has reason to believe that this property is connected to the illegal drug activities of Cassian Moreau."

My stomach dropped, but I refused to let it show. I unfolded the paper, skimming the legal jargon that seemed to scream guilt without evidence.

"This is a mistake," I said, my tone cold. "There are no drugs here. This is a flower shop, not some criminal operation."

The agent didn't flinch, his gaze unyielding. "We'll be the judge of that," he said. "Please instruct your guests to cooperate while we secure the building."

Julian appeared at my side, his service dog pressing close to his leg as his gaze swept the room. "This is ridiculous," he said, his voice smooth but edged with steel. "You're disrupting a legitimate business and its clients. On what grounds?"

The agent ignored him, signaling to his team. They began moving through the shop, their gloves snapping on as they inspected every corner.

I turned back to the agent, my eyes narrowing. "You won't find anything here," I said. "And when you don't, I expect a public apology for this baseless accusation."

The agent didn't respond, his attention focused on his team as they moved through the shop. One of them began prying open a crate of floral supplies, while another carefully examined the coffee station.

The murmurs of the guests grew louder, their confusion and fear palpable. My mind raced, the weight of the moment pressing down on me. This wasn't just about Ivy & Bloom—it was a calculated move. Another nail in Cassian's coffin, another step in dismantling everything he'd built.

And as I stood there, surrounded by flashing lights and uniformed agents, I couldn't help but feel like the trap wasn't just for him.

It was for me, too.

The sound of breaking wood and clattering objects filled the air as the DEA agents tore through Ivy & Bloom. Shelves were cleared, boxes ripped open, and floral arrangements tossed aside without care. The vibrant beauty of the shop—the very heart of what I had built— was being reduced to chaos, and I stood helpless in the middle of it all.

Guests were huddled near the far end of the shop, whispering nervously among themselves. Some had already slipped out the back exit, led by Marcus and Sierra, while others lingered, their curiosity mingling with fear. Julian stood close by, his service dog sitting alertly at his side, his face unreadable.

Outside, the flashing lights of police cars and DEA vehicles drew even more attention. I spotted the first journalist just beyond the window, her camera aimed directly into the shop. She was quickly joined by others, microphones in hand, eager to capture the commotion. The click and flash of cameras became relentless, their lenses trained on every move the agents made.

"Keep them back," Sierra hissed, but I stopped her mid-step toward the door.

"No," I paused, "Let them come. Let them all see this."

An agent ripped open a crate of floral supplies, sending packets of seeds and gardening tools scattering across the floor. Another yanked open drawers, tossing ribbons and decorative materials aside as though searching for something hidden beneath.

"That's enough!" I snapped, stepping forward despite the tight grip of anxiety in my chest. "You've made your point. There's nothing here!"

The lead agent turned to me, his expression impassive. "We'll stop when we've searched every inch of this place," he said coldly. He gestured to two other agents, who moved toward the back room where Lena had stored additional supplies.

"This is a flower shop!" I shouted, my composure slipping. "You're tearing apart my business, my livelihood, for nothing!"

The agent ignored me, his attention shifting to the commotion outside. More reporters had arrived, their cameras now filming the shop's dismantling through the windows. A few guests tried to slip past them, shielding their faces from the flashing lights.

Julian stepped up beside me, his voice low but sharp. "This is a circus. They've made their point, Rosalie. If they don't leave soon, it's going to spiral out of control."

"I know," I whispered, my nails digging into my palms. "But they're not stopping."

CHAPTER THIRTY-THREE

Minutes dragged on like hours as the agents continued their rampage. The shop was unrecognizable—flowers crushed underfoot, shelves emptied, displays toppled. Every carefully curated detail of the grand opening was in ruins, and I could feel my composure fraying with each passing second.

Then, finally, the lead agent stepped toward the door, pulling his phone from his pocket. He dialed a number, his posture stiff and agitated as he brought the phone to his ear.

"There's nothing here," he said, his voice loud enough to carry through the shop. "No drugs, no paraphernalia. It's clean."

I caught the words, and so did everyone else. A few guests exchanged glances, the tension in the air shifting slightly. The journalists outside leaned closer to catch every word, their cameras still rolling.

"Understood," the agent said curtly before ending the call. He turned back to his team, his jaw tight. "Wrap it up."

The lead agent began to turn, his face a mask of indifference as his team started filing out of the shop. Rage burned in my chest, hot and unyielding, as I watched them walk over the ruins of Ivy & Bloom without a second glance.

No. Not like this.

"Wait!" My voice rang out sharply, cutting through the heavy silence. The agent paused, his back stiffening as he turned to face me.

"Don't go yet," I said, stepping forward. My heels crunched against shattered glass and crushed petals, the sound loud in the stunned quiet. Every eye in the room turned to me. Guests whispered, reporters leaned closer, and the air grew charged with anticipation.

The lead agent's eyes narrowed. "Ms. Quinn, this is over. We've completed our search."

"Oh, it's far from over," I replied, my voice calm but sharp enough to slice through the tension. I stepped onto a piece of broken furniture—a toppled wooden display that creaked under my weight—and stood tall, commanding the attention of the room.

"Ladies and gentlemen," I began, my voice carrying with a strength I barely felt. "You've all seen what's happened here tonight. My shop—my business—was torn apart under the guise of justice. The DEA stormed in, claiming they were searching for drugs tied to Cassian Moreau, but what did they find?"

I turned, my gaze locking on the lead agent. "Nothing."

The crowd murmured, their unease rippling through the room. The journalists outside pressed closer to the windows, their cameras catching every word.

I gestured toward the ruined shop around me. "This wasn't just about me. This wasn't just about Ivy & Bloom. This is about corruption—corruption that's spreading through this city like a disease, infecting even those sworn to protect us. Even DEA agents."

The lead agent's jaw tightened, his posture growing rigid. "Watch your accusations, Ms. Quinn."

"Oh, I plan to do more than watch," I replied, my tone steady. I pointed to the large TV screen mounted in the corner of the room. Its black surface reflected the shattered remnants of the shop, but it held the attention of everyone present.

"This city deserves the truth," I said, my gaze sweeping

the crowd. "And the truth is that corruption thrives when no one is willing to expose it. Tonight, that changes."

I reached into my pocket and pulled out a small remote, holding it up for everyone to see. "What you're about to witness proves tonight wasn't about a simple, tax paying citizen's flower shop or a baseless raid. It's about power, greed, and the lengths some people will go to protect their secrets."

The murmurs grew louder, the anticipation thick enough to cut with a knife. I pressed the button, and the screen flickered to life.

The screen flickered to life, the grainy image sharpening into clarity. The familiar interior of Nocturne filled the frame—the dim lighting, the pulsing shadows of the club's crowded corners. The camera's perspective was slightly angled, discreetly hidden, but its view was undeniable.

The scene showed Cassian standing tall, his posture commanding but calm, as the man now standing in front of me approached him. The lead DEA agent, dressed in a dark suit, moved with practiced ease, leaning in as though to speak. But the footage revealed something far more sinister.

The agent's hand slipped into his pocket, emerging with a small, unmistakable object: the neon pink pills. With a quick, deliberate motion, he pressed them into Cassian's pocket, his expression neutral, his movements almost imperceptible to those nearby.

The crowd gasped.

I let the footage continue for a moment longer, showing the agent stepping back, his hand brushing his jacket as if to wipe away any lingering evidence. The room was silent now, the weight of the revelation sinking in as people exchanged wide-eyed glances.

"This," I said, my voice carrying through the stillness, "is how justice is served, apparently. Not with truth, not with evidence—but with deceit."

I turned slightly, letting my gaze sweep the room before gesturing toward the TV again. "And if you think it stops there, you're wrong. Watch."

I pressed a button on the remote, fast-forwarding the footage. The grainy image blurred for a moment before settling on a new scene—an industrial underpass bathed in the harsh glow of headlights.

It was the shipment.

The camera's perspective was shaky but clear, capturing the chaos as armed figures swarmed the convoy. The sound of gunfire crackled faintly, and the screen showed bodies falling, blood pooling on the pavement. But it wasn't just the carnage that held everyone's attention.

The camera zoomed in, focusing on one of the men as he turned slightly, his face briefly illuminated by the harsh glare of a flashlight. The same lead DEA agent.

I hit the pause button, freezing the image. His face stared back at the room, undeniable and damning.

The journalists surged forward, their cameras flashing as they captured the screen. Questions erupted from the crowd, their voices overlapping in a chaotic symphony of disbelief and outrage.

The chaos in the room was palpable, the weight of the evidence on the screen rippling through the crowd like a tidal wave. Cameras flashed, journalists shouted over one another, and the guests who hadn't yet fled whispered furiously among themselves.

But I wasn't done. Not yet.

"This," I said, gesturing to the paused screen, "is not the end, ladies and gentlemen." My voice cut through the noise, commanding the room's attention once more. "You've seen how Cassian Moreau was framed. You've seen the brutal ambush orchestrated to undermine his network. And now, you're about to see what they planned to do to me."

I pressed the button on the remote again, and the screen flickered back to life. The footage changed, shifting to a high-definition view of Ivy & Bloom's interior. The timestamp in the corner showed the early hours of this morning, long before the grand opening.

"This expansion was our idea," I began, my eyes flickering to Lena, my voice steady, "but Cassian Moreau wanted it to have more than beauty—he wanted it to have protection. What you're seeing now is part of the state-of-the-art security system he insisted on installing. Cameras in every corner, discreet and almost undetectable, recording everything, no matter what."

The screen displayed two figures entering the shop through the back door. Their movements were deliberate, their faces obscured at first by caps and jackets. But as they stepped further into the frame, their features came into focus.

Markson.

And the lead DEA agent standing in front of me.

Gasps erupted from the crowd, followed by a flurry of camera flashes. The footage continued, showing the men planting small bags of neon pink pills in strategic locations: under a display case, inside a decorative vase, even tucked into the coffee station.

"I knew," I said, turning to face the room, "that they might try to use this shop to frame me. To smear my name and, by extension, Cassian's. So, I took precautions."

I nodded toward the German Shepherd sitting calmly at Julian's side. The dog's eyes were sharp, its posture poised. "This is Thorn. He's a retired drug detection dog. I asked my friend to bring him in this morning to ensure the shop was clean before the grand opening. And, unsurprisingly, he found the drugs they planted."

The screen showed Thorn in action, sniffing out the hidden stashes with methodical precision. The footage captured me removing the bags, placing them into sealed evidence containers, and handing them to Marcus for safekeeping.

"You see," I said, my voice rising slightly, "justice isn't served by people like this. It's manipulated. Twisted. Turned into a weapon to destroy lives." I turned back to the screen, pausing the video on a clear shot of Markson and the DEA agent working together. "And this is who you're trusting to uphold the law."

The room erupted. Journalists surged forward, their questions overlapping in a cacophony of disbelief and outrage. Cameras flashed wildly, their lenses capturing every detail of the damning evidence.

The DEA agent's face turned a deep shade of red, his composure unraveling with each passing second. "This is a smear campaign," he barked, his voice strained. "That footage is fabricated!"

"Is it?" I asked, tilting my head. "Because we both know it's not. And so does everyone else, but if you have doubts, I'll hand over a copy to anyone in this room who would like one."

Markson, standing near the back of the room, looked frozen, his usual smug confidence replaced by something closer to panic.

Julian stepped forward, his hand resting lightly on Thorn's harness. "If it's fabricated," he said smoothly, his voice cutting through the chaos, "then I'm sure you won't mind an independent forensic analysis of the footage. After all, you have nothing to hide... right?"

The agent didn't respond, his jaw tightening as the cameras focused on him.

"Cassian Moreau was framed and arrested under false charges—let that be your headline in the morning," I continued, my voice sharp. "This is about the truth. And now, thanks to all of you," I gestured to the journalists, "the world will finally see it."

The room buzzed with energy, the story unfolding in real-time as reporters scrambled to capture every angle. The DEA agent turned abruptly, barking orders to his team, but the damage was done.

As the agents filed out, their faces pale and tight with fury, I allowed myself a moment to breathe. The shop was in ruins, the night a disaster in many ways—but the truth was out.

And now, it was their turn to run.

CHAPTER THIRTY-FOUR

The night air was crisp, a faint chill brushing against my skin as I stood outside the police station. The hum of the city was a distant backdrop, its usual chaos muted by the anticipation thrumming in my chest. The streetlights above cast a soft glow on the concrete, their light pooling around me as I shifted on my heels, my nerves refusing to settle.

I glanced down at my phone, the screen glowing with the time. *Any minute now,* I thought, my grip tightening on the device.

Harrison's words still echoed in my mind.

"They had no choice, Rosalie," he'd said over the phone, his tone calm but tinged with satisfaction. "After the stunt you pulled, the District Attorney dropped all charges. They're scrambling to save face. Cassian will be out tonight."

The roar I'd caused—the truth laid bare for the world to see—had done its job. The images of the DEA's corruption, the planted evidence, the ruthless ambush on the convoy... It had been enough to turn the tide, enough to force even the most stubborn of officials to fold.

The doors of the station finally opened, and my heart leapt as Harrison stepped out, his silhouette sharp and confident against the bright light spilling from inside. Behind him, another figure emerged—taller, broader, moving with a deliberate grace that was unmistakable.

Cassian.

My breath hitched as our eyes met. He looked tired, his usual sharp demeanor softened by the weight of the past weeks, but there was no mistaking the fire that still burned in his gaze. He was free.

As they approached, the world around me seemed to slow, the noise of the city fading into a distant white noise. Harrison's faint smile and swinging briefcase were peripheral details, barely registering. My eyes were fixed on Cassian, his movements purposeful, and determined as he made his way toward me.

When he stopped in front of me, everything else vanished. His gray eyes, shadowed but piercing, locked onto mine, and I felt the breath catch in my throat. He looked... different. The sharp edges of his presence were still there, but now there was something raw beneath it— something unguarded that made my chest ache.

"You did this," he said, his voice quiet but rough, each word carrying the weight of exhaustion, relief, and something I couldn't yet place.

I nodded, my lips parting as I tried to speak, but the lump in my throat made it difficult. "It wasn't just me," I managed, my voice barely above a whisper. "But... I couldn't let them take everything. Not like this."

For a moment, he just looked at me, his gaze roaming over my face as though he were memorizing every detail. The air between us was thick with unspoken words, and I felt exposed, like he could see every crack in the armor I'd tried so hard to hold together.

A flicker of something passed through his eyes— something I couldn't quite define but felt all the same. Gratitude, pride, relief—maybe all of it, maybe more.

Then he stepped closer, and the space between us dissolved. His presence was overwhelming, his warmth a quiet force that made my pulse race. My breath hitched as his hand lifted, his fingers brushing gently against my cheek before tucking a strand of hair behind my ear.

"You never cease to amaze me," he murmured, his voice softer now, almost reverent.

Cassian's lips twitched, but the faint smile didn't last long. His eyes darkened, the storm behind them crashing into me with full force. Before I could say another word, he stepped closer, his presence overwhelming and all-consuming.

"Rosalie," he murmured, my name a rough whisper on his lips.

I barely had time to process the way his hand gripped my waist, pulling me toward him. The world around us disappeared, swallowed by the sheer gravity of his proximity. Then his lips crashed into mine—fierce, commanding, like he was claiming a piece of me that had always been his.

The kiss wasn't gentle; it was powerful, unapologetic, filled with a fire that left me breathless. My hands instinctively found his chest, gripping the fabric of his shirt as if it could anchor me. But even as I tried to ground myself, my knees buckled under the sheer intensity of it all.

Cassian's other hand slid to my lower back, steadying me, his grip firm and unyielding. He didn't let me fall—not physically, not emotionally. His lips moved against mine with a precision that left no room for thought, no space for doubt. It was raw, consuming, and utterly him.

I melted into him, my body responding before my mind could catch up. Every nerve, every sense, was attuned to him—the heat of his touch, the possessiveness in the way he held me, the taste of him that lingered like a promise.

When he finally pulled back, it wasn't because the fire had dimmed—it was because he wanted me to feel its burn even in his absence. His forehead pressed against mine, his breath hot and uneven as it mingled with my own.

"You're mine," he said, his voice low and commanding, the words sending a shiver down my spine. "Never forget that."

My chest heaved as I tried to catch my breath, his hands still anchoring me in place. "How could I?" I whispered, my voice barely audible, but the words carried every ounce of truth I had.

Cassian's thumb brushed against my cheek, his touch softer now, though his gaze remained as intense as ever. "Good," he said simply, as though that was all that needed to be said.

And maybe it was.

As his hand slipped from my waist, I felt the absence of his touch like a loss, but the fire he'd ignited burned fiercely in its place. The car waited at the curb, Marcus standing by the door, his eyes carefully averted but his presence a reminder that the world hadn't stopped for us.

Harrison cleared his throat behind us, the sound cutting through the moment like a sharp blade. "As much as I hate to interrupt," he said, his tone light but pointed, "we should really get out of here. The press is already catching wind, and I'd rather not give them a photo op on the station steps."

Cassian's jaw tightened slightly, a flicker of irritation crossing his features before he turned back to me. "He's right," he said, his voice steadier now, more composed. "Let's go."

For a second, I didn't move. My body felt frozen, my emotions a tangle of relief, exhaustion, and something else I couldn't name. Then I nodded, taking a shaky breath as the reality of the moment began to sink in.

As we walked toward the waiting car, his hand brushed against mine, his fingers curling briefly around mine in a touch so fleeting it felt almost imagined. But it wasn't. And it was enough to keep me grounded in the storm that still raged in my chest.

The car doors closed with a quiet click, sealing us inside. The steady rythm of the engine vibrated faintly beneath me as Marcus started to drive, his eyes fixed on the road ahead. The city lights blurred past the window, but I barely noticed them. Cassian was beside me—too close, yet not close enough.

His lips brushed against the shell of my ear, so close I could feel the warmth of his breath. It sent a shiver cascading down my spine, pooling heat low in my stomach. When he spoke, his voice was a dangerous, lust-filled whisper, every word dripping with raw, unrelenting intent.

"You have no idea how long I've waited for this," he murmured, the sound wrapping around me like velvet, smooth but laden with an edge that made my breath hitch.

I turned to face him, my chest rising and falling in uneven rhythm, the air in the car heavy and charged. His gray eyes burned into me, molten and unwavering, the intensity making me feel both trapped and utterly consumed.

"Cassian," I whispered, my voice trembling, though I wasn't sure if it was from anticipation or the sheer force of his presence. It was supposed to be a warning—a reminder that Marcus was just a few feet away, driving silently—but it came out soft, like a plea I couldn't control.

His smirk was faint, predatory, as his lips hovered against my ear, close enough that I could feel every syllable as he spoke again.

"When we get home," he whispered, his tone dipping lower, each word deliberate and sinful, "I'm going to make you forget everything but me. Every word I say. Every touch. Every sound you make."

I felt the tension coiling in my stomach, sharp and undeniable, as his hand trailed along my thigh, his fingers grazing the soft fabric of my dress.

His lips moved slightly, brushing my earlobe as his voice dropped even further. "I'm going to take my time. Make you shiver, make you beg. And when you think you can't take anymore..." He paused, his teeth grazing my skin just enough to make me gasp. "That's when I'll make you mine all over again."

My breath hitched, my pulse roaring in my ears. The car felt impossibly small, his words wrapping around me, sinking deep into my chest and settling there like a weight I didn't want to let go of.

"Only if you promise..." I whispered again, this time with no attempt to mask the desire in my voice.

His lips curved into a wicked smile, though he didn't pull

away. "Good girl," he murmured, his voice still soft but brimming with satisfaction.

I closed my eyes, my hands gripping the seat beneath me as he leaned back slightly, his hand still resting possessively on my thigh. The penthouse couldn't come fast enough, and by the look in his eyes, he knew it too.

CHAPTER THIRTY-FIVE

The elevator ride up to the penthouse was a blur. Cassian's arms wrapped around me with an ease that made the world outside disappear. He didn't ask, didn't wait—he simply acted, his strength enveloping me as though I weighed nothing.

By the time we reached the bedroom, my pulse was a steady roar in my ears. He pushed open the door with his shoulder, the motion fluid, confident, before crossing the room and setting me gently on the edge of the bed.

Cassian didn't step back immediately. Instead, he hovered for a moment, his hands resting on my waist, his gray eyes boring into mine. The hunger there was undeniable, but beneath it, there was something deeper— pride, admiration, something that made my chest tighten.

"You've been busy," he murmured, his voice low and edged with something dangerous. "I should've known you'd find a way to turn this city upside down."

I opened my mouth to respond, but the words never came. Cassian stepped back, and my breath caught as his fingers went to the knot of his tie. He pulled it loose slowly, deliberately, the movement as commanding as any he'd ever made. His gaze never left mine, sharp and unrelenting, as he slipped the tie from around his neck and tossed it carelessly to the floor.

The soft thud of fabric against the hardwood made me shiver.

Next came his jacket. His hands moved with precise intent, shrugging out of the tailored material as though it were an inconvenience. He tossed it to the side without a second thought, leaving him in a crisp white shirt that clung to his frame in all the right places.

"You're full of surprises, Rosalie," he said, his voice quiet but laced with something almost predatory. He began unbuttoning his shirt, each motion slow, deliberate, calculated. "When Harrison told me how everything unfolded... I didn't want to believe it. But then again..."

The last button came undone, and he slipped the shirt from his shoulders, revealing the taut muscle beneath, the scarred strength of a man who'd fought for every inch of power he held. He let the shirt fall to the floor, standing before me in only his slacks, the dim light casting sharp shadows across his chest.

"I should've known," he finished, his lips curving into a faint smirk.

My breath hitched as he stepped closer, his hands finding the edge of the bed on either side of me. He leaned down, his face inches from mine, his eyes dark and full of heat.

"Not just anyone could pull off what you did," he murmured, his voice a soft growl. "The footage, the timing, the precision... It was perfect. *You* were perfect."

I swallowed hard, the intensity of his gaze pinning me in place. "I just... I couldn't let them take everything, and I had a great teacher." I said softly.

Cassian's smirk faded, replaced by something deeper. "You didn't just stop them. You turned the tables, Rosalie. You gave them a reason to fear you."

He leaned closer, his lips brushing against my ear, his voice dropping to a whisper. "And that's why I can't keep my hands off you."

A shiver ran through me, every nerve in my body igniting at the promise in his tone. His hands moved to my waist, firm but gentle as he pulled me closer to the edge of the bed.

"Tonight," he said, his voice steady and commanding, "I'm going to remind you exactly what happens when you take control."

The words settled over me like a challenge, and as he straightened, his gaze roaming over me hungrily, I knew this was just the beginning.

Cassian's lips crashed into mine with a ferocity that stole my breath. There was nothing tentative about the way he kissed me—no hesitation, no softness. It was raw, consuming, and utterly dominating, like he was reclaiming something he'd lost the moment he was taken from me.

His hands gripped my waist, pulling me flush against him as his body pressed mine into the edge of the bed. The heat of his bare skin radiated through the thin fabric of my dress, and I couldn't hold back the shiver that ran down my spine. His tongue slid against mine, each movement deliberate, coaxing, commanding.

When he pulled back, I was left gasping, my chest heaving as his gray eyes burned into me. "You have no idea how much I've missed this," he murmured, his voice low and rough as his hands trailed up my sides, his touch leaving a trail of fire in its wake.

He didn't wait for me to respond. His lips found my neck, his teeth grazing the sensitive skin just below my ear. I arched into him, my fingers tangling in his hair as the sharp pull of his teeth gave way to the soft, wet heat of his tongue.

His hands moved with purpose, sliding over the curve of my hips before gripping the hem of my dress. He pulled it up slowly, the fabric sliding against my thighs, and when he finally tugged it over my head, his sharp intake of breath sent a thrill through me.

"You're perfect," he growled, his hands tracing the curves of my body as his lips returned to mine. The press of his chest against me was firm, grounding, his skin hot and slick against my own.

When he guided me back onto the bed, I went willingly,

my legs parting instinctively to accommodate the weight of him. The mattress dipped under us, and for a moment, all I could feel was him—his heat, his strength, the steady, rhythmic thrum of his pulse against mine.

Cassian's hands roamed freely now, mapping every inch of me as though committing me to memory. His mouth followed, his lips brushing over the curve of my shoulder, the swell of my breast, the hollow of my throat. Each kiss sent sparks shooting through my veins, a heat that pooled low and deep, pulling me closer to the edge of reason.

His hips pressed against mine, the hard, insistent weight of him making my breath hitch. He didn't ease into me—not Cassian. When he pushed forward, it was a single, deliberate motion, filling me completely and leaving me gasping at the intensity of it.

The sensation was overwhelming, every nerve in my body lighting up at once. I clung to him, my nails digging into his back as he moved, each thrust deliberate and deep, sending waves of pleasure coursing through me.

"Rosalie," he murmured against my lips, his voice a reverent growl that sent a shiver down my spine.

Our bodies moved together, a perfect rhythm that felt inevitable, like we'd been made for this—made for each other. His hand tangled in my hair, pulling gently as his lips found mine again, his kiss searing and demanding.

Every touch, every motion, felt like a reclamation—a reminder of what we were, of what we meant to each other. The rest of the world faded into nothingness, leaving only us, our bodies entwined, our breaths mingling, our hearts beating as one.

When I finally shattered beneath him, his name was a cry on my lips, the sound swallowed by his kiss as he followed me over the edge. The moment stretched on, endless and all-consuming, leaving me trembling in his arms as the heat between us began to ebb, replaced by the steady, grounding warmth of him.

Cassian held me close, his breath heavy against my skin, his hand tracing lazy circles over my back. He didn't say anything, but he didn't need to. In the silence, in the aftermath of our connection, there was nothing left unsaid. We were whole, if only for this moment, and that was enough.

Cassian's hand remained on my back, his touch steady as his breath evened. The weight of him, warm and grounding, was a comfort I hadn't realized I'd craved until now. His lips brushed against my temple, a surprisingly tender gesture that made my chest tighten.

He shifted slightly, propping himself up on one elbow to look down at me. His gray eyes, usually so guarded and calculating, were bare now—raw with an emotion that made my heart stutter.

"I've been fighting this for too long," he murmured, his voice low but firm. His fingers traced a slow, deliberate path along my jaw, his touch light but reverent. "I thought I could keep you close without letting you in. That I could protect you without... without letting you take all of me."

My breath hitched as he paused, his gaze locking on mine. "But you're already there, Rosalie," he continued, his voice thick with emotion. "You've been there from the moment you walked into my life and turned everything upside down."

His hand cupped my cheek, his thumb brushing gently over my skin. "I love you," he said, the words heavy with certainty. "I've never been more sure of anything in my life. And I don't want to waste another second pretending otherwise."

My chest tightened, a swell of emotions rising so quickly it left me breathless. Tears pricked at the corners of my eyes, but I refused to let them fall. Instead, I reached up, my fingers tangling in his hair as I pulled him closer.

"I love you too," I whispered, the words spilling out with a conviction I hadn't allowed myself to voice until now. "I think I always have. And I want this—us. All of it."

Cassian's eyes softened, a rare vulnerability breaking through the sharp lines of his features. He leaned down, his lips brushing against mine in a kiss that was softer this time, unhurried but no less consuming.

When he pulled back, his forehead rested against mine,

his voice dropping to a tender murmur. "I want to spend the rest of my life with you, Rosalie. Whatever it takes, whatever it costs, I want you by my side."

I exhaled shakily, my fingers tightening in his hair as I let the weight of his words sink in. "Then we'll figure it out," I said, my voice steady despite the tears threatening to spill. "Together. Always."

His lips curved into a faint smile, one that felt impossibly rare and precious. "Always," he echoed, his voice a quiet promise.

As he gathered me into his arms, his warmth enveloping me completely, I knew with unwavering certainty that this moment was the start of something unbreakable. Together, we could face anything—even the shadows still looming over us.

CHAPTER THIRTY-SIX

The soft crackle of the fire in the hearth filled the drawing room, its warm glow casting flickering shadows across the walls. Outside, the sky was a soft gray, the first hints of autumn creeping into the air. The place was ours now—a world away from the chaos of the city, nestled in the peace of the countryside. It felt surreal, sitting here with Cassian, far removed from everything that had once felt like an impossible weight.

The chessboard between us held my focus, though I wasn't sure I stood a chance. Cassian sat across from me, his posture relaxed but his sharp eyes scanning the board with the same precision he applied to everything else. His fingers tapped the edge of a rook, his smirk faint but infuriatingly confident.

"Your move," he said, his voice carrying a teasing edge.

I stared at the board, my brows knitting together as I considered my options. "I think you've been playing mind games this entire match," I muttered, my lips curving into a small smile despite myself.

"Mind games?" he echoed, leaning back in his chair with a mock look of offense. "I'm simply playing to my strengths."

I rolled my eyes but reached for my queen, sliding it into

position with a deliberate motion. "Well, let's see how your strengths hold up now."

Cassian's smirk widened, but he didn't immediately counter. Instead, he studied me, his gray eyes softening in a way that made my chest tighten.

"You've changed," he said quietly, his tone devoid of the teasing from moments ago.

I glanced up at him, my fingers still resting lightly on the edge of the chessboard. "What do you mean?"

"You're stronger," he said simply, his gaze unwavering. "More certain. It suits you."

A warmth spread through me at his words, and I let out a soft laugh. "I had to be. I didn't really have a choice."

Cassian leaned forward, his hand brushing against mine, sending a familiar shiver up my spine. "No, you didn't," he agreed. "But you didn't just survive, Rosalie. You thrived. You made them see you for what you are—unstoppable."

The intensity of his words left me momentarily speechless. I turned my hand over, letting my fingers intertwine with his as I gave him a small, grateful smile. "It helps when you have someone in your corner," I said softly.

He lifted my hand to his lips, pressing a kiss to my knuckles, his gaze never leaving mine. "Always," he murmured.

The decision to move in with Cassian hadn't been easy. I'd fought against it at first, insisting on keeping pieces of my independence. But in the end, we'd found a compromise—*our* place. This house, with its sprawling landscape and quiet seclusion, was a fresh start for both of us. It held no ghosts, no shadows of Cassian's father, just the promise of a life we were building together.

The drawing room was my favorite part of the house. Its high ceilings and large windows made it feel open, but the fireplace and dark wood accents gave it an inviting warmth. Bookshelves lined one wall, filled with a mix of Cassian's meticulously organized collection and my own haphazard additions. A small stack of gardening books rested on the coffee table, a nod to the flourishing garden I'd started just outside.

"I think I've had enough losing for one night," I said, glancing at the chessboard with mock disdain.

Cassian's grin widened as he leaned back, his hand still intertwined with mine. "Admitting defeat already?"

"Not defeat," I corrected, standing and tugging him up with me. "A tactical retreat."

His laugh was low and rich as he followed my lead, letting me guide him to the sofa. He settled beside me, his arm draping over my shoulders as I curled into his side. The warmth of the fire and the steady rhythm of his breathing created a cocoon of comfort I hadn't realized I needed.

For a while, we sat in silence, the weight of the past months hanging between us, not as a burden but as a reminder of how far we'd come. The shadows of The Broker, the arrests, the betrayals—they felt distant now, dulled by the passage of time and the strength we'd found together.

"Do you think we'll ever have peace?" I asked quietly, my gaze fixed on the flames dancing in the hearth.

Cassian's arm tightened around me, his lips brushing against my temple. "We'll make it," he said firmly. "No matter what comes, we'll face it together."

I turned my face up to his, my hand resting lightly on his chest. "Together," I echoed, the word a quiet promise.

His lips found mine, slow and lingering, a kiss that held all the certainty in the world. When we pulled apart, his gray eyes were softer, his smirk replaced by something more genuine.

"Now," he said, a playful edge returning to his voice, "about that tactical retreat. Are you planning to win next time?"

I laughed, the sound light and easy as I rested my head against his shoulder. "Just you wait, Cassian Moreau. I'm full of surprises."

And for the first time in what felt like forever, the future didn't feel daunting—it felt like ours.

The fire crackled softly as I leaned against Cassian, my

thoughts drifting to Ivy & Bloom. The expansion had been more successful than I ever imagined. The grand opening—despite the chaos—had drawn crowds larger than I dared to hope for. And in the weeks since, the shop had flourished.

People came not just for flowers but for what Ivy & Bloom represented: resilience, beauty, and the defiance to bloom in the harshest of circumstances. The mural on the back wall, *Where Beauty Grows,* had become an emblem, a beacon for clients who walked in looking for more than just a bouquet.

Lena had become a force of nature, managing the day-to-day with a precision I deeply admired. She'd even started hosting workshops in the expanded space, teaching everything from arranging bouquets to crafting wreaths. The coffee nook was a hit, too—regulars often lingered, filling the air with the hum of conversation and the scent of freshly brewed lattes.

I smiled softly, my mind replaying moments of laughter and creativity that had filled the shop in recent weeks. Despite the storm we'd weathered, Ivy & Bloom had become stronger, brighter. It wasn't just a business anymore—it was a sanctuary, for me and for everyone who walked through its doors.

Cassian's voice broke through my thoughts, pulling me back to the present. "What's that look?" he asked, his tone teasing as his fingers idly traced patterns on my arm.

"What look?" I asked, feigning innocence.

"That one," he said, tilting his head to study me. "The one where you're plotting something or thinking so hard I can practically see the wheels turning."

I laughed softly, shaking my head. "Just thinking about Ivy & Bloom," I admitted. "How far it's come. How far we've come."

His lips curved into a slow smile, the kind that sent a familiar warmth spreading through me. "You turned that place into something extraordinary, Rosalie. It's a reflection of you—strong, beautiful, and utterly unforgettable."

My cheeks flushed at his words, but I didn't have time

to respond. Cassian shifted suddenly, his movements swift and deliberate as he scooped me up into his arms.

"Cassian!" I squeaked, my arms looping instinctively around his neck as he stood, holding me effortlessly.

He smirked down at me, his gray eyes glinting with mischief. "I think you've spent enough time daydreaming for one night," he said, his tone low and teasing. "Now, I have far more deliciously naughty plans for you."

My breath caught, the playful edge in his voice sending a thrill through me. "Oh, do you?" I managed, my tone wry despite the fluttering in my chest.

He winked, his smirk widening. "You'll find out soon enough."

With that, he strode toward the bedroom, his steps confident and unhurried, as if he had all the time in the world. I laughed softly, the sound light and carefree as I let my head rest against his shoulder.

For the first time in a long while, I felt weightless—free from the shadows of the past, lost in the warmth of the present, and ready for whatever came next.

THE END

ABOUT THE AUTHOR
LINDSEY FINCH

Lindsey Finch is a devoted mother, loving wife, and self-proclaimed hopeless romantic who has been crafting heart-pounding love stories for over a decade. Her passion for storytelling began with a simple idea: love, no matter how dark or twisted, has the power to transform and heal. This belief shines through in every one of her novels, where strong heroines meet brooding, complex heroes, and happily-ever-afters are anything but conventional.

A ten-year veteran of the romance genre, Lindsey has penned multiple bestselling series, including *The White Lotus* and *The Citadel*, captivating readers with her signature blend of emotional intensity, steamy chemistry, and richly imagined worlds. Her stories often explore the fine line between love and danger, drawing readers into tales of power, betrayal, and unrelenting desire.

When she's not writing, Lindsey enjoys spending time with her husband and children, sipping wine over a cozy dinner, or getting lost in her ever-growing library of romance novels. Whether she's dreaming up her next dark and twisty romance or indulging in a guilty pleasure binge-watch, Lindsey's heart always gravitates toward love stories that push boundaries and defy expectations.

Stay connected with Lindsey Finch for updates on upcoming releases, sneak peeks, and exclusive content:

Author Page: **www.amazon.com/author/lindseyfinch**
Instagram: **@AviaryPublications**
Goodreads: **Lindsey Finch**

With each book, Lindsey invites readers into a world where passion cuts deep, love is worth the risk, and even the darkest hearts can be redeemed.

www.ingramcontent.com/pod-product-compliance
Lightning Source LLC
Chambersburg PA
CBHW020052180626
46812CB00006B/2290